THE GHOST SEEKERS

DEVON TAYLOR

Swoon READS

NEW YORK

A Swoon Reads Book
An imprint of Feiwel and Friends and Macmillan Publishing Group, LLC
120 Broadway, New York, NY 10271

Our books may be purchased in bulk for promotional, educational, or business use.
Please contact your local bookseller or the Macmillan Corporate and Premium Sales
Department at (800) 221-7945 ext. 5442 or by email at
MacmillanSpecialMarkets@macmillan.com.

Library of Congress Control Number: 2018955584
ISBN 978-1-250-16833-7 (hardcover) / ISBN 978-1-250-16832-0 (ebook)

Book design by Carol Ly

First edition, 2019

1 3 5 7 9 10 8 6 4 2

swoonreads.com

This one is for my girls,
Rylan and Norrie,
the protectors of my soul.

THEY ARE CALLED THE
DEAD WHO LIVED THROUGH
THEIR DEATHS . . .

—FRANK STANFORD

PART

ONE

ONE

His ghost was cold.

It was frozen, down to the last string of whatever incorporeal ooze it was made of. Whatever else changed around it—and things were always changing—the cold was a constant, unwelcome thing.

For most of it, there was a house around him. It was small—just a couple of bedrooms, barely a kitchen, a cozy fireplace that he could never warm up with. The single hallway was long and empty, sometimes swept clean, sometimes cluttered with dust and leaves and bits of trash. He could stand in the living room and blink and it would be different every time he opened his eyes.

Outside the windows, seasons snapped in and out of place like slides in an old projector. In one moment there were long, luscious blades of grass waving at him from the yard. In another there was a blanket of clean white snow, untouched and unbroken. And then it would go back to summer, then to spring, then to winter again, then to fall. In the trees, he could see leaves stuttering in and out of existence, as cardinals dripped through the branches in streaks of bloodred.

He couldn't remember ever having been here, in this house, but he was sure that it was a part of his memories. He felt lucky just to have that one little bit of confidence. There was a lot about his life—and everything that came after it—that he couldn't pin down. It shifted in his mind as sporadically as the seasons outside.

Sometimes he wasn't sure. Sometimes his memory would slip and he would lose it all, and he would slump to the floor, cold as ever. He would sit there with his head in his hands, staring between his feet, trying to ignore the unhinged passing of time.

It was a joke to think that he could ever eat or sleep or do anything that seemed even remotely normal. Normality was so, *so* far gone. He just sat on the floor, against the wall, letting the world flicker around him, watching tiny dunes of dirt and dust build themselves up and break themselves down along the floorboards.

Occasionally the house would unbuild itself, becoming a sturdy wooden skeleton standing in the bright sun atop a freshly laid concrete foundation. Then it would be gone entirely—or never there at all—and he'd be sitting in the empty field. He liked those moments the best. He could see the sky, the clouds rocketing across it. He could see blue fade into black and the stars chasing one another above the atmosphere in swarms of light. Given enough time, he might have been able to will himself to stay there with the wide-open sky above him. Every now and then, he'd even try to do it.

And that was usually when time shifted in the opposite direction.

The house would become a ruin, clothed in darkness, slumping against itself. Broken beams poked down out of the tattered ceiling;

the floorboards rolled and snapped from the damp and the cold. It was empty and lonely and forgotten.

He would see her then, in the deepest shadow of the farthest corner. There was only ever the unfocused outline of her body—her knotted hair, her too-thin arms and legs. And, of course, her eyes. Black with just the tiniest white pinpricks for pupils, staring out at him with something that could have been curiosity or barely withheld rage.

He didn't know or care. What he knew was that even here, in a place that should have been just his, cursed as it was, she had found him. She had *found* him, and clarity would slam into him like an alarming gust of wind, and he'd be afraid. For his friends, for the ship that he abandoned, for the souls that he had been made to protect. What had she done to them?

How had they lost?

"Because you were foolish enough to think that you could not," she said once, somehow hearing the question that he never spoke. Her voice was the same as it had always been, a force of its own, thrumming with a thousand other voices. Only now, here, it was more subdued, somewhere between a rumble and a whisper.

"What do you want from me?" he asked her, forcing himself to meet her gaze.

"All the parts of you that you could never hope to understand," she said. *"The power that you've only just scratched the surface of."*

"So why don't you just take it? Take *me*?"

Her grimy teeth shone in a horrid grin. *"It is a game, Soul Keeper. And the only way to win is if everyone keeps playing."*

Time cycled forward, and then it cycled back. Furniture appeared and then vanished. The sun came and went in violent flashes of light from the windows. Except for the darkest days of the future, when the demon girl was there watching him, he was alone.

And he had never been more terrified.

When he finally heard the voice, he wouldn't allow himself to believe that it was real. The voice that called to him was one he hadn't heard in so long, and missed so deeply, that if he believed he was really hearing it and it turned out to just be another trick of his awful prison, his mind would snap like a dry twig under a heavy foot.

But it persisted. Calling to him. Searching for him.

Mate.

That voice.

Mate, are you there?

He was sitting against the wall, watching the trees outside judder and flail, growing leaves and shedding them over the course of minutes instead of months.

It was the same as it had been every second of every minute of every hour since he arrived here. But when the voice spoke, the sound of it exploded into the room like a firework going off. It shook against the floor and the ceiling, and he swore he saw a sprinkling of plaster come falling down from somewhere.

Mate. Rhett. It's me.

He knew that voice, but it couldn't possibly be real. Yet the sound of his own name was such a sweet thing to hear that he couldn't help but pull himself off the floor, cocking his head to listen. He thought about a time that felt like centuries ago, when he'd stood on the side of a highway in New York, talking to the owner of that voice.

My name is Rhett, he had said. *Rhett Snyder.* While nearby, his dead body hung within the wreckage of the car accident that had ultimately landed him here.

The voice spoke again, thunderous within the tiny house.

It's me, mate. It's Basil. Can you hear me?

Rhett opened his mouth to respond, but nothing came out. He realized he'd barely spoken the entire time he'd been here.

He tried again. Standing in the middle of the room, he cupped his hands around his mouth and yelled from the deepest part of his gut.

"I'm here!" he barely croaked. "Basil, I hear you! I'm *here!*"

Beneath him, the floorboards shuddered. The walls groaned deeply, menacingly. As Rhett watched them, tiny cracks began to form, snaking their way across the paint like slow bolts of lightning.

Hang on, mate! We're going to try to bring you to us!

What the hell did *that* mean?

The house rumbled and shook around Rhett. Outside, he could still see the sporadic passing of the seasons. But everything inside the house had given way to chaos.

More cracks formed across the walls. The floorboards bowed upward. Doorframes leaned in haphazard directions. Some of the windows exploded, sprinkling the floor with shards of broken glass.

Okay, Basil said from . . . wherever he was. *We're ready to go. Rhett, are you ready?*

"Ready for *what?*" Rhett yelled back.

Here we go. One.

The walls buckled.

Two.

Rhett shut his eyes, listening to the destruction as it happened.

Three!

There was a rush of air and a crackle of electricity. The house roared around him briefly—sounds of blowing dirt and snapping wood and collapsing reality.

Then it was quiet.

He could feel a change in the atmosphere. The world was silent . . . but it was also still. That feeling of time flickering around him like a constant, inextinguishable fire was gone, replaced by a smothering ache in his chest and a tingling in his limbs. He could barely breathe. And for the first time in a long time, he could feel it. He struggled to pull air into his lungs and got barely a gasp.

Rhett opened his eyes. The first thing he noticed was that they burned. Not just in a dry, itchy way, but in a way that made it feel as if someone had thrown acid into his retinas; keeping his eyes open at all was a struggle.

He fought through the pain, waiting for his vision to clear. Once it did, he wasn't disappointed.

He was in the same house, his prison for who knew how long now, but time had finally settled. The place had long been abandoned, leaving a coating of dust across everything like a blanket of dull, gray snow. The paint on the walls was so faded and flaked it looked like dry skin after an awful sunburn. There were a couple pieces of old furniture—a caked-over mirror on one wall, a fraying wicker chair in the corner, a lone end table with a vase that still choked on a bouquet of brittle, bone-like flower stems—and it all stayed put. Nothing sputtered in and out of existence. Outside, the trees were naked and the sky was clear. A faint ray of cold sunshine angled in through one of the windows like a spotlight. Rhett stared at it for a moment, waiting for it to start rushing across the room, waiting for time to unstick itself again . . . until he noticed the figure standing just outside that spotlight of sun.

He would have recognized that damn blazer anywhere.

Basil stepped forward, allowing the sunlight to fall over him, and that slanted grin blew away any doubt that Rhett may have had: He was really here. They had come back for him.

"Hello, mate," Basil said, his gaze darting up and down, staring at Rhett with wide, uncertain eyes. No, not uncertain—unbelieving. It was the same look that Rhett imagined he was giving Basil. "Don't take this the wrong way, but . . . you look god-awful."

Rhett couldn't help but laugh. Except it didn't sound like much of a laugh at all. It was a horrid, choked sound. He watched the muscles in Basil's face twitch slightly.

"Listen, mate," Basil went on. "We're here to help you, okay?"

Why was Basil putting his hands out like that, like he was talking to a child or a stray animal about to run away? And who was *we*?

For the first time, Rhett noticed other shapes lurking in the shadows of the house. And until they began coming into the light, each one gave him an unpleasant jolt of fear. Fear that they might be *her*.

Rhett also realized that there were lines crossing in front of his field of vision, forming a grid. Not just lines—bars. Metal ones. When he focused on them, he could see speckles of rust.

He was in a cage.

"Basil . . . ," he started, but he couldn't go on. The sound of his own voice was too jarring. It sounded distant. It sounded broken. It sounded . . . haunted.

He put a hand up to try and grab hold of the cage and had to force back a scream.

His hand was barely there, made mostly out of roiling gray smoke, shedding flecks of what could have been ash or skin with every motion. When he balled his fingers into a fist, any indication of his fingers vanished, leaving only a fist-shaped bulb of churning matter. His arm was the same way. And when he looked down at his feet, he realized that he had none. There was only a slowly boiling mass of gray, like a miniature storm cloud clinging to his body, infecting him somehow.

Rhett looked up, panic rising inside him, and found Basil had come closer to the cage. His hands were still outstretched, but his face was relaxed and confident.

"Stay calm," he said. "You have to be cool, Rhett."

Rhett put a cloudy hand up again, reaching for the cage, but the bars buzzed with electricity when he got too close. Sparks sprayed out and he felt a strange current roll through him, like slowly dipping into a pool of water.

He didn't want to speak, didn't want to hear the unnerving sound of his own voice again.

It still hurt to breathe. It still hurt to see.

What was happening to him?

"Okay, so, here's the deal," Basil said, obviously spotting the panic on Rhett's face. Did he even have a face? He didn't want to know. He just focused on Basil's voice. "You're . . . still a ghost."

Rhett gave him a look that was meant to say *You think?*

But it had never been like this. How had they pulled him out of the prison of his haunting?

He glanced around the inside of the cage and then looked beyond it. Electrical wires curled and twisted along the splintered floorboards, connecting to what looked like old car batteries and a white, plastic desktop computer from the nineties.

He returned his gaze to Basil, who had finally moved across the room so that he was standing just beyond the cage. There was somebody else beside him: a shorter, skinnier guy with a baseball hat that was still just the faintest shade of red twisted up in his hands and a jagged, unkempt head of hair.

Basil motioned to him. "This is Jon," he said. "He set this up for us. I'll let him explain all the . . . I'll just let him explain. Jon?" Basil took a small step back.

The other guy—Jon—took an equally small step forward.

"Uh . . . h-hi," Jon said.

Rhett just stared at him, trying not to imagine how horrifying he must have looked in that moment—a vaguely human-shaped cloud of smoke and ash floating inside an electrified cage, staring out with a dead face and impatient eyes.

Jon's eyes widened slightly, but he went on. "S-so, the idea here is that you need energy to . . . to manifest . . . in order for us to be able to see you. The . . . uh . . . cage provides that energy. If we were to shut the power off, then you'd go back to . . . wherever it is that you came from."

Rhett listened, feeling the slightest thump of panic at the thought of going back. From the other side of the room, near the front door, he heard what sounded like the squawk of a walkie-talkie. After a moment, one of the other syllektors—a woman with wavy brown hair—stepped up beside Basil and leaned toward him.

"Captain," she murmured, but Jon spoke over the rest.

"I understand you have . . . um . . . an ability?" he asked. He stared at Rhett hopefully.

Rhett knew what he was referring to, but he didn't know if he really had the ability or not. He had only used it once . . . and it had cost them all everything. He gave Jon what he hoped was a shrug.

Jon nodded.

"Okay," he said. "Fair enough. Well, if you do have the . . . ability and you *can* bring yourself . . . back, you're going to need a lot more energy for that." He gestured at the car batteries, maybe a dozen of them, lined up at his feet. "Right now, we're drawing power from two of these. In order for you to . . . do what you can do, we're going to need all twelve."

"Jon," Basil said, putting a hand on his shoulder. "We need to hurry this along."

Jon looked back, and Rhett watched as they communicated silently. Something was wrong.

"Aye, Captain," Jon said. When he looked back at Rhett, his face was even more unnerved than it had been before. But he got back into his explanation. "Once you start . . . doing your thing," he said, "these puppies won't last long. You'll have to use up all the juice and then be quick. Because as soon as the energy level in the cage starts to drop, your window of opportunity will close."

Basil stepped forward again. "We've got one shot at this, mate," he said. Then that devilish grin spread across his face, smooth and sarcastic as ever. "Don't screw it up."

Rhett took little comfort in Basil's humor—which was usually the case when Basil tried to crack a joke in the middle of something serious, so this shouldn't have felt any different. But it did. It felt like the end of the line, like one last wink of hopeful light before Rhett was to be cast back into the hell that he'd been existing in.

He closed his eyes, momentarily thankful for the relief it brought—now all he had to do was focus on the ache in his chest. He let the images flicker around in his head for a moment. Endless days of constantly moving time that gave way to those last moments aboard the *Harbinger*, right before she sank, right before he told Basil and Mak to do this to him, to keep him and his power away from the souls, away from *her*. Urcena.

He saw those piercing, deadly eyes watching from the corner. The power was what she wanted; using it was dangerous. But the souls that she intended to use the power on were at the bottom of the river in the afterlife, still tucked inside the monstrous hull of the *Harbinger*. Rhett's parents were among those souls. He had promised himself that he'd protect *them* if nothing else, because he hadn't been able to do that in life. She had come for them, too.

Urcena had caused *all* of this. He wanted to end her.

Around him, electricity hummed and snapped along the bars of the cage. He heard Jon's voice, along with what sounded like the clacking of computer keys.

"Okay," Jon said, raising his voice over the sound of the electrified cage. "We're up to full power! It's now or never!"

"Always the optimist, aren't you, Jon?" Basil cried.

The energy rushing through the cage was stronger, louder. Rhett felt it mixing with the tingling sensation in his ghostly limbs. He felt the weight pressing into his chest, crushing his lungs.

He saw the girl from the apartment building, surrounded by flames and sparks of purple lightning. He remembered hearing her heart beat in time with his own . . . and he could hear it now. It thumped in his ears, just once. At the same time, something beyond the cage popped and sparks fizzled against the vibrating metal.

"Shit," Jon hissed.

"It's okay," Basil said. "I . . . I think it's working . . ."

It was.

Rhett could feel the surge of life coursing through him. Well, not life exactly. But the fibrous extensions of his soul were reconnecting themselves, turning him back into what he'd been on the *Harbinger*.

His heartbeat sounded in his ears again. *Whump-whump.*

And again.

Again.

He opened his eyes.

Veins of purple electricity snaked their way around the cage, weaving in and out of the bars. One of the car batteries was a smoldering husk of melted black plastic, spewing noxious smoke. Another one popped as Rhett watched, launching a wave of glowing sparks into the air. Everything was charged. Light bulbs in the house that probably hadn't been lit in years flickered violently.

Whump-whump.

Rhett took a step forward, putting his nose right up against the metal of the cage . . . and then he stepped through it.

Basil and Jon took a few stumbling steps backward, watching Rhett pass through the solid, electrified bars.

Rhett moved through them, feeling the density of the steel. He left the bubbling cloud of smoke and ash behind, let it dissipate along with the energy in the cage. He stepped onto the wooden floor as if breaking through the surface of water, gasping for air.

As he fell forward onto his hands and knees, Basil tried to catch him, and they ended up on the floor together amid the dirt and the dust. But Rhett was there. He was back.

He was a syllektor again.

TWO

"Whoa," Jon said, staring down at them.

Rhett and Basil knelt on the hard floor together, both of them panting—Rhett from the exertion of un-ghosting himself, and Basil from what must have been fear. They looked at each other sidelong . . . and then they both burst out laughing.

Rhett felt a strange warmth, something that he never realized had been there when he was aboard the *Harbinger*. Even though the sensations in his body were numb, there for him to switch on if he needed to, he wasn't cold. He didn't think that there could ever be a cold as punishing as what he felt . . . back there. He had been a ghost; he could admit that much to himself. But the place where his ghost had resided—some kind of sublevel of reality—he had no idea what to call that.

People were still staring at Rhett. Not just Jon, but the handful of other syllektors who were there as well. They watched him as he sat up, examined him like some kind of specimen. He assumed they all knew what he was, that he had the ability to bring people back from the brink of death. And if they didn't before, they definitely did now.

He tried to ignore the stares and glanced up at the cage: a tall, hastily constructed cylinder. It still smoldered along with the car batteries and the computer, which had a blank screen now.

Rhett cleared his throat before speaking, even though he was sure that his voice would work just fine.

"This is . . . different," he said, gesturing toward the equipment. And he was right—his voice did sound fine. Slowly, he allowed himself to relax.

"Yeah, well, we had to go a bit analog since . . . well, you know," Basil said, pulling himself up off the floor. He reached down to help Rhett up, and there was a strange look on his face. He was choking back more laughter. "I'm sure it's a side effect of what just went down, but Anderson Cooper called, mate. He wants his hair back."

Rhett didn't understand. He let Basil pull him off the floor, and then stepped across the room to the grimy mirror. He smeared away some of the muck with the sleeve of his shirt.

As he stared at his reflection, his mouth dropped open. He wasn't focused on the fact that the skin on his face was more sunken and deathly looking than ever, or the fact that his clothes from the *Harbinger* had somehow gotten darker. What he stared at was his hair, which had been a standard shade of brown before but was now a shocking, perfect white.

"Jesus . . . ," Rhett murmured, running a hand through what could have been a stranger's hair.

"Yeah," Basil said from behind him. "I feel you. But I'm more confused about something else."

Rhett turned to face him, giving him a questioning look.

"Why aren't you . . . alive?" Basil said. "Like, *alive* alive."

"I . . . don't know," Rhett replied. He thought about it. "Maybe it doesn't work like that. Especially not on myself. I'd probably need a corpse for that."

Basil looked horrified.

"*Blegh!*" he said. "No offense, mate, but I'd rather not see you as a zombie."

Rhett opened his mouth to try and explain what he *thought* the logic was, but someone else cut him off. It was the woman from before who had whispered in Basil's ear.

"Captain Winthrop," she said. When Basil glanced in her direction, she simply tapped her wrist with her index finger. *Tick-tock.*

"Yes," Basil responded. He gave his head a shake and seemed to bring himself back into the moment, standing up straight. Rhett realized that Basil looked different, too. Not older, because syllektors could never look older than they were when they died, just more severe. Exhausted, maybe. "Thank you, Liz. Everybody back to the truck. We have to be gone before they show up."

Rhett didn't have to ask, but he did anyway. "Psychons?"

Basil nodded. "Psychons."

Rhett looked around. "Where's Mak? Is she okay?"

"She's fine," Basil replied, glancing down at his boots. "She's working on something else at the moment." The look on his face told Rhett not to question the issue further. As long as Mak was all right, he didn't care where she was or what she was doing.

"What about all this?" Rhett asked, pointing at the hulk of the cage and the equipment.

"Leave it," Jon said before Basil could reply. "It's toast."

Rhett glanced at Jon, then extended his hand toward him.

"Thank you," he said. "I owe you my . . . *after*life, I guess."

Jon smirked, taking Rhett's hand and shaking it. "Don't mention it. You're the Twice-Born Son. If you're going to save us, someone had to save you first, right?" And then he secured his baseball hat on his head and walked out into the cold day with the others, leaving Rhett and Basil alone in the house.

Rhett shot an accusing look at Basil, who cringed.

"I'll explain later," he said.

"You better." Rhett took a look around the house one last time, still seeing it as it had been to him.

"Your parents . . . ," Basil started.

"I know," Rhett said. "They lived here when I was a baby. Probably right after I was born. After my dad lost his license for saving me."

Basil nodded, his face suddenly solemn. "It seems like they were trying to lie low. Lots of nosy press people and all that."

Rhett took a deep breath as Basil slipped into an overcoat that hung down to his knees.

"So," he said, grinning. "Captain Winthrop, huh?"

"Oh, shut up," Basil said, but he was smiling, too. "I'd much rather talk about your hair."

"Ugh."

They moved together toward the door, leaving the ruined equipment behind, stepping out into the crisp winter air. They stopped when they nearly ran into the other syllektors, all of them grouped against the steps that led up to the front door.

In front of them, stretched across the long field of dead grass, were at least a dozen psychons. They stood tall and gruesome in the bright light, their tattered cloaks swaying slightly in the frigid breeze, their hot breath puffing in front of their constant grins. They kicked at the dirt with their bony feet, watching the syllektors with their hungry skeleton eyes, like a pack of wild dogs.

Between the psychons and the syllektors, Urcena stood waiting.

She stood in a patch of dead weeds that had gone from brown to an ashen gray under her bare feet. She sneered at Rhett, locking eyes with him over the tops of the other syllektors' heads. He wanted to look away, wanted to avoid that gaze. Her black eyes were emptier than ever, the tiny white pinpricks of her pupils reduced to barely a speck.

She was here for Rhett, and he could just as easily have given himself up. But before that idea could even take root, madness erupted around him.

The psychons sprang forward, thundering around Urcena's narrow shape and across the field, kicking up dirt and the few remaining patches of snow.

The syllektors, who had still been grouped at the bottom of the front steps, fanned out, unsheathing weapons. The woman with the wavy hair—Liz—yanked a hatchet out from under her leather coat, and in one fluid motion she let it loose, flinging it toward the nearest psychon. Rhett could hear a low whistle as the hatchet spun through the air, followed by a nasty, wet crunch as it collided with the psychon's head. The creature dropped at once and didn't move again.

The other syllektors followed suit. They revealed their own weapons, blades mostly, and didn't wait around for the psychons to come to them.

Jon planted his feet, flipped his red hat around so it sat backward on his head, and pulled a short metal stick from the inside of one of his sleeves. The stick didn't seem that intimidating to Rhett at first, but when Jon twisted it a certain way, the stick extended from both ends and turned into a staff that was almost as tall as Jon himself. He spun the staff around his body, impossibly fast. And when it came to a stop, locked firmly in both of Jon's hands, Rhett saw it come to life with tangles of white electricity dancing along the metal.

Of course the genius inventor guy would have an electrified staff, Rhett thought.

Even before he moved to join them, Rhett could see how outnumbered the syllektors were. There were only seven of them, including himself and Basil. There were almost twice as many psychons, and they were blocking the way to a pickup truck that had seen better days, what Rhett assumed was the getaway car.

He stepped down onto the hard, frozen earth, with Basil at his side, and put a hand out.

"Give me one of your scythes," he said to Basil. Nearby, Jon swung his staff into a psychon's ribs. It fell to the ground, spasming from the jolt of electricity.

When there was still nothing in his hand, Rhett looked over and found Basil cringing back at him.

"They're in the truck, aren't they?" Rhett said.

Basil lifted his shoulders to his ears and cringed even more.

"You're the worst."

Across the field, metal clanged with bone, and one psychon let out a screaming roar that rolled away into the trees, sending birds fluttering in terror. A few feet away, one of the syllektors—a short, stocky guy who *looked* like he was in his thirties (but of course had probably been around a lot longer than that)—had lost hold of his katana. It fell backward, the open sky flashing across its gleaming metal face, and stuck into the ground. The psychon that the guy was fighting wasted no time. It planted both of its massive claws into his chest and ripped them away from each other. The syllektor tore apart, breaking down into a cloud of ash that swirled across the field, carried by the wind.

Rhett saw his chance and took it. Basil followed his lead.

They sprinted through tufts of dead grass and patches of frozen weeds. Rhett got there first and yanked the ghosted syllektor's katana out of the ground. He dropped to a knee and spun. The blade cut through the air with a metallic *schinnng* . . . and then it sliced through the psychon. Shards of bone and threads of gristle broke off under the force of the katana. The top half of the psychon tumbled off the bottom half, and both pieces thumped to the ground.

Basil darted past Rhett and the downed psychon, running for the truck. There was another psychon there to meet him, lunging forward with its horrid skull face, which dripped with the white sludge that was its saliva. Basil leaned back and kicked it in the teeth with the hard sole of his boot. The thing stumbled backward, emitting a whining growl and clutching its face with one bony claw. Rhett was there with his borrowed sword. This time he swung it downward, cutting through the ragged hood of the psychon's cloak and burying the blade in its stooped head. The skull cracked like an egg, splitting open to reveal black, steaming ooze. The psychon slumped to its side and lay still.

Rhett glanced up and found Urcena staring back at him. She was as terrifying as ever—her ratty hospital gown swayed around her too-thin legs, her body coated in grayish skin and blue veins that twisted across her limbs. Her hair was a knotted black mass that hung off her head like a dead animal, and as always, she was sopping wet, dripping fat globs of water that quickly turned to ice in the cold air, creating icicles that hung from her fingers and nose and ears and the bottom of her pointed chin. The she-thing stepped toward Rhett, the white dots in the blacks of her eyes all but burning a hole into him.

"*You should have stayed in your prison, Soul Keeper!*" Urcena spoke, and the crash of a thousand voices exploded inside Rhett's head. It left him unsteady.

Her voice ripped through his mind—and the minds of all the other syllektors, it seemed, who were wincing and putting their hands over their ears, even in the midst of their fights. One psychon took advantage of the distraction and dove its claw right into Liz's chest. For a single second, she was a statue of ash, and then she was a cloud of it, and then she was nothing.

"*You were safer while you were there!*"

Rhett looked back to Urcena, who was still striding toward him.

"So were you," he said. He bent his arm over his shoulder and then threw the katana with as much force as he could. He had a brief mental image of Basil doing the same thing with one of his scythes back in the engine room on the *Harbinger*, the moment when he'd inadvertently ghosted Treeny. Rhett pushed the image away and focused on the sword as it flipped through the air, end over end, aimed right at the place where Urcena's heart should have been, if she had a heart at all.

Urcena smirked, her lips twisting into something not even close to humor. The air around her rippled and then she blipped out of existence, leaving only a few icicles behind that fell to the ground where she had been.

The katana flew through the vacancy where Urcena had been standing and landed harmlessly on the ground a couple of feet beyond that.

Rhett straightened and peered around the field. Urcena couldn't have shown herself on her own. When she'd first appeared to Rhett on the Golden Gate Bridge what seemed like eons ago, she'd used Treeny as a conduit, although he hadn't known it at the time. She had to be using one of the syllektors in their group . . .

But then he saw something else at the very edge of the field, in the uneven shadows of the bare trees. A tallish man who couldn't have been much older than Rhett, maybe late twenties. He had jet-black hair and a nose that was canted at an awkward angle. His hands were stuffed into the pockets of a black coat, and even from this distance, Rhett could see his eyes—black with little pinpricks of white. The stranger grinned at Rhett, then stepped backward into the brush and the cover of the trees.

"*Rhett, look out!*" That was Jon's voice.

Rhett tore his eyes away from the trees just in time to see the gnarly mass of a psychon bearing down on him. It leaped, claws extended, and Rhett ducked. He rolled beneath the psychon as it lunged over him. It hit the ground and skidded through the dirt, more pissed off than ever.

"Everybody get in!" Basil yelled. He'd made it to the truck. He was leaning out the open driver's-side door as he turned the key. The truck may have looked like a pile of junk, but the engine roared to life. The sound was extra loud in the emptiness of the field.

Rhett and Jon broke for the truck at the same time, psychons racing after them. Jon swung his staff behind him, nearly catching one of the monsters across the face. The metal sung as it swept through open air, buzzing with its electric charge.

The last two syllektors were still fending off two psychons each. One of them was a girl with straight, short black hair that gleamed hints of purple in the wintry daylight. Her weapon was a sword that appeared to be made mostly of glass. It caught the faint light of the sun and splattered it across the grass in speckles of pearlescent colors. The girl swung her blade in a wide arc, keeping both of the psychons circling her at a distance. She spun one way, then stopped and twisted quickly in the opposite direction. Her sword left her hand, shooting perfectly straight, like an arrow made of light, and sank to the hilt in the gut of one of the psychons. The beast fell, clutching at its midsection as it gushed hot black slime.

The other syllektor was a middle-aged man with dashes of gray in his hair and his short beard. He was caught between the two psychons he was trying to fight, lashing at them with a long dagger in each hand. The man tried to break away, but one of the psychons caught his heel and dragged him back across the dirt. He yelled once before the psychons fell on him and turned him to dust.

Basil already had the truck in gear as Jon pulled himself into the bed and Rhett climbed into the passenger side. The remaining psychons were closing in.

"Damn!" Basil yelled, slamming his hand on the steering wheel. "Damn, damn, damn! I thought we'd have more time!" He pushed the pedal to the floor. The engine revved and the tires spun before catching traction. The truck lurched forward.

Basil pointed the truck at the girl with the purplish hair, who now had a third psychon pouncing on her. She had retrieved her sword from the stomach of the first. The blade sliced through the air in a long arc, taking off the left arm of the second psychon and just missing the third, who galloped past the point of the girl's weapon and turned to come back around, charging at her yet again.

"Hang on, Jon!" Basil called through the open cab window.

Just before he was about to plow into the girl and all three psychons, Basil hit the brakes and spun the wheel. The truck drifted, kicking sprays of dirt up behind it, and the back end slammed into the charging psychon with a metallic crunch. The thing vanished beneath the truck.

In the rearview mirror, Rhett watched Jon try to pull the girl up over the tailgate, jabbing at the other two injured psychons' upturned grins with his staff. But before she could climb all the way in, the gnarled arm of the psychon they'd just run over exploded up through the bed of the truck. There was a sound of shearing metal as the limb scrambled around, looking for anything it could hold on to. It found the one leg that the girl had managed to get over the tailgate. The deadly claws of the psychon's bony hand wrapped around the girl's leg and pulled. She screamed and lost hold of her sword. It tumbled out of the truck bed and disappeared.

Jon turned around and saw what was happening just in time for the psychon to shred the girl's leg. She held tight to the tailgate even as the muscles and bones of her leg were split apart. If she hadn't, Rhett was sure that he'd be watching yet another syllektor be reduced to a pile of ash. The girl gritted her teeth—not from the pain, Rhett knew, because she wouldn't feel any of that if she didn't want to, but from the struggle of fighting off the psychon and watching it take her leg.

The charged end of Jon's staff came down on the psychon's arm, and there was rage in Jon's eyes as he held it against the creature's flimsy muscles. The limb spasmed, smacking against the metal truck bed. It released the girl's ruined leg, and Jon was able to push the arm back down through the hole it had created.

"Go, go!" Jon yelled as soon as the claw was gone.

Basil threw the gearshift down into drive and hit the gas again. The truck launched forward and bucked over the top of something that could only have been the psychon that had tried to take a souvenir. Ahead of them and behind them, more psychons were heading toward the truck. Their cloaks billowed around them like bat wings, and the little bit of sinew that stretched across their skeletal bodies strained and flexed. They looked more like wild, rabid dogs than ever with their hungry, grinning skulls.

The truck gained speed, headed for a narrow opening between the trees.

Rhett glanced over at Basil, who only stared straight ahead, the steering wheel tight in his hands. In the mirror he could see Jon's red hat and the girl's purple-black hair; both of them desperately hung on to the sides of the truck.

There was only one psychon that seemed brave enough to take the truck head-on; the others had skirted away, forming groups on both sides. The lone psychon gained speed, its head low and its jagged shoulders working like pistons beneath the thin veil of its cloak.

Basil locked his arms against the steering wheel and a low yell bubbled out of him. The yell grew louder and louder . . .

The psychon slammed into the front of the truck, buckling the metal and crushing one of the headlights, and then it flew into the air. It didn't even connect with the top of the truck. It disappeared for a moment and then plummeted back down behind them, its cloak making a sound like frantic wings. It slammed into the earth and stayed there.

Jon and the girl cheered in spite of her severed limb, which lay in the truck bed, slowly oozing blood instead of gushing it, as only a syllektor injury could. Basil grinned slightly as Rhett slapped him on the shoulder.

But they weren't safe yet.

The truck dipped onto a narrow dirt road that was mostly two rivets with a bunch of weeds growing down the middle, regaining speed, making its way toward what looked like an interstate a mile or so away.

And the psychons followed.

The truck tore down the dirt road, and the four syllektors inside it lurched and bobbed, trying their best to hang on. Scrawny Jon was nearly thrown out completely.

Behind them, there were still seven or eight psychons hurrying to catch up. They dug in with all four limbs, galloping like a drove of horses. To Rhett, they seemed even more awful in the bright daytime light, nightmares normally reserved for the shadows that had come out into the sun anyway.

The truck's tires spewed a cloud of yellow dirt behind them. The engine growled.

A minute later, the truck flew off the dirt track and screeched onto asphalt, turning into oncoming traffic. There were plenty of other cars on the highway, some of them honking and swerving out of the way as the truck drifted onto the road. Its back end smashed into the guardrail on the opposite side, scraping and grinding across it, showering Jon and the purple-haired girl with sparks. Basil spun the tires again, and Rhett was suddenly choking on the smell of burning rubber, his senses triggered by the panic of being here, in a vehicle, on a highway, where all of this had started. Just before the tires caught purchase, Rhett saw the pack of psychons come bursting onto the road. If only the living people driving along the highway could see the terrors that surrounded them.

Basil nearly lost control as he yanked the truck into the correct lane and sped up.

"You really suck at this," Rhett said, grabbing the "oh shit" handle above his door so hard, he thought he might rip it off.

"You're one to talk," Basil griped.

Rhett ignored the jab. "I don't get it. We don't even have any souls on us."

"Oh, they don't need that excuse to come after us anymore, mate," Basil replied. Rhett felt a surge of panic.

The highway wasn't jam-packed, but it was still crowded. Basil maneuvered the truck around the other vehicles, gaining speed, weaving between lanes. Drivers were gaping at the truck that must have appeared empty, driving itself recklessly along the interstate. Rhett watched the speedometer climb from seventy to eighty.

And yet the psychons were keeping up. They dashed around some cars and vaulted over others, gaining on the syllektors.

A big semitruck was coming up on the right. Basil swerved to the left. Rhett watched in his side-view mirror as a psychon hopped on top of an SUV and used it to leap on top of the semi, keeping pace with Basil's driving. The psychon clawed across the top of the semitruck . . . and then jumped off the front of the cab, falling toward Jon and the girl.

In one quick motion, Jon stood, propped his leg up against the tailgate, extended the ends of his staff, and swung. The staff connected with the psychon, zapping it with jagged bolts of electricity, and the creature became dead weight, crashing back into the asphalt.

Rhett watched in what felt like slow motion as a second psychon caught hold of the truck, stabbing its claws into the metal right behind the purple-haired girl's head. As soon as she heard it, she lurched forward, just out of its grip. She swung around with something long and thick. For a split second, Rhett was convinced that it was her own severed leg. But it turned out to be an oversize monkey wrench that she'd found somewhere in the truck bed. She had it by the narrow end and smashed the wide, toothy mouth of it into the psychon's face. It was enough to throw the thing off-balance. It lost hold of the truck and plummeted back down to the highway. Rhett could see it in the rearview mirror, scrambling to get back up, but it was shrinking fast.

Basil had his foot to the floor. The truck zigged and zagged between traffic, and slowly the remaining psychons began to get smaller, unable to close the distance. They dove over and around the other vehicles on the road, but they couldn't match the truck's speed. Eventually they became specks dancing across the uneven stretch of cars and trucks. After that they disappeared entirely.

Jon and the girl finally allowed themselves to relax, lowering their weapons and settling back down into the truck bed.

Rhett watched the woods as they flickered beside the truck, waiting for another attack. When none came, he decided that maybe this was the last they'd seen of the psychons.

For now.

THREE

Eventually traffic thinned out and they had the road mostly to themselves. No living people to potentially witness a truck that seemed to be driving itself at almost ninety miles per hour, no psychons to come rushing after them, and best of all, no Urcena.

Everybody relaxed. For the first time, Rhett let reality sink through him. He had escaped the horror of being a ghost, had escaped the torment of haunting a house that he had barely known but which had been his miracle home. It was the home that his parents had fled to when they'd given up everything else so that he could live. A debt that he would never have the chance to repay.

But he hadn't escaped it alone.

Shaking thoughts of his parents away, Rhett turned to Basil.

"So, what's the plan?" he asked. "Where are we going?"

"In due time, mate," Basil replied without taking his eyes off the road. He looked shaken and hollow, his cheekbones more pronounced, his eyes ringed with shadowy bruises. Or maybe that was just Rhett's imagination.

"Where have I heard that before?" Rhett said, managing to get a tilted smirk out of Basil.

In the rearview mirror, Jon and the girl sat staring past the tailgate at the road as it came spewing out from beneath the truck. Jon's hat was still firmly fixed on his head, and the girl's dark violet hair flapped in the wind.

"So . . . Jon . . . ," Rhett started, knowing he didn't have to finish his thought for Basil to get the meaning.

"I know," Basil replied. "He's nonstop. A captain couldn't have asked for a better crewman."

There it was again. That word. *Captain*. And Rhett understood why Basil looked so unsteady. He was the captain now. It was a weird thing to say when there was no ship, but the crew were trained to follow the commands and decisions of one person, no matter what. And this captain's decision to come and save Rhett had cost him three crew members.

Rhett didn't know what was going to happen next, but he hoped he was worth that decision.

They kept driving.

Rhett's mind finally cleared enough for him to pick up on the license plates of the few cars they passed. As far as he could tell, they were in Pennsylvania. And even though they drove for what felt like a couple of hours, they didn't appear to leave the state.

The trees were all leafless and clawlike, reaching out of the hardened earth at a sky that had been clear and pale with winter when they'd first emerged from the house but was now collecting gray clouds, threatening fresh snow. The day was fading away, the sky growing darker every minute, and Basil eventually switched on the truck's headlights.

The four of them were quiet the whole way.

Not long after it got dark, they came to a tiny side road tucked behind a low hill. Rhett wouldn't even have noticed it was there if Basil hadn't slowed down and turned onto it. It was barely a road at all, mostly packed dirt and petrified leaves. A few feet up, there was a rusted orange gate that appeared to be padlocked. Basil pulled the truck up to it and switched off the headlights.

"Jon," he called over his shoulder.

But Jon was already hopping out of the bed of the truck, staff in hand, though he had shortened and disarmed it for now. There was still a thread of bluish-purple light in the sky, peeking out from between the gathering clouds, just enough for them to see by.

Rhett watched as Jon pulled a set of keys from his pocket and used one to remove the padlock from the gate. He swung the gate open with a pained squeal, and Basil drove through. After Jon had secured the gate with the padlock and gotten back into the truck, they continued down the road.

They followed the path that had been crushed into the terrain as it wound around a few hills and carved its way through a couple of jagged rock formations. Basil never turned the headlights back on but seemed to know where he was going even in the growing dark.

How many times has he been down this road? Rhett wondered.

It must have been close to three hours by the time they completed their entire journey, and their destination was even less inviting than the house Rhett had been haunting. All shadows and metal and dread, like when Rhett had first seen the *Harbinger* cutting through those churning waves, black and monstrous. But he had come to learn that the *Harbinger* was a place of protection, of good work and good people, of hope.

The place that stood before him now looked as if it hadn't seen any hope in a long, long time.

There were several buildings and outhouses, all of them made of old brick and rusted iron. One long structure in particular must have been a factory building at one time, with a slanted metal roof crawling with dense patches of rust and broken by ragged holes. That fed into another, slightly larger building—taller, but not quite as long, and mostly brick but smeared with soot, as if there had been a fire. And from that building there was a tall, narrow smokestack made entirely out of red brick. There was no smoke coming out of it, though, and Rhett was starting to understand that there was probably a reason for that.

The whole thing was positioned practically on top of a river that rushed with the sound of winter runoff. Rhett could hear it even before Basil parked the truck.

"The Holiday Inn was all booked up?" Rhett asked, squinting into the darkness as Basil put the truck in park and switched it off. The silence left behind by the purring engine was abrupt and unsettling. Not a sound except for the shushing of the river.

"Well, it was as close to home as we could get," Basil replied. He reached under the bench seat and pulled out his twin scythes, which used to look identical but were now almost imperceptibly different— a slightly more pronounced curve of the blade on one, as well as a difference in the wood that made the handle. They were different because Basil had lost one back on the *Harbinger*, when he'd ghosted Treeny.

Rhett shook the thought away, wanting to avoid thoughts of the *Harbinger*'s sinking for as long as possible.

What Basil had said was true, Rhett realized. This place may have been bleak and abandoned, but it definitely had characteristics that reminded him of the *Harbinger*. The river, the smokestack, the metal . . . It was certainly no replacement, but it was a good reminder of home.

"It's a steel mill that closed up three or four decades ago," Basil continued as he came around the front of the truck. "We were on the run from the psychons, trying to lie low. We found this place tucked away back here."

Jon disembarked and helped the girl onto her one good foot. He half carried her as she hobbled across the lot, still carrying her dismembered leg. The four of them moved slowly toward the factory. It was dark and shapeless in the cloud-covered night, blending with the near-black clouds that hung low in the sky. And as the four of them trudged across gravel and weeds, new snow began to fall.

Rhett caught sight of two other trucks parked under a precariously leaning awning near the factory's main building. There were license plates on both, but Rhett doubted that they really belonged to the vehicles. The only way the syllektors would have been able to get their hands on the trucks was if they stole them from the living, which brought with it its own risks.

The river swept across its banks just beyond the factory, and as they got closer to the building, Rhett could hear murmuring voices and the crackle of fire.

Basil stepped up to a big rolling metal door and knocked three times quickly, three times slowly. A moment later, something beyond the door clicked, and it rolled up with a clatter. There was a group collected there, several dozen syllektors waiting to see who was return-ing, Rhett guessed, and he felt a pang of guilt at knowing half of the original party that had set out was not coming back because of him.

"Captain," one of the women at the front of the group said, nod-ding at Basil, and then she scanned the rest of their faces. Before she even got to Rhett, she put her arms out toward Jon. "Jon," she said, her voice relieved and elated and almost scolding at the same time.

"Mom," Jon replied. He put out his free arm, still helping to hold the injured girl up. The woman embraced him and squeezed him tightly.

Rhett gave Basil a curious glance.

Basil leaned in and whispered, "They died separately. Years apart. Both just happened to end up on the *Harbinger.*"

Rhett shook his head, amazed that after everything he'd seen, there was still something to surprise him.

As Jon's mother let him go, a group materialized out of the crowd and took the girl, along with her leg. Rhett wanted to thank her, but she was carried away before he got the chance, the last glimpses of her dark hair bobbing between the bodies of the gathered syllektors.

Jon and his mother watched the girl go as well, wincing slightly. Then his mother turned to Rhett, her face beaming.

"You must be the Twice-Born Son," she said. "We've been waiting for you."

"Mom," Jon said, elbowing his mother in the side.

The rest of the group stared at Rhett with that same look of fascination and some species of reverence. Some of them were faces that Rhett recognized just from passing them aboard the *Harbinger*. Others were complete strangers to him. He felt the weight of their gazes pushing into him.

"All right, everyone!" Basil called. "I know you've got a fandom going here, but let's clear the way!"

The group began to break apart, opening up the doorway into the factory. Jon's mother, with her arm still draped over her son's shoulders, looked past Basil, peering out into the dark expectantly.

"The others?" she murmured to Basil.

Basil only shook his head at her and continued on inside.

Rhett followed him . . . and then had to stop short before he could go any farther.

The inside of the factory was even more miserable and forgotten than the outside. The high ceiling sagged, the metal beams twisted and stretched, and the corrugated roof eaten through by rust let flakes of snow come fluttering inside. The floor was all concrete, cracked and buckled and wet. Thick iron support beams placed every few feet or so were the only things that kept the building upright, and among them stood empty barrels with fires burning inside, crackling

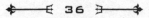

and hissing, combatting the invading snow and the constant sound of the river outside.

The syllektors themselves—only a couple hundred of them, as far as Rhett could tell—looked nothing like the syllektors that he remembered from the *Harbinger*. Of course, some of them *were* syllektors that he recognized. But aboard the *Harbinger*, they all had work to do, they all had purpose, something to keep them moving. Here, now, they looked lost.

Some of them sat with their backs up against the walls, staring across the factory floor at nothing. Others paced or busied themselves with silly tasks, like the man in a far corner who was poking at one of the fires with a stick, apparently stoking it even though it burned powerfully. And some of them, Rhett noticed, were far worse than he could ever have imagined. While most of the syllektors looked calm and comfortable for the most part, their bodies reactionless to the cold and the elements, there were several groups among them that looked frozen and hungry. They huddled around the fires, bundled in thick coats, their lips shivering, their faces shriveled and sunken. They looked like they were starving. They looked like they were *dying*.

But how could that be when they were already dead?

"Mate!" Basil called. He had crossed the entire length of the factory floor and was waiting by a set of rickety metal steps. They led up to an office that was wrapped in cracked, dirty windows. He seemed impatient, and again Rhett couldn't help but notice the difference between this Basil and the Basil who had originally brought him aboard the *Harbinger*.

"Coming," he said quietly, taking one last look around at the syllektors. Some of them glanced his way and rolled their eyes. Some gave him quick, wondering glances. The rest were indifferent, lost in their own misery. It was like some kind of post-apocalyptic world captured just inside the walls of this factory. And that made sense, didn't it? The sinking of the *Harbinger* had been their apocalypse, and now they were trying to exist in the world after it.

A hand smacked against Rhett's shoulder, startling him. Jon was standing behind him.

"It's not great," Jon said, looking around, matching Rhett's gaze. "But hopefully you can help us fix it. Basil has a plan. You've got your power. I believe we can get out of this."

Rhett could only nod, remembering what he'd told Basil and Mak right before he let them ghost him. He'd said something very similar. But now . . .

Basil was climbing the steps to the run-down office, leaving him behind.

Jon gave Rhett another nudge.

"Go on and save us," he said.

Rhett climbed the metal steps, listening to them creak and rattle beneath him, trying not to think about how much it reminded him of that first time he set foot on the bridge aboard the *Harbinger*. The first time that his parents' death had really sunk in. The first time he'd had a conversation alone with Captain Trier, who was gone now, ghosted like so many others. The image of the captain disintegrating in front of him, breaking down in his arms and being swept away by wind and rain, was still fresh. To Rhett, it felt as if it had happened only hours ago.

He stepped inside the office, wrapped in its dirty windows that looked out over the entire factory floor, where fires burned and syllektors meandered and hulking pieces of machinery still sat crouched in corners and along walls like rusty tombstones.

The inside of the office was even more depressing. Everything was lit by a few dripping candles that were placed around the room. There was a wooden desk in the center that was splintered and swollen with water damage but still stood on its own. A couple of folding chairs on either side of the desk, a moldy carpet that filled the room with must. The walls were mostly bare, except for an oversize corkboard that was cramped with papers: newspaper clippings overlapping one another, a couple of maps with red thumbtacks poked into them, and a calendar that Rhett didn't dare look at. He took his eyes away from the wall and forced them to find Basil's. Rhett wanted to hear everything from him, and he wanted it straight.

"Tell me," Rhett said quietly.

Basil had lowered himself into one of the chairs, tossing his scythes onto the desk as if they were just a set of keys or a stack of junk mail. He put his head back, with his hands laced in front of him, and closed his eyes.

"What do you want to know?" he said.

"Everything," Rhett replied.

Basil grinned without opening his eyes. "I feel like we've had this conversation before."

"I'm serious, Basil. What the hell is happening out there? Why do some of the crew look so . . ."

"Tired? Hungry?" Basil asked. "Cold?" He opened one eye and looked at Rhett.

Rhett just nodded.

Basil sighed and finally leaned forward again, resting his elbows on the edge of the desk. He stared through a hole shaped like a warped stop sign in one of the windows.

"Some of the crew have started calling it the Ash," Basil said.

"I . . . don't know what that means," Rhett said.

"When we left the *Harbinger*, we took as much as we could," Basil continued, as if Rhett hadn't spoken at all. "Most of us already had our weapons on us. Some of the other crew who joined up with us later had raided the armory and grabbed everything they could carry before fleeing the ship. They were bloody brilliant for doing it, too. Otherwise we wouldn't be nearly as armed as we are."

Rhett stood with his arms folded across his chest, watching as Basil reached into one of the desk drawers. It opened with a wooden groan. Basil pulled out something that glinted in the unsteady candlelight and tossed it to Rhett.

"Somebody somewhere picked up this ridiculous thing," Basil said. "And here I thought we'd seen the last of it."

Rhett caught the item by its handle—smooth, polished wood with metal rings for him to slip his fingers through. He caught it deftly, relishing its comforting weight in his hand. His knuckle blade. He couldn't help but grin.

One side of Basil's face jerked up in a half grin for just a few seconds, but then he went on.

"We abandoned the ship just as it went down. Actually, we had to swim our way out because all the doors were completely underwater by the time we got out of the steam room. It was . . . a mess. But we escaped. There was just a handful of us at first, Jon included. You've already noticed how brilliant that kid is. After we got settled—and avoided a few psychons—he came up with a way to broadcast a signal to other syllektors who were left stranded in the living world, to put out a call for them to join us. He actually rewired the thing to help us communicate with you while you were in spookyland. Calls it the 'spirit radio,' but whatever. To each their own, right?" He chuckled, but it didn't sound right. It sounded more like he was gagging.

"Anyway," Basil continued, "we got off the *Harbinger* with as much as we could. Some of us have met up here, and we've fought to be able to continue with our plan, which was to find you and somehow get back to the ship so that you can . . . do whatever it is you think you can do. We've stolen things from the living, but mostly we've tried to stick to ourselves, stick to using everything we were able to get from the *Harbinger*. But there's one thing we couldn't take with us when she went down." His voice was low, almost agitated.

"What's that?" Rhett asked.

"Her power," Basil replied, finally locking eyes with Rhett. And what Rhett saw in them was not just a sad, broken kind of determination, the kind that comes when you have nothing left to lose, but a white-hot rage. "*Our* power. The thing that keeps us from feeling, from hurting, from falling apart." He paused and scrubbed his hand over his face. "It starts with the cold. Bone deep. So cold you can barely think straight. And then there's the hunger. *Real* hunger. Hunger that most syllektors haven't felt in ages. After that there's aches and pains, stiffness. Then there's the rash. And eventually . . ." He looked up at Rhett again, and Rhett understood. Eventually, the syllektors were ghosted by it—the Ash, Basil had called it.

"There's a . . . rash?" Rhett asked.

Basil nodded. "Black as night. Comes across your skin and hardens and then breaks apart into what looks like . . . well, ash. Basically, it's just a very, very slow way of being ghosted."

"But . . . what causes it?"

"As far as we can tell, simply being away from the *Harbinger* for too long."

Rhett looked at the uneven wooden floorboards, listened to them creak as he swayed from foot to foot. The question that he'd been dreading lurked at the tip of his tongue. He couldn't put it off any longer. He had to know.

"Basil," he said. "How long has it been?"

Basil didn't look at him, didn't even acknowledge that a question had been asked. But his eyes flicked to the calendar on the wall.

"Basil," Rhett said again. "Tell me how long it's been."

There was a long pause, bloated and heavy and uncomfortable. And then Basil sighed, burying the heels of his hands into his eyes, forcing the words out through gritted teeth.

"It's been two years, mate."

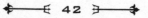

If Rhett had flipped his senses on in that moment, he would have puked all over the floor. Instead, he sank into one of the hard metal folding chairs, feeling his eyes go wide and his mouth fall open. Two years? *Two years?*

"Jesus . . . ," he whispered.

The silence drew out between them, and Rhett felt the weight of all that time collapsing on top of him. Had he really been stuck in that awful prison for two years? It had felt like an eternity. And toward the end he had been sure that he would never see anything other than those constantly changing shadows, the ceaseless flickering of the seasons. But to truly know how long he had endured that . . . It made his mind want to implode.

Rhett glanced up at Basil, who was now sitting back in his chair, his overcoat still on, wrapping his arms around himself. He was shivering.

"Oh my God," Rhett said. "How long have you had it?"

Basil shook his head. "What are you talking about?"

"Don't dick me around, Basil. *How long have you had it?*"

Basil stared at him for a moment, searching his face for any way around the question. But Rhett wasn't backing down. Basil sighed loudly and yanked up the sleeves of his coat and blazer.

There, stretched across Basil's forearm like an ugly, lopsided tattoo, was a black splotch maybe the size of a small book. It was malformed and faded into the veins of his arm in dark squiggles. Rhett wanted to reach out and touch it but was too afraid. Afraid for his friend, afraid for the crew of the *Harbinger*.

"Mak?" Rhett asked.

Basil shook his head, pulling his sleeve back down again.

"She doesn't have it," he said. "And she doesn't know that *I* have it, so you better keep it to yourself."

"You haven't told her?"

"No. We aren't exactly on the greatest terms right now."

"Why? Because you wanted to come find me?" Rhett knew that Mak had never been his biggest fan. By the time Urcena attacked the *Harbinger*, though, they had become almost friends. He knew how logical she was. She wouldn't have wanted to waste resources on a wild goose chase.

"No," Basil replied quietly. "Because I *wouldn't* come find you."

Another enormous silence thudded into the room.

"Oh" was all Rhett could think to say.

"Oh c'mon, mate! It's not like I didn't want to. It's just that . . ." Basil searched for the words. "It's just that we were never going to have a hope in hell of getting our ship back if we couldn't regroup and strengthen our morale. I mean, the *Harbinger* spit us out in bloody Indonesia, for God's sake! It's been one setback after another. For two fucking years. And when we couldn't find you where you died, on the highway . . ."

"You gave up," Rhett said.

"No. Not then. I gave up after we went to your *apartment* and you *still* weren't there. We got attacked by psychons there, too. Lost two more syllektors. That's when I gave up. But Mak . . . She hasn't stopped believing. And I shouldn't have, either."

Rhett stood and pushed a heavy breath out through his teeth.

"Well, don't get your hopes up just yet," he murmured. "We still don't even know if I can do . . . I don't even know. Resurrect the entire *Harbinger*? And for what? So Urcena can turn around and sink it again? It all sounds so impossible."

"It probably is. But you don't have any other choice, mate. We have to get the fight out of the living world as soon as possible."

Rhett turned back to him. "What do you mean?"

Gesturing to the corkboard filled with the newspaper clippings and maps, Basil said, "Psychons are killing the living. And there are syllektors helping them."

Rhett kept on staring at his friend but with eyes that were steadily growing wider. He turned those eyes back to the board, and he let the information there flood over him.

It was crammed with overlapping articles about tragic accidents caused by "strange" or "mysterious" circumstances—fires starting out of nowhere, buses flipping over in stand-still traffic, windows shattering forty floors up and the falling glass slicing into groups of tourists—things that looked like accidents but felt like something else. The most recent article was about a cruise ship that was overrun by chaos in the middle of the Baltic Sea, with several of the few survivors claiming to have witnessed people being torn apart by some "invisible force" right in front of them. The cruise ship eventually capsized after an explosion on board blew a hole in its starboard side. There were one hundred and nine casualties.

"Oh my God . . . ," he whispered.

"This is what we know," Basil said after Rhett was finally able to tear his eyes away from the corkboard. "We know that when the *Harbinger* was attacked, it was a coordinated effort led by our favorite unholy-monster-child," Basil went on. Some of his humor had resurfaced, and Rhett was glad to see him looking a bit more animated. "And *she* had Treeny's help. Or, as the case turned out to be, she was using Treeny. And then she was using Theo."

A chilly drop of guilt ran through Rhett at hearing Theo's name. He'd inadvertently ghosted the big guy, and the thought of it still made his heart feel heavy and sore.

"Right," he interjected, if only to get his mind off Theo. "I think she needs to use someone as a . . . a conduit or something."

Basil cocked a finger at him. "Righto, mate. The thing is, Urcena may seem all-powerful, but she needs some kind of soul to latch on to in order to manifest herself."

"Back at the house," Rhett said, "there was someone in the trees. Some guy. I only saw him for a second, but I knew he was a syllektor."

Basil nodded. "That's the leader of the other group of syllektors who survived. And he's almost definitely Urcena's new . . . conduit, as you called it. His name is Anton Markeski."

"Great, so he's a Bond villain."

Basil genuinely chuckled for the first time since they had escaped the house.

"How many are there in this *other* group?" Rhett asked, still trying to wrap his head around the idea that there were syllektors out there helping the psychons. Helping *Urcena*.

"We're not sure," Basil said. "One or two hundred, maybe. Could be more. Most of them probably aren't even aware that Markeski is being used by Urcena. They're just following him because they're against us and what we stand for."

"Which is?"

"You, mate." Basil looked away uncomfortably for a moment, trying to find the words in the grain of the wooden desktop. "You heard Jon's mom out there. You're the Twice-Born Son. We had to talk you up a bit to get people behind the cause, behind the idea that the *Harbinger* could somehow be saved. Problem is, nobody's actually seen you do what you can do. So what we mostly succeeded at was pushing people away. Markeski took advantage of that, started doing the opposite of what we tried to do. He and his whole group blame *you* for the sinking of the *Harbinger*."

Rhett stepped up to the windows that lined the outer walls of the office and stared out at the factory floor, where by now most of the crew were hunkered down, either willing their bodies to sleep or not bothering and just sitting, watching the fires burn in their barrels.

He understood why they would want to blame him. He understood that his power, his revival—it was all cause to be suspicious. The power really was the thing that Urcena had been after. She would have torn that ship apart to get it. But the crew didn't understand that. All they saw was one syllektor who stood out from the rest, who was a target for this evil thing that had destroyed their home.

"So Markeski's group, the ones that don't know the full story, they're helping the psychons attack the living because . . . why?" Rhett said quietly.

"Because right now they don't have any other choice. Urcena and Markeski ghost any syllektors that get in their way. Urcena's promised to leave the crew alone so long as they do what she wants until she can get her hands on you. All she's wanted up until today is to keep her army fed and happy."

"And they really believe that once Urcena has me she'll go away? Just like that?"

Rhett could see Basil nodding in the smudged reflection of the window.

"That's the gist of it. Their group doesn't believe that the *Harbinger* is ever going to be resurrected. They're trying to start a new way of the afterlife. One where syllektors remain on this plane with the living and have a twisted partnership with the psychons. For every soul that's gathered and protected, another one is sacrificed to the big bad creepies. It's sick, but they're convinced it's the only way to keep on existing. They'll do whatever they have to in order to get there. But first they have to get rid of Urcena. In order to do that . . ."

"They have to help her get rid of me," Rhett finished. *The only way to win is if everyone keeps playing.*

Basil didn't respond, but the pause was answer enough.

After a few minutes, Rhett said, "Jon told me you have a plan. What is it?"

There was a clock hanging above the door. Rhett had been listening to it tick during their entire conversation. Now Basil looked up at it, and Rhett followed his gaze. His body wasn't tired, but his mind was exhausted.

"We can go over it in the morning, mate," Basil said. He stood and stretched out his arms. Rhett could hear crackling in Basil's bones, and halfway through the stretch, Basil put the back of his hand to his mouth and yawned. It was almost as if Basil weren't dead at all. And

Rhett knew that somewhere under all those layers, his friend was deteriorating. He had to help him.

"Mak should be here in the morning," Basil went on, obviously ignoring Rhett's concerned stare. "We can all get together and talk then."

"Okay." Rhett turned away, ready to head down and join the rest of the crew where he belonged.

"Oh, mate, there's one other thing," Basil said.

Rhett looked back.

"I need a first mate." Now Basil was grinning the same old idiotic grin that Rhett hated and also kind of loved. "Mak won't do it. Neither will Jon, which was kind of a surprise. And nobody else is really . . . qualified."

"You mean trustworthy?" Rhett asked, smirking himself now.

Basil chuckled again. "Exactly."

"Glad to know I was number three on your list," Rhett jabbed.

"Listen, I'll put you right back where you came from," Basil said. Even though it was meant to be a joke, the gravity of everything fell in on top of them again. They just couldn't escape it.

"I'd be honored," Rhett finally said.

"Good lad," Basil replied, and stuck out his hand.

They shook and then, without another word, they hugged. Because what else was there to do when their entire world had fallen apart around them, when the last little slivers were about to slip through their fingers, but hold on to each other?

FOUR

His dreams were infected by memories.

Of the house and the broken motion of time. Of the *Harbinger*, tilted and plunging into the waves. Of Urcena, staring at him with her deadly white pupils from the shadowy corner of his haunting ground.

For a few horrible moments, he was sure that he was back there, that everything else—his rescue, his conversation with Basil—had been a dream. He was so sure, he started to scream inside his own head, begging for it not to be true, begging to be set free again, until . . .

. . . until he jerked awake and nearly fell out of his cot.

He sat up, feeling the panic fade as his senses retreated back into their dormancy. The thud of his racing heart drifted away like the drumbeat of a rock song fading out into silence.

From where he sat, Rhett could see most of the factory floor. It was early; bright sunshine angled in and stretched across the entire facility, but most of the syllektors were already pulsing through the building, keeping busy with morning tasks. There was a group making breakfast—scrambled eggs and canned fruit, it looked like. There were a few that paced back and forth just outside the roll-up door, heaving shovelfuls of fresh snow away from the entrance. There was a team of three working at an old furnace that glowed with fire and heat, apparently forging new weapons. It was almost as well operated as things had been aboard the *Harbinger*. Almost.

Rhett stood, folding his scratchy blanket and setting it back on top of the cot. Before he could walk away, he froze. Across the floor, tucked behind one of the steel pillars, was a man lying on a cot of his own. He was withered and shivering, and his neck was smeared with the same black rash that Rhett had seen on Basil's arm the night before. It traced its way up the veins along the man's throat. There was a woman with him, squatting beside the cot, holding a mason jar.

Trying not to look too obvious, Rhett squinted in that direction, wanting to see what was going on. As he watched, the woman lifted the mason jar to the man's lips. Within the glass, a cloudy mist swirled, pulsating, glowing slightly between the woman's fingers. A soul. The soul of a person who had died and had been captured there, in a common jar. And as Rhett watched, the man on the cot inhaled, pulling the soul out of the mason jar and into his own lungs. He took it in like cigarette smoke, closing his eyes and putting his head back in relief. He scratched at his neck, and even though flakes of ash came peeling off, Rhett was sure that he saw the rash recede just slightly, slipping back down his neck, below the line of his collar.

They were using souls to treat the Ash.

It made sense. The *Harbinger* was not only a place of protection for the souls the syllektors collected; it was also powered by them. Which meant that the energy that maintained the syllektors' existence came more from the souls than it did the ship itself. If the Ash was caused by prolonged separation from that energy, using souls to try to fend off the symptoms was the most logical thing to do.

But Rhett still felt an unpleasant throb of anxiousness at the back of his mind.

He turned from the scene and stepped away from his cot, feeling on edge. The concrete floor was slick with melted snow and streaked with smears of orange rust and mud. He sidestepped a group of crew members who were carrying big crates full of canned food and bottles of water toward the back of the factory, where there appeared to be storerooms.

He was almost all the way to Basil's office when a voice called out to him.

"Hey, slacker!" the voice yelled, ringing against the iron support beams.

Rhett grinned, turning. Mak was walking toward him. The sun pouring in from the open door lit her dark hair like a sheet of bronze, and her long legs took equally long strides to close the distance between them. Rhett couldn't help but notice that she was wearing a genuine smile of her own.

When she reached him, she surprised him with a hug, wrapping her arms around him tightly, right there among the rest of the crew. Rhett hugged her back, as happy to see her as he had been to see Basil. Another surprise, if he was really being honest.

After a moment, Mak whispered in his ear.

"Dude, what the hell happened to your hair?" she said, and burst out laughing as she pulled away.

"I really don't want to talk about it," Rhett replied, though he was still smiling. He had a feeling that every time he was on the verge of forgetting about the new lack of color to his hair, someone was going to remind him.

"Oh, I don't ever want to *not* talk about it," Mak said. She stifled even more laughter as she reached up and tousled his hair.

When her giggles had run their course, Mak looked at him seriously.

"It really is good to see you," she said. "It's been . . . a while. Did Basil bring you up to speed?"

"For the most part," Rhett replied. "Everything except for this mysterious plan I keep hearing about."

She nodded, staring at the floor, her arms crossed.

"And Mak?"

She looked at him.

"It's good to see you, too."

A tiny smile played across her lips as she tilted her head in the direction of the stairs that led up to the office.

"Let's go find Jon and el capitán himself, and we'll go over everything," she said. "And, just a warning? You're not gonna like it."

He didn't reply, but Rhett had already figured that much out for himself.

They convened outside, by the river.

Today was different. Still cold but brighter, Rhett thought, and he suddenly missed the constant storm clouds and unsettled waves of the river in the afterlife. That river looked more like an ocean, vast enough for the *Harbinger* to have been sailing it for eternity with no end in sight. *This* river was spilling over its banks from the runoff of melting snow and dripping icicles. Its edges were frozen, bits of ice continuously gluing themselves together and breaking apart as the water rushed past.

Behind them, the factory cut into the bright white of the snow-covered trees, its dark mass like a splotch of ink on an otherwise flawless page. In the daylight, Rhett could see hulking metal tanks and pipes twisting around one another at the far end of the factory's main building, and he could see the smokestack more clearly, empty and crumbling but still reaching for the cloudless sky.

Rhett stood with one foot propped up on a rock, arms folded across his chest, watching the stones at the bottom of the river. Mak was beside him, facing the other way, staring up at the dark walls of the steel mill. Jon was there, too, sitting on a boulder, clanking his metal staff against the side of it in a slow rhythm. *Clink . . . clink. Clink . . . clink.*

They had been waiting on Basil, but now he was trudging down from the factory, his overcoat swishing around his knees. He was carrying a steaming ceramic mug.

"Did anybody else want some tea?" he asked, looking mostly at Jon and Rhett. "I asked for English Breakfast, but all they could find was Earl Grey, which between you and me tastes like straight piss and oil. But it'll have to do."

Rhett watched him take a sip from the mug and try to hold back a shudder, which he didn't do very well. If Basil was trying to keep

Mak and everyone else from knowing that he had the Ash, he was doing a less-than-spectacular job of it.

"Are you done whining about your beverage?" Mak asked. Her voice was cold and even.

Rhett blinked back and forth between Mak and Basil. He could see Jon out of the corner of his eye doing the same thing, no longer clanking his staff against the boulder.

Basil stared at Mak through the rising steam of his tea, and Rhett thought he saw hurt in his eyes.

"Carry on, then," Basil said quietly. He set his mug down in the snow and left it there without taking another sip.

Mak had an item in each of her hands. The first Rhett recognized at once. It was the lantern from the bridge on the *Harbinger*, its compass, the flame designed to guide the ship to whatever its destination was. The other item was a file folder, stuffed with an uneven stack of papers. Mak held the lantern up. It had gone out on the day the *Harbinger* sank and was still dark now, the charred wick behind the glass cold and stiff.

"We all remember what this is?" she asked, her eyes darting between the three boys and lingering for just a hair longer on Rhett.

They all nodded.

"Good. Because this is what we need to get back to the *Harbinger*." Mak looked down at the rough metal and glass of the lantern. "Even though the ship went down and we haven't been able to find any active doorways back to the afterlife, if we can get this flame lit, it will guide us back to the *Harbinger*."

"Wait. How do we know that?" Rhett asked. "If there's no ship to guide, how is it supposed to help us?"

"It doesn't just guide the ship," Basil said. "The flame in that lantern guides the person who possesses it."

"To where?"

"Wherever they need to be," Mak said.

"So, when the lantern is on board the *Harbinger*, it's guiding the whole crew?" Rhett still wasn't following.

"No," Jon interrupted, getting up from his boulder and moving to stand with the group. "You forget that the *Harbinger* has a very specific power source running through her. The lantern doesn't guide the crew . . ."

"It guides the souls," Rhett finished. He had been on board the *Harbinger* for almost a year before Urcena arrived and wrenched it away from them, and yet he was still learning new things about how it really worked.

"But now," Mak went on, "those souls are at the bottom of the river in the afterlife. And *we* need to get to *them*."

"Which means that the lantern will take us there," Rhett said. "I get it. But how do we get it lit again? You guys have obviously tried, right?"

"Well, you can't just light a match and hold it away from the wind, mate," Basil said. "The lantern is ancient. It's powerful. It won't light for just anybody."

There was a pause. The river shushed beside them, indifferent to the struggles of the dead. Rhett thought that the day was too bright and peaceful for a conversation like this. He wanted to just sit near

the water and let the quiet chatter of the forest roll over him. Still and calm and undisturbed.

But he had to press on.

"Okay," he said. "If the lantern won't light for us, then who?"

Mak and Basil exchanged a glance. Rhett watched it pass between them, a silent discussion. He was happy that they weren't staring daggers at each other, but were they really debating whether to tell him every detail of their plan? Judging by the way that Jon was eyeing the two of them, Rhett could tell that he was out of the loop, too.

Finally, Basil and Mak looked away from each other.

"This is going to sound . . . unbelievable," Mak said.

"Like, every-urban-legend-rolled-into-one unbelievable," Basil added.

"Guys, just spit it out," Rhett snapped. "You think I can't handle unbelievable at this point? The fact that we're even standing here having this conversation is unbelievable."

Mak sighed, and Basil nodded at her to go ahead.

"The only way to get this lantern lit again is to find the person who created it in the first place," she said. Her eyes were shut and her shoulders were tense, as if she couldn't believe she was saying any of this.

"You've got to be kidding me," Jon said. He let his arms flop to his sides in exasperation.

"I know how it sounds," Mak said.

"I really don't think you do," Jon shot back.

"I don't understand any of this," Rhett interrupted. "What's the big deal?"

"The big deal," Basil said, "is that the creator of the lantern was also the original captain of the *Harbinger*, back when it was just that lowly rowboat. Remember?"

Rhett felt his mouth drop open. He forced it shut, but it fell open again. He remembered his Greek mythology. He knew about Charon and the ferry across the River Styx. He thought about his conversation with Captain Trier on his second night aboard the *Harbinger*. They'd talked a little bit about that story. And now they were going to seek out its main character?

When Rhett found his voice again, he said, "And this person still . . . exists?"

"As far as we know, yes. There's no record of him ever being destroyed," Mak said.

"In the literature aboard the ship, he's referred to as *ploigós ton nekrón*," Basil said, botching his Greek.

"Navigator of the Dead," Jon translated.

Rhett tried to let all of it sink in. The idea of a person who was as old as the *Harbinger* itself, who had created the ship and was thereby responsible for the continued existence of everyone standing in the group right now, was more than a little daunting.

But maybe that wasn't it at all.

The Navigator had created the ship, yes. But had he created its purpose? Rhett supposed they were going to have the opportunity to find out.

He looked at Basil and said, "You probably already know what my next question is going to be, but I'll ask it anyway. If the Navigator is still out there, how do we find him?"

Basil was staring at the ground, poking at a few pebbles with the toe of his boot. The brightening sunlight cast long shadows across his gaunt face, deepening the hollows of his features. With his head tilted that way, his face looked almost like a bare skull, and Rhett felt a twinge of panic rumble through his mind. For a second he let go, and his senses came alive. He felt the cold air biting against his skin, he could smell the pine trees and the melting snow, and he could feel that panic, like an earthquake in his heart, at the thought of losing Basil.

Rhett didn't care what they were planning; he would do it. He would do whatever it took, and not even necessarily for the sake of the entire crew. Right now, he was only really interested in saving his friend.

Mak stepped forward, her feet crunching into the snow, and held out the file folder for Rhett to take. He took it and flipped it open to the first page. Beside him, Jon was craning his neck to see the contents himself, and Rhett repositioned so that they could both look together. Jon had already done so much for him in the short time they had known each other, and clearly Basil trusted him.

The page that sat on top of the stack of documents was a printout of an old news article. It was from a Pennsylvania newspaper, and the headline read: LOCAL SURGEON LOSES LICENSE AFTER DANGEROUS PROCEDURE TO SAVE SON. Rhett didn't even have to scan the article to know that it was about his father, about the surgery he'd performed to remove a tumor that Rhett had developed as a baby, still inside his mom's womb. It was that very procedure that had led Captain Trier to believe that Rhett was a so-called Twice-Born Son. It was easy logic to follow but a harder reality to grapple with.

Below the news article, there were a few other documents with information about Rhett. He found a copy of his birth certificate alongside a copy of his own death certificate (which gave him the creeps). There was a copy of the lease to his family's apartment in New York, with notes scribbled in the margins in what could only be Mak's perfect, boxy lettering. Information about where Rhett's parents had both worked, where Rhett had been going to high school, the names of a few close relatives. It was amazing to think that all this information was years old, when it still felt like yesterday to Rhett.

"This is how you found me," he said quietly, flipping through the documents.

"It was a pain in the ass," Mak replied. "Thank God we can't be seen by the living, because it could have been *way* more complicated than it was. That's not the part you need to be looking at, though. Keep going."

When Rhett got through all the documentation that pertained to him, he flipped to the next page. He found another printout, this time of a grainy photograph from a newspaper article dating back to 1947. The copy alongside the photograph was almost illegible, and the faces in the photo itself were mostly blurred, but Rhett could make out what he needed to. The photo showed two rows of stoic, fearsome-looking men. They were mobster types, dressed in pinstriped suits and fedoras. One guy on the end even carried a tommy gun. These were legitimate gangsters from the 1940s, and there in the back row was a face that Rhett would have recognized anywhere, a face that he still saw grinning maniacally back at him whenever he closed his eyes: Theo. The big lug was impossible to miss, and he looked as if he had been plucked right off the *Harbinger* and stuck into the photograph.

Behind the article was a death certificate for Theo, with an empty address box circled in red ink. After that were a couple more news articles, all pertaining to the same group of gangsters as the first one. These articles had a few lines highlighted, with more of Mak's notes in the margins. Rhett didn't need to read everything to understand where this was going.

If she had been able to locate Rhett's ghost, she had clearly been able to locate Theo's. And if she had been able to locate Theo's . . .

He turned one more page and found her staring back at him, her red hair pulled into a tight ponytail, her cheeks smattered with freckles, her glasses sitting too big and heavy on her nose. It was a full-size yearbook photo, and in it she was smiling, innocent and happy and alive. But this was not the version of Treeny that Rhett had known. It never would be.

"Nope," he said, snapping the folder shut with one hand. "No way." Beside him, Jon took a step back, a hand rubbing at the side of his face.

"Just hear us out—" Mak started.

"I don't need to hear anything," Rhett shot back. "Were you not both there when Treeny betrayed us all? When she ghosted Trier? When she tried to take *that*?" He pointed a finger at the lantern that was still in Mak's hand, dangling at her side.

"It wasn't all her, mate," Basil said.

"Of course you would say that," Rhett said, his voice rising. "You would say anything to justify what happened to her." The words slipped before he could hold them back, and the image of Basil's scythe colliding with Treeny as she leaped to protect Urcena assaulted his mind.

"*And you don't think I've paid for it?!*" Basil roared, stepping toward Rhett. "I didn't ask for this. I didn't ask to be captain. I didn't ask to be put in charge of this entire crew. But here we are. Two bloody years later, and I've had enough of hiding, of just surviving until tomorrow." His voice went low, dangerously quiet. "If I'm going to be captain, I want my goddamn ship back."

Rhett could only stare. He had never seen Basil this angry. The silence hung heavy between them. The only sounds were the river and a steady clanking from inside the factory. More weapons being forged, Rhett was sure, but from here it sounded almost as if the factory were operating again.

"You're right," Rhett said after a moment. "That wasn't fair. I'm sorry. I just . . . I still don't understand the plan. As much as I would love to have Theo back, and as much as I want to hope that we can still trust Treeny, how is bringing them back going to help?"

Mak let out a long breath, then said, "Treeny's the only person with enough knowledge about the *Harbinger* and its history to be able to tell us how to find the Navigator. She spent so much time in the library, compiling information in that damned tablet of hers. She knew that ship inside and out. The only person who would have known it better than her was Captain Trier."

"So why don't we track *him* down instead?" Rhett asked.

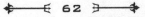

"We tried. But he was on board the ship for a really, really long time. I couldn't find a record of him anywhere."

"And Theo?"

"You saw him in action," Basil said. "We need his muscle if we stand any chance of defending ourselves along the way."

"Yeah, but I also saw him snap a syllektor's spine with his bare hands when Urcena had control of him," Rhett said. "How do we know the same thing won't happen again?"

"We don't," Mak replied simply. "But we're hoping that Urcena's connection with Markeski has grown strong enough at this point that she wouldn't want to just abandon it. We don't know how it works exactly, but in the last year or so, we've only ever seen her connected to him. If she had wanted to take control of any one of us, she could have. But she hasn't."

Rhett opened the folder again and stared at the pictures of Theo and Treeny. He turned over the pages of Treeny's information. She had been a middle schooler in Nebraska when she died. Her death certificate said "blunt force trauma/drowning." He could only wonder what happened.

"There's another reason we need Theo," Mak continued. "Treeny was close to him. She trusted him. He was like a big brother to her. We have no idea what state of mind she's going to be in. We need Theo there to help calm her down. And besides that . . . he's kind of a test run."

"Test run?" Rhett asked. But the meaning was clear as soon as the words left his mouth. "You mean to make sure that I can actually do this."

"Yes," Mak replied. "But also to make sure that Treeny won't automatically be compromised by Urcena. If we revive Theo and he's already susceptible to Urcena, then we know we can't revive Treeny."

"And then we have to start over," Basil added quietly.

The four of them stood in silence for what felt like the hundredth time during this conversation, which seemed to be taking years instead of minutes. The plan that Basil and Mak had come up with was so far beyond what Rhett had imagined, beyond what he thought was even possible.

"Okay." Rhett sighed. "Let's say we do all of . . . *this*." He shook the file folder that was still in his hand. "Do we even know *why* we're doing it?"

"What do you mean?" Jon asked.

Rhett glanced back at him. "I mean, what's Urcena's plan? Her *real* plan. We know she wants me and my power. We know she has an army of psychons and syllektors at her disposal. What's stopping her from marching in here right now and wiping us all out? I . . . I saw her. When I was haunting that house."

"You *what*?" Mak cried.

"She came to me," Rhett went on. "I asked her why she didn't just take me if I was all she wanted."

"Did she give you an answer?" Basil said.

"Not really." Rhett paused. "If she has this ability to bring people back to life, then she has leverage over the living world, right? She has trillions of souls that she could revive and use however she wants. But . . . that doesn't feel like everything. It feels so . . ."

"Simple," Jon finished.

Rhett gave him a grateful look. "Exactly."

A few branches above them quivered in the chilly breeze.

"If we can bring Treeny back," Basil started, "then that's something else she can help shed some light on." He didn't sound excited at the prospect.

Mak nodded. "He's right. We don't know how long Urcena was attached to Treeny, but it was long enough. If anyone knows what Urcena's plan really is, it'll be Treeny."

Rhett groaned, pinching the bridge of his nose. After a moment, he looked up.

"So let me get this straight," he said. "We're going to find Theo's ghost and revive him, hoping that he doesn't rip us all apart as soon as we do. And then, as long as Theo isn't possessed by any demons, we're all going to find Treeny's ghost, revive *her*, get her to tell us what she knows about Urcena and how to find this Navigator person, and then . . . what? We're a big happy family again, off to see the wizard?"

"No," Basil said, and something in his voice stopped Rhett cold. "Theo is still up in the air. Who knows if he'll even want to be a part of this after what he's been through. But we need Treeny for one thing and one thing only. After she gives us the information we need . . ." He trailed off.

Mak flinched at the implication that followed.

But Rhett blinked back and forth between them, incredulous. "Then what? What, Basil? Then we ghost her again? Just like that?"

Basil wouldn't look at him. He stared out at the river.

"These are monstrous days, mate," he said. "And monstrous days call for monstrous deeds."

FIVE

Rhett couldn't take anymore. He left the others on the riverbank and trudged back up to the factory. He didn't know where he was planning on going. The factory wasn't like the *Harbinger*—he didn't have his own cabin to escape to. Even if he went back to his cot and sat staring at the wall for a couple hours, he would still be able to feel the curious and accusing eyes on his back.

But he couldn't stand another second of talking about ghosts and resurrection, not to mention what they were planning on doing to Treeny. Yes, she had betrayed them. Some could argue that she was single-handedly responsible for bringing down the *Harbinger*— if not for her distracting Rhett and the others on the bridge, they might have been able to warn the rest of the crew in time. But how much of that had been Treeny and how much of it had been Urcena? How much of it had been both? There was too much gray area for Rhett to say for certain that Treeny deserved the fate she got.

Instead of going back into the factory, he cut into the forest. The quiet of winter had settled down among the low hills—no animal sounds, no buzzing bugs, no whisper of leaves. There was the occasional *pat-pat* sound of dripping water, but that was it.

Rhett knew that wandering out into the woods alone, dressed in all black amid the blanket of snow, was not a great idea. He just needed a minute. To gather himself. To remind himself a few thousand times that Mak and Basil's plan was the *only* plan. They could never be like Markeski and these "new world" syllektors. They weren't about to stand by and let Urcena reign over death.

How much did they still have to lose before they got everything back?

Something snapped behind him.

He swung around, yanking his knuckle blade out of its newly refashioned sheath on his thigh. The blades sent curved strips of light sweeping across the snow.

"Whoa there, Wolf Man." It was Jon, standing with his hands up as if Rhett had just pulled a gun on him. "Didn't mean to catch you midtransformation." He grinned, crossing his arms. His hat looked extra red in the bright light, despite how ratty and worn-out it was.

Still confused about Jon's comment, Rhett cocked his head at him.

"Your claw," he said in response, tilting his head toward the knuckle blade.

"I cannot catch a break with this thing," Rhett said, rolling his eyes. But he laughed a little bit just the same, remembering training days with the others back on the ship and how they would rag on him constantly about his choice of weapon.

"How are you feeling?" Jon still had his arms folded, and Rhett couldn't help but notice how much he clung to himself, how noticeably cold he seemed to be.

"Okay," he said. "So far." He fiddled with the handle of his blade, picking at it. "Actually . . . I've been better."

"I think we all have," Jon replied. He took a step closer and leaned against a tree. Rhett noticed the distinct shake of his fingers as a shiver ran through him.

"Some of us are worse off than others, though, right?" Rhett said, raising his eyebrows.

Jon laughed. It was thin and missing any kind of humor.

"Is it that obvious?" he asked.

"Kind of."

He sighed. "It's only been a few weeks since I started to feel the cold. It's worse every day, but . . ."

"But what? You can't bring yourself to use a person's soul as your medication?" Rhett fought to keep the bitterness out of his voice, but failed.

Jon stared at him.

"This is why I knew they were right about you," he said. "You catch on quick."

"Yeah, well . . . sometimes I think it'd be easier if I didn't have to. If I was just another crew member."

"That was pretty rough back there." Jon peered up at the naked blue sky for a moment. "I'd like to say I'm still skeptical, but . . . I saw what you did back at that house. I know the circumstances aren't great. Your power, though, or whatever you want to call it, is something to believe in. We need that right now." He paused, then said, "And to answer your question, no. I won't use the souls to help my . . . condition. It's not right."

"What do you mean?"

"It's against our nature to use the souls directly like that, without the filter and distribution of the *Harbinger*. At this point the only reason we're even still collecting souls is because of the Ash. If we keep going this way, we're no better than the psychons." He shivered again.

Rhett couldn't argue with his logic. He had been appalled earlier that morning, watching the sick syllektor take in that soul, watching its power heal him, if only temporarily. What would he have done if that was one of his parents' souls?

"Besides," Jon went on, "there are . . . risks to using the souls as treatment. Even though, theoretically, it doesn't harm the soul at all, it could do some pretty serious damage to a syllektor if they hold on to one too long."

"Like?"

Jon waved him off, though. "I've had enough depressing talk for one day. Let's just say it gets weird."

They were quiet for a while.

"Does your mom know?" Rhett asked Jon. "About you and the Ash, I mean."

He nodded. "I didn't even bother trying to hide it. Nothing gets past that woman."

Rhett smiled, then said, "I never really thanked you. For everything you did back at the house. I might not be standing here if not for you having my back, Jon. And you did that before you even really knew me, so . . . thank you."

Jon shrugged. "No need to thank me. You don't always have to know exactly what you're fighting for. You just have to believe that it's good. Or at least better."

"How am I looking so far?"

Jon cocked an eyebrow, thinking about it.

"TBD," he said finally, and they both laughed.

They made their way back to the factory together, and Rhett was glad for the distraction. Jon tried to catch him up on the last two years of pop culture and news, but most of it went over his head—other than music, he hadn't really been that connected to the world in the first place.

When they stepped back into the dim light of the factory together, Jon's mom was working over one of the fires, turning hot dogs that were hanging over the flames on skewers. She looked up and saw Rhett and Jon. She smiled.

"It's nice to see you again, Rhett," she said as they approached.

"You too, Miss . . . ?" Rhett said.

"Marta, please. Just Marta." She gave him another lovely smile. Almost as lovely as his own mother's. "Care to join us for dinner, Rhett? We like to go sit out by the river and eat sometimes."

Rhett opened his mouth to say that he would love to join them, but before he could, he spotted Basil. He was standing up at the top of the stairs leading to his office, gripping the metal railing, staring out over the crew as they milled about. He looked drained and withered and alone.

"Actually, I'll have to take a rain check," Rhett said to Marta. "But could I have two of those to go?"

He gave Jon and Marta another smile and then he took his two hot dogs and climbed the steps to where Basil stood.

"Thought you might be hungry," he said, holding one of the hot dogs, now wrapped in a stale bun, out to Basil.

Basil shook his head.

"Eat something," Rhett pushed. "You'll feel better. I promise."

"I don't need to eat something," Basil murmured. "I need a new bloody plan."

Rhett closed his eyes and sighed.

"No, you don't," he said. "The plan you have is the only option. I've been over it and over it."

"Tell me about it," Basil replied, finally taking a hot dog and looking genuinely relieved. "Listen, mate. I'm not any happier about it than you are. I just . . ."

"It's okay. We don't have a choice. I get it."

They were quiet for a minute, both of them taking bites out of their hot dogs.

Through a mouthful of crumbling bun, Basil said, "This could use some tartar sauce." Flecks of moist bread and meat went flying as he spoke.

"You're disgusting," Rhett replied, laughing. Then, with his own mouth full of food: "Wait . . . *tartar sauce?*"

And for the first time all day, Basil was the one to laugh.

Over the next few days, they finalized their plans.

Finding Theo's and Treeny's ghosts was going to be the most difficult part; they'd proved with Rhett that the most obvious place isn't always where the haunting occurs. Mak was certain that she had their locations locked down, though.

"We had nothing to go by when we started looking for you," she told Rhett. Then she waved her file folder of stolen information at him. "With them, we have plenty."

Theo was (hopefully) haunting a graveyard in New York City, where he was buried. But Treeny was nowhere nearby. According to what Mak had been able to dig up, Treeny's ghost was at her parents' house in Nebraska.

"So we pick up Theo first," Mak said. They all stood around the desk in Basil's office, with maps and paperwork spread out across its entire surface. "New York's just a couple of hours away from here. We can take one of the trucks the whole way."

"Then what?" Rhett asked. "We road-trip halfway across the country in a single pickup truck?" They knew for certain that the four of them—Rhett, Mak, Basil, and Jon—were going. With the addition of Theo, that would be five syllektors—though Theo probably counted as two—crammed into one vehicle for at least a couple of days.

"Nope," Basil said. "I wish."

Mak grunted.

"This is the part that Basil can't stand," she said. When Rhett raised his eyebrows at her, she explained, "From New York to Nebraska, we hop a train."

Basil groaned.

"What's so bad about that?" Rhett asked him.

"He died in a train accident," Mak said, cocking her thumb in

Basil's direction. Her tone was so nonchalant. "Hasn't been much of a fan since."

"You should've seen him on a plane," Jon murmured, glancing at Rhett.

"There's more to it than that," Basil said, putting his hands up defensively. "But . . . yes. I don't particularly enjoy modern forms of transportation."

"Well that explains a lot," Rhett said.

Basil gave him a confused look.

"I saw you behind the wheel of the truck," Rhett replied. "Your driving sucks."

Basil stuffed his hand into the inside of his blazer. "Hang on, mate, I think I have something for you," he said. And when his hand reemerged from the blazer, one of its fingers was sticking up at Rhett.

The four of them laughed, and they took a moment before diving back into their preparations to let it linger. Rhett couldn't help but feel a pang of regret that Treeny and Theo weren't already here with them. This was what they had done back on the *Harbinger*—train and prepare and poke fun at one another—back when they were still a team. Now Rhett didn't know what they were. And if things went the way they were supposed to, Treeny would never see the inside of the *Harbinger* again. They were going to use her for information and then betray her the way she had betrayed them. Rhett still didn't know if he was okay with that. But it didn't matter what he was okay with. This was bigger than him, bigger than all of them. This was the entire afterlife resting on their shoulders, on Rhett's ability to revive. There were souls out there that had either been eaten by psychons or had been left to float away into the atmosphere, full of fear and regret and anger and confusion, until they were just more stardust. They couldn't let that continue.

They had their plan. They would get back their lost team members, track down the Navigator, find the *Harbinger*, and restore the ship so that the next time Urcena wanted a fight, they would have something to fight with.

Rhett could do little more than hope that it would work.

And hope that they were all strong enough to go through with it.

Rhett slammed the tailgate on the truck shut. He and Mak would be riding back there, but they were also bringing a few things with them. Mostly their weapons—Basil's scythes, Mak's machete, Jon's staff. They had a crate full of canned food, a box of Mak's research, a bunch of maps, some extra coats, and some kind of AM/FM radio with extra wires and tubes attached to it: Jon's "spirit radio." They had used it to talk to Rhett before manifesting his ghost via electrified cage. Hopefully they could use it to talk to Theo's and Treeny's ghosts, as well.

And of course there was the lantern, the thing they needed to fix before they could start to fix anything else.

Before Rhett could head back inside, the lantern-keeper herself appeared beside him, carrying one last box of bottled water. Mak reached into the bed of the truck and set it down before turning back to Rhett.

"Listen," she said. "I know I wasn't too fond of you when you first joined up, but . . . Well, I just hope you know we're past that now. You don't have to get all stiff every time you see me coming."

"I know," Rhett said, nodding again. "I appreciate it, but that's honestly not what I'm tense about."

"Treeny?" she asked after a moment.

"Treeny," he said.

It was her turn to nod. "I know. I don't think I have any good way to justify it, other than—"

"It's what we have to do," Rhett finished for her. He put a hand on her shoulder. "I know."

She smiled at him, and even though it was a worn-out, exhausted smile, it was still full of appreciation. Rhett tried to smile back but couldn't come up with much more than a grimace. He turned away quickly, hoping Mak hadn't seen how pained that look had been.

It was another clear day, though not quite as crisp. The sun wasn't just bright today; it was hot, too. It was beginning to cut through the ice and snow, leaving behind sagging wet branches and strange outlines of the trees in the snow that had survived in their shade.

Rhett and Mak didn't say anything for a while. They just stood by the truck and let the weight of what they were about to do cling to them, wishing it would just melt and drip away like the snow. It wasn't just Treeny. It was the whole mission. Of seeking out the ghosts of their friends and bringing them back from that horrible reality. There were so many unanswered questions, so many *maybe*s and *what-if*s. They didn't even have proof that the Navigator was still out there. Their entire existence and the future of the world rested on a hunch.

A few minutes later, Basil and Jon emerged from the factory . . .

with most of the crew trailing behind them. Rhett stared at the crowd. They were here to send them off, he knew. But they were interested in more than that.

Basil shambled through the muck alone, his overcoat wrapped tightly around him. Marta was hovering nearby, but Jon had someone else with him, a guy with short-cut blond hair who looked around the same age as Jon and Rhett. He was holding Jon's hand, and while the others continued to the truck, Jon and the blond guy stepped aside for a moment.

"Ready to go?" Basil asked as he and Marta approached.

"I think so," Mak replied. Rhett nodded in agreement.

And before they could say anything else, the crowd of syllektors swarmed them. More accurately, the crowd swarmed *Rhett*. They took turns shaking his hand or patting him on the shoulder. He heard murmurs of "Twice-Born Son" and "savior of the *Harbinger.*" They thanked him. Over and over again, they thanked him. He wanted to tell them that he hadn't done anything yet, that he might not be able to do anything at all. But before he could even open his mouth, Rhett caught sight of himself in the truck's side-view mirror, standing as tall and as strong as he could, his hair the same color as the dwindling snow, and the syllektors, some of them clearly afflicted with the Ash, staring at him not just in hopeful appreciation but in reverence. He was more than just a syllektor to them now. He was their ticket home.

"All right, all right," Basil called. "Let's give the man some space, yeah?" He flapped his arms at the crew like wings, gesturing for them to step back. They obliged, though Rhett could still hear their whispers.

Beside the truck, Marta had her arms wrapped tightly around

Mak, murmuring something in her ear. Mak listened, patting the older woman on the back, clearly trying to reassure her. Rhett watched them for a second, until his eyes drifted over to where Jon and the blond-haired guy were standing. They held on to each other, hand in hand, talking emphatically. Rhett could tell that if either one of them had switched on their senses in that moment, they'd be crying. And after just a few more words, they quit talking, leaned in, and kissed.

Rhett nudged Basil, who was checking the gear in the back of the truck, and cocked his head in Jon's direction.

"How do you get lucky enough to have your mom *and* a boyfriend in the afterlife?" he asked.

Basil looked up, and a tiny grin settled along his lips.

"That's only been going on for a year or so," he said. "They met while we were hiding out here. They're pretty good together."

Rhett nodded, and they both continued to intrude on Jon's moment a little longer, watching as he and the blond-haired guy put their foreheads together, eyes closed.

"It's pretty amazing," Basil nearly whispered.

"What is?"

"Love after death. The idea that you could live your whole life without finding the person you belong with, only to stumble into them after you're both dead."

Rhett looked over at his friend, but Basil was no longer watching Jon and the blond; he was staring at Mak. She was standing on the other side of the truck, fingering the rusted edges of the metal. Maybe she felt Basil's eyes on her, maybe not. Either way, she didn't look up.

As he watched them not watching each other, Rhett's eyes began to shift, sweeping across the faces of those who had come out to see them off. They all had their own histories, their own tragic reasons for being members of this crew. Whether they'd wanted to go on existing after death or not, they were all here, and they had all found something in the afterlife that made them want to keep fighting, to keep surviving. All of it was in Rhett's hands now.

"Take care of my son," Marta said from beside Rhett. He hadn't even noticed she was there. "Please."

"I'll do my best," he replied, nodding. And he wasn't just talking about Jon.

Basil left Marta in charge and made sure she was clear on where she was supposed to lead the crew after Rhett and the rest of the team were gone. There was a rendezvous point set up in a whole other state, and the only two people who knew where it was were Basil and Jon's mom.

If all went according to plan, Basil's team would be able to open a door on the *Harbinger* that connected directly to the meet-up spot. When the *Harbinger* was destroyed, every door from the living world was cut off from the endless river. The only way to finally reunite the crew with the ship would be to get the lantern lit and use it to reestablish the connection from the other side.

After the details were discussed one last time, Basil drove the truck away from the steel mill, around the curved bends of the road that was barely a road, which, according to the rust-speckled signs Rhett saw, led out to I-78.

When they hit the highway, Basil opened it up, the beat-up old engine revving the way an elderly man clears his throat, and for a while they aimed simply for making good time instead of being discreet. They flew down the road with the sun winking off the truck's windows and the clean air blowing their hair into wild tangles. Rhett was glad that Jon and Basil were tucked away in the cab of the truck, away from the chill that hung in the air despite how bright and warm everything looked. He and Mak were doing just fine in the back. In fact, Mak was leaning back into the corner of the truck bed, her eyes closed, her hair pulled out behind her in long, fluttering ribbons. She was smiling. Rhett felt himself smiling, too, in spite of everything. He flipped his senses on, letting the sensation of actual feeling wash over his numbed body, and the slap of the cool air on his face felt amazing. It felt like the first real thing he'd experienced in a long time. Everything else might have just been some horrible dream.

It was just the four of them for now. With any luck, there would be five soon. And then six, if only briefly. Rhett almost wished that they'd brought more people, knowing what a handful of syllektors looked like against even a dozen psychons. But the more syllektors they risked for this wild goose chase, the stronger the possibility that the syllektors could be wiped out entirely.

Rhett tried to imagine what a world without syllektors would look like. Souls lost to oblivion or devoured by psychons. Urcena reigning over death as some sort of queen. Even if Rhett wouldn't allow her to use his power—and he never would, not for anything—she would find a way to take it from him. If she was capable of all the other terrible things she'd done, it was in her to do that. And in that same world, the *Harbinger* would still be gone, and the souls trapped within her hull would still be left unprotected, Rhett's parents among them.

It was a world that Rhett could not allow to be realized, even if it meant being ghosted again and having to carry on haunting that tiny house in the void of time forever. Like the rest of the crew that they'd just left behind, Rhett had found so much that was worth fighting for in his life after death.

He would fight until there was nothing left.

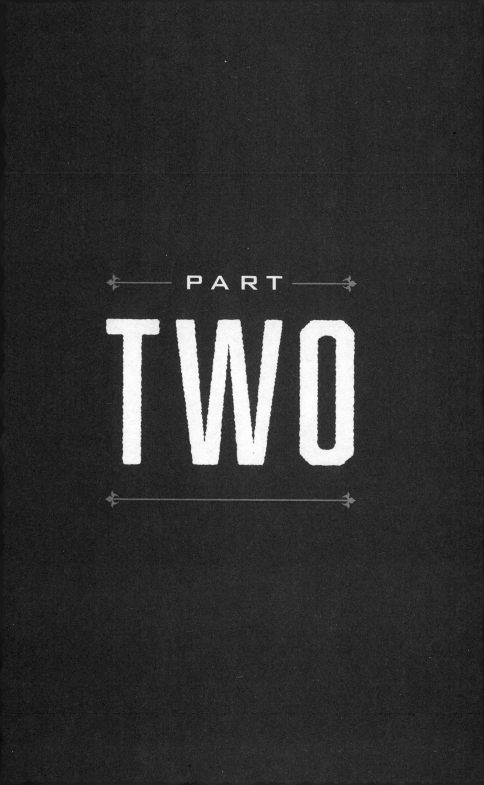

PART

TWO

SIX

It was only a couple of hours before the spires and high-rises of New York City began to jut up over the horizon. The city grew in the distance, more and more of it bubbling up as they got closer. Rhett felt a surge of homesickness at the sight of it. The sunlight winked off all the glass and metal, and the buildings stood tall in the clear winter air. He'd been back to New York a couple of times since his death, but only to gather souls—he hadn't had any time for visiting his old spots. He didn't now, either, but even with the confusing sadness that it brought, seeing the city in its entirety was enough to boost his spirits.

They drove through the shipyards of Newark, passing stacks of shipping containers and boat cranes on either side, and the occasional airplane growled past overhead on its way to the airport. Basil had told Rhett that their group of syllektors had spent some time out here, trying to hide among the shipping containers. That had ended rather quickly when they started to spot psychons lurking nearby.

"Heading into the tunnel!" Basil called out the open window. "Be on the lookout!"

The Holland Tunnel swallowed them up, bathing them in its murky yellow light. They had discussed the possibility of an attack here. If there was any decent place for Urcena and the psychons to try something, it was where Rhett and the others could be blocked in from all sides. Just like on the Golden Gate Bridge. That time, Urcena had only been interested in giving Rhett a message. This time, she would be here to destroy them.

But they passed through the tunnel without incident. It was late in the day and traffic was slow. Rhett saw a couple of drivers in the other lane do a double take at their truck, knowing that it probably looked as if the truck were driving itself, the syllektors inside not visible to the living eye. Otherwise, there were no problems.

When they emerged from the tunnel, Mak leaned in through the window from the back and gave Basil directions.

The city hummed and throbbed around them, and Rhett couldn't help but relish it—these were sounds that he thought he'd never hear again after he was ghosted. He sat back in the truck and listened to Mak and Basil argue over which street to turn down, to the raging cries of car horns, to the murmur of voices along the sidewalks, to the exchange of music from places all over the city. New York was an easy place to get lost in and an even easier place to fall in love with.

After another half an hour, Basil finally maneuvered the truck off the main thoroughfare. Mak guided him down narrow side streets lined with boarded-up houses and dilapidated apartment buildings. Weeds sprung up through cracks in the buckled asphalt and gnarled trees reached out from the sidewalks like bony claws—like psychon claws.

At the end of one of these streets, the asphalt and concrete stopped at a leaning wrought iron fence, coated entirely in rust and missing most of the points that were supposed to be on top. Beyond the fence were dead tangles of overgrown grass and a few old, black trees. Mixed in with the yellowed grass were tombstones, all of them at least fifty years old, all of them cracked and canted in odd directions like broken teeth. Between the distance and the weeds, Rhett couldn't make out any of the inscriptions on the tombstones, but he was sure that he probably didn't want to—even for someone who was already dead, old cemeteries gave him the shivers.

"This place rocks," Jon said as the truck came to a stop. He threw open his door and got out. He stood with his hands on his hips, surveying the cemetery from alongside the truck.

"This is really the place?" Basil asked Mak.

Mak rolled her eyes. "After everything else, you're really not going to trust me on this?" she said.

Basil pursed his lips and slammed the gearshift into park.

The three of them hopped out and stood along the fence. Jon was carrying his spirit radio. Above them, the sky was beginning to glow a deep pink, the sun fading. A tiny breeze whistled through the stiff grass. Rhett thought the whole place seemed alive in a very unpleasant way.

"Eyes peeled," Basil said quietly. "We know who we're looking for. Let's find him."

They jumped the fence, which wasn't difficult given that it was barely standing on its own, and dropped down into the cemetery as

the daylight began to fall apart. The lights of the city hung not far behind them, permanent stars that helped to light their way through the tombstones.

Rhett peered at the grave markers, trying to read the faded, weather-worn inscriptions. Most of them were illegible; he could make out part of a name here and there, but that was it. The others began to spread out, wading deeper into the overgrowth. Jon was still close by, though, and as he clicked on the spirit radio, the entire cemetery filled with a warbling static noise, like the white noise that normally came from a radio between stations, but intermingled with a moaning gurgle. When Jon moved the antenna around, the static and the moaning changed with it, fading in and out, cut with other sounds, sounds that Rhett could have sworn were voices . . . but not ones that belonged to disc jockeys or car salesmen.

Before Rhett could ask, Jon was already stepping away, crunching through the weeds like a bloodhound following a scent.

The rest of them carried on the old-fashioned way, bending down to read each tombstone, hoping every time that it was the one they were looking for.

Rhett stumbled through the cemetery, the scraggly weeds catching on his jeans. He kneeled down next to a few markers, staring at each one for a long time, waiting for anything familiar to appear. But as the light dwindled and night took over, it became harder and harder to make out even anything *un*familiar.

He opened his mouth to suggest that they camp out for the night (although the idea of sleeping in the cemetery was less than appealing) and start over tomorrow, when Jon called out.

"Over here!" he yelled, his voice carrying across the cemetery in a haunted sort of way.

The shadows of the others began to move in Jon's direction, and Rhett did the same. When Rhett reached Jon, he was standing perfectly still, staring down at the spirit radio in his hand. A little red bulb lit his face with a deep crimson glow. He looked like a red phantom hiding out among the graves. The radio itself was no longer just emitting static; there was a voice coming through, one that Rhett recognized—the thick New York accent was impossible to mistake.

Rhett was the first to get to Jon. "What's he saying?" he asked. Mak and Basil fumbled through the grass together a moment later, coming from the same direction.

Rhett strained to hear the voice coming from the radio.

"Billy . . . ," the voice was saying. "Billy, stay with me, pal . . ." It sounded urgent, but it also sounded plaintive, like an echo.

"Who's Billy?"

Jon shrugged. "A friend, maybe?" he said. "The radio seems to pick up signals from important moments in the subject's life. Stuff that's . . . well, haunting them."

Rhett wondered what they'd heard on the radio when they finally found *his* ghost. He couldn't help but think that *haunting* was the most accurate word. Because as much as his ghost had haunted that tiny house back in Pennsylvania, that tiny house had also haunted *him*.

Before Rhett could ask anything else about the spirit radio, Jon took a few steps forward. He seemed to lose the signal briefly, took a couple steps back, shuffled to the left.

"This way," he said.

They followed Jon deeper into the cemetery, watching the little red light on the radio as it bobbed above the grass, casting its glow across Jon's concentrated face and the rough outlines of the stone grave markers. The farther in they went, the more intricate the gravestones became, growing from simple slabs of concrete to full-on statues of angels with crumbling wings. They crouched atop their pedestals and stared down at the syllektors trudging past.

As the signal on the spirit radio became clearer, the distant, anguished voice becoming easier to make out, Rhett felt something shifting within *him* also. It was kind of like the push, which he hadn't felt since the day the *Harbinger* sank, but not as insistent. It pulsed inside him like a radar, thumping in time with the heartbeat he was supposed to no longer have. He thought of the girl in the fire and the purple electricity that revived her. He thought of the house in Pennsylvania, the ghost that he'd been. That heartbeat was a memory of his living self, the extra life that had been given to him by his parents. Without it, none of this would even be possible. Rhett reached for it, let it fill him up.

He followed it.

A few minutes later Jon stopped, and Rhett stepped up beside him. The darkness was heavy and smothering now, coating the cemetery in swaths of shadows that never quite seemed to stay still. Jon turned the radio so that the faint red light fell at their feet.

There, among ancient curls of thorns and dead grass, was a simple grave marker, worn down by the years but still mostly untouched. It lay flat across the ground like a stepping stone. And the name carved into it was clear and readable:

THEODORE SAMPSON TINDERBUFF III
1925-1943

Mak and Basil joined Rhett and Jon around the grave, all of them staring down at it, faces slack, eyes worried.

"We don't have to . . . you know . . . dig him up, do we?" Mak asked.

"I don't think so," Rhett said.

It was hard to concentrate with the beating of that powerful heart in his ears. It was stronger than ever, pummeling into the middle of his very being. If he stood here long enough without doing anything, it would probably knock him out cold.

Theo was down there, right under their feet.

A flash of the battle on the *Harbinger* stuttered across Rhett's vision—Theo's horrible grin as he stared up at Rhett, holding the sword between his palms, his eyes replaced by Urcena's. What if this all went wrong? What if Rhett wasn't meant to bring anybody back? What if the *Harbinger* had been doomed from the start and was doomed even still? Was he playing God? Was he following the rules or breaking them?

All of this rushed through Rhett's mind as he knelt down beside Theo's grave marker and placed a palm against it. He shut his eyes and let his senses come on. His body was attacked by the cold air, sending goose bumps across his skin. The cool stone beneath his hand was firm and unmoving, rough but still solid. The coarse concrete scraped against his fingers.

The heartbeat hammered in his ears like a violent drum until . . .

"Theo," Rhett whispered.

The heartbeat fell away instantly. The shushing tide of the city's orchestra went with it. The uneasy shuffling of the other three behind him. The gentle murmur of the wind through the cemetery. All of it gone. Replaced only by a tiny, static hum. "Theo," Rhett said again. "I know you're here."

In Jon's hands, the radio squawked loudly, startling all of them.

"Yes," Rhett continued. "That's it. Talk to me, buddy. Give me a signal that you want to come back."

"Screech once for yes, twice for no," Basil mumbled under his breath, and Mak elbowed him hard in the ribs.

"I can't bring you back unless you want me to, Theo," Rhett said. It was something that he hadn't known until this moment, but he knew it was true; if Theo really wanted to remain a ghost, there was nothing Rhett could do. "It's your choice. But we could really use your help."

The spirit radio sounded off an alarming series of whines and static bursts, cycling through several stations in a blabbering mess of voices. Rhett couldn't tell if this was Theo trying to communicate or if it was just the radio itself acting up. He kept his hand firmly against the gravestone.

A second later, the radio died completely, the little red bulb fading away, taking what little light it cast with it. The cemetery was left in silence and darkness, both of them total and devastating.

Rhett almost took his hand away from the stone. He had no gauge for what was happening: no heartbeat, no push, no electricity. Until the heartbeat returned, a single thump of it—*whump*—that sent a shock wave through Rhett's chest, down into his fingers. Tendrils of purple electricity darted along the ground like luminescent worms and rode upward along the curves of two blades of grass. They lit the tiny graveyard from within, an epicenter of life in a prison of death.

Whump-whump.

Again. The entire earth seemed to lurch beneath Rhett's hand.

"C'mon, buddy," he muttered.

Whump-whump.

A cloud of gray and black smoke burst up from the grave, lit with bolts of purple electricity, some of which stabbed out into the empty air. It bubbled and frothed and began to form a shape. Of broad shoulders silhouetted against the star-filled sky. Of long, powerful arms and legs.

Then, all at once, it was Theo, standing there in front of them as if he'd never left, with a few final, thin wisps of gray smoke curling out of his mouth and nose. He stood tense for a moment . . . before collapsing onto his hands and knees, nearly crushing Rhett in the process.

Mak and Jon fell in beside Theo, trying to keep him steady.

"Whoa there, big fella," Jon said. "Stay with us."

Theo stayed where he was, on all fours, head down between his muscular arms, one of which was easily as big as Jon's entire body.

Rhett fell back and sat hard in the dirt. He couldn't feel it, but he knew he was drained. Whatever source inside him that made Theo's revival possible was now exhausted. It cried out in the back of his mind, aching for rest.

"Theo?" Mak whispered into the big guy's ear. "Is that you? Are you okay?"

Everything was quiet, but not in the way it had been right before the cloud erupted from Theo's grave. Rhett could still hear the city, and the breeze had returned to rustle the grass around them.

Finally, after several long moments, Theo's voice spoke up, heavy with his thick New York accent.

"Yous guys didn't happen to bring a pizza, did you?" he asked.

They ended up camping in the cemetery after all. Theo was in no shape to travel, not yet. But it seemed fitting, messengers of death sleeping among the dead. It wasn't all that different from what they had done on the *Harbinger*, though the cemetery wasn't nearly as comfortable.

There was no pizza, but they ate from a few of the cans that they'd brought from the mill. He watched Basil inhale a can of pork and beans, looking even more gaunt than usual.

They sat in a rough circle, all of them staring somewhere else to avoid staring at one another. Mak sat with Theo, across from Basil, Rhett, and Jon, who was tinkering with his radio. Theo focused on the ground at his feet, tiny lights from the city hiding in the depths of his wide, almost fearful eyes. He looked like he was in shock, and Rhett knew the feeling. He didn't know what was more terrifying, existing as a ghost for so long or coming back to the reality of being a syllektor on the run from monsters and demons.

Basil brought Theo up to speed. When he was finished, Theo, without taking his eyes off the spot he'd fixed on, said, "I remember Markeski. He was an ass even before any of this creepy stuff went down. I ain't surprised the demon lady latched on to him." He looked down at his hands, massive and fumbling with themselves. "I ain't surprised she latched on to me, neither," he said quietly.

Mak put a hand on Theo's shoulder. "It's not your fault," she said. "It's not anyone's fault but hers."

Suddenly, Theo stood, his eyes locked on Rhett. He took two enormous strides across the circle. Rhett stood to meet him. They faced each other, Theo towering over Rhett. The image of Rhett's hands plunging the sword into Theo's chest replayed itself over and over in Rhett's mind . . . until Theo put his hand out.

"Thank you, guy," he said. "We got put in a crappy spot. Thank you for making it right."

All the tension went out of Rhett, and he shook the big lug's hand, sure as he had been the first time they met that he could hear bones crackling in his fingers from the force of Theo's grip.

"Anytime," Rhett said. "Let's just not make a habit out of it."

Theo grinned.

"All right," Basil said from his spot, hunched over himself, struggling to stay warm. "Let's get some rest. Tomorrow morning, we have a train to catch."

They all spread out, with Theo taking up one giant chunk of their makeshift camp. Jon went a couple of feet away and propped himself against one of the tombstones, leaned his head back, and shut his eyes. Rhett put his head down on a folded-up blanket and lay on his back, staring at a sky that was still smothered with light from the sleepless city.

Basil lay down with his back to the group and his blazer draped over him like a blanket. He had his arms wrapped around himself, and as soon as his head touched the soft pillow of overgrown grass, he was snoring. The Ash and the journey had taken their toll.

When Basil was out cold, Rhett looked over just as Mak went to him. She lay down with her back toward his, her arms wrapped around herself just like his were. She scooted herself across the grass until her back was just barely touching Basil's. A look of heartbreaking relief filled her face, and Rhett suddenly felt guilty for staring.

In a matter of minutes, they were all sleeping. Except for Theo and Rhett, who just stared at the dirt and the sky.

The former ghosts didn't sleep at all.

SEVEN

Rhett was quiet until the others started to stir. He watched the stars blink out one by one and the sky fill up with a milky blue color. When Basil sat up, blazer still clinging to his one shoulder, he was shivering.

It wasn't just him. Jon shook against the hard surface of the tombstone until he startled himself awake, his eyes bleary and miserable-looking.

Rhett felt a pang of guilt. They could have made a fire or something, but that might have given their location away—to psychons or demons, at least—and of the five of them, Rhett was the only one who knew that Basil and Jon had the Ash. It would have given *them* away to be huddled over a campfire all night. Rhett wished that he could hold them, give them his warmth. But the truth was that he had no warmth to give. Even with this strange power fluxing inside him, his body was still a frozen echo of what it used to be.

Carefully, Rhett pulled himself up to his feet. Jon glanced up at him, his hat sitting at a canted angle on his head, and offered Rhett a sleepy grin. He tried to return it but wasn't very successful.

Basil was stumbling to his feet, barely keeping his balance. Rhett caught one of his elbows before he could fall . . . and before Mak could really notice the way Basil was acting.

"You look like hell," Rhett whispered into Basil's ear.

"Huh," Basil mumbled in response. "Same as the way I feel."

Rhett guided him away from their little camp, trying to make it look as inconspicuous as possible.

"I'm serious," he hissed when he thought they were out of earshot. "You're in bad shape, Basil, and—"

"It's *Captain*," Basil interrupted, his words tired and slurred. "Captain Basil, if you please." He was acting like he was drunk.

"C'mon, man, snap out of it." Rhett looked at his friend. Then he slapped him across the face.

Basil's head jerked to the side from the force of it, the smacking sound rolling across the cemetery. Rhett could see the others look up at them out of the corner of his eye.

Basil gently rubbed the spot on his cheek where the dull purplish outline of Rhett's fingers stood out. When he caught Rhett's stare again, his eyes were focused, present.

"Sorry, mate," he said, his voice low. "The mornings are . . . rough sometimes. The cold doesn't help."

"Maybe we should just go back," Rhett said. "You're not in good enough shape . . ."

"No." Basil's eyes were hard, determined. "We're not going back. Do you understand me? There's a reason I made you first mate, and it's not just because you're my friend."

Rhett flinched at what Basil was trying to say. He had no words in response.

"Listen, mate," Basil went on, turning now to face the others, who had gone back to gathering their things and loading them into the truck. "I don't care what happens. This isn't about you or me. Or any of them. It's more important than that. I need you to promise me something."

Rhett watched Basil watching the others.

"Okay . . . ," he said, the hesitance clear in his voice.

"No matter what happens," Basil said, "promise me you'll carry on. Promise you won't give up even if . . . even if this thing takes me." He turned, his eyes boring into Rhett, silently pleading.

"But . . . ," Rhett tried.

"Promise me."

Rhett could only nod, a slow dip of his head.

"And don't you go out of your way to find my ghost, either." Basil tugged at the sleeves of his overcoat. "Not until the job's done. Got it?"

After a pause, Rhett said, "Got it." His voice sounded defeated even to himself.

"Guys!" Mak called. They'd broken down the campsite and looked like they were ready to get going. They had a train to catch and . . . Rhett glanced at the cab of their beat-up truck and stopped cold.

Sitting there in the driver's seat, grinning ferociously, was Urcena. Her matted and twisted hair clung to her pallid face, dripping water down her neck and arms, both lined with dark, bulging veins. Her eyes were locked on Rhett, the white pinhole pupils cutting into him. But she didn't look like she was in a fighting mood. She simply sat back against the worn leather seats and drummed her grotesque fingers against the steering wheel. It seemed to Rhett that she was only here to observe. And if *she* was here, then . . .

He came wading out of the thick brush of the cemetery, coming from the far side, where they'd found Theo. His hair looked long and greasy, slicked back over the top of his head with a few stray pieces dangling across his forehead; it gave him a crazed, unpredictable look that Rhett didn't like at all. He was dressed in slacks and a creased button-down shirt, both of which could have contained different shades of color at one time but were now completely black, the vibrancy sucked out of them by the afterlife. He came closer, followed by two other syllektors, and when they were near enough, Rhett realized that none of them were armed.

"Markeski," Basil said to the guy in the slacks. He had stepped up to their camp, hands behind his back, examining the patches of dirt and weeds as if looking for some kind of message hidden there.

"Winthrop," Anton Markeski replied.

The other two syllektors who had come with Markeski stayed close but weren't on top of them. This wasn't like the matchup at the house in Pennsylvania—they weren't here to fight. They were here to talk.

And while they talked, Rhett kept his eyes on Urcena in the truck, who kept *her* eyes on *him*. There was a streetlight near where the truck was parked, still lit in the early pre-dawn hours. The bulb flickered, alternating the glow that fell upon Urcena's face between a dull orange and complete shadow. When there was only the shadow, her grin disappeared, leaving only the ruthless white pupils floating in the blackness of her eyes. Rhett wanted to look away, but he couldn't do it.

"Theo," Markeski continued. His voice was leering, toying, laced with an undercurrent of something that sounded almost human but not quite. "Nice to see you on your feet again."

Theo grunted.

Markeski flashed a toothy smile, showing off a set of too-perfect teeth. "Never were much of a talker, were you?"

"What do you want, Markeski?" Mak asked. She stepped up to him, with Basil and Rhett coming in behind her. All of their weapons were still in the back of the truck. If they wanted Markeski to feel threatened, they were going to have to bluff.

But Markeski raised his hands, palms out.

"Just to talk," he said. "You know my only interest is in the survival of our species, Makayla."

"Watch it," Mak said. "And we're not a species, we're—"

Markeski cut her off. "Yes. We are. And we're the last of it. Us. Your crew. My crew. We're all the syllektors that are left." He jerked his chin in Rhett's direction. "*He* made sure of that."

"You don't know what you're talking about," Basil said. Any exhaustion that had been plaguing him was replaced by anger now, his voice low and gravelly.

"Don't I?" Markeski said. Behind him, Jon and Theo closed in, while his own goons continued to keep their distance, obviously unbothered by the fact that their leader was being surrounded. "So you're saying that your boy couldn't have prevented all of this if he'd just given himself up in the first place? That's all she wanted. She just wanted *him*."

"She's lying to you, Anton," Mak said. "She wants more than that. She wants the souls, too."

Rhett's eyes were still on Urcena, sitting in the front seat of the truck, watching him back. Between flickers of the streetlight, her grin vanished. What took its place was a sneer that would have sent chills through Rhett's entire body if he had his senses plugged in. Filling his head now was the same old fear, what he'd felt on the Golden Gate Bridge the first time he saw her, on the *Harbinger* right before she drove it into the water, in the corner of the house as she watched him haunt its halls. He didn't know if he'd ever stop being afraid of her and what she was capable of. But he knew that he would never stop trying to keep her from getting the one thing she desperately wanted: his power.

"Just tell us what you want," Rhett said, finally dragging his eyes away from the truck and leveling them at Markeski. "Or get out of our way."

Markeski turned his attention to Rhett and his face flickered for a moment, his eyes becoming *her* eyes. The sneer that he wore mirrored hers, and it was almost just as terrifying.

"He speaks," Markeski said, slowly and quietly. Then, after a pause: "We know what you're doing. Where you're going. And it won't work."

Rhett didn't move or blink. He waited to see what else Markeski had to say and hoped that the others kept their mouths shut.

"You can bring back as many syllektors as you want," Markeski went on. "You can dig up syllektors from centuries past. You can bring

back Trier himself. It doesn't matter. She'll just rip his heart out all over again."

Basil took a lurching step forward, but Mak held him back, blocking his path with her arm without taking her eyes off Markeski. His goons still didn't move.

"You can bring back an entire army and it won't make a difference. Urcena has promised our crew sanctuary in return for our help to bring an end to this chaos. Chaos that *you* started." He was still speaking at Rhett. "This is your last chance. Join us. Or be destroyed."

"She's using you," Rhett said. He stepped in Markeski's direction, and for the first time, Markeski's syllektors came closer, lowering their balled-up fists to their sides. "She's in your head. She did the same thing to Treeny. Theo, too. *She's* the reason the *Harbinger* sank. You have to know that. Deep down."

There was the briefest flicker of recognition in Markeski's eyes, the smallest indication that he believed what Rhett was saying. And then it was wiped out by the warbling of her possession, twisting his features into something barely like his voice, something not quite human.

In deadly hushed tones, Markeski said, "What I know is that you destroyed our home. Ghosted hundreds of syllektors. Put the souls that we were sworn to protect at risk. And put all the future souls of the dead in danger for the sake of keeping your parents' souls safe. Tell me what you're really fighting for, Rhett. Tell me the truth."

Behind Markeski, Jon was watching, his guard up, his empty hands closing and opening, probably yearning for the weight of his staff. Rhett caught his stare and held it. Deep in Jon's eyes, he was asking

Rhett the same question, the question that he was also asking himself. *What are you fighting for?*

"I'm fighting for life," Rhett said, shifting his gaze back to Markeski. He stepped up beside Mak and Basil, and again Markeski's goons followed suit. "And for death. For the balance of both. The souls of the dead are alive in a way that none of us will ever understand. And yeah, my parents are with them. But if I had to give them up to save all the others, to save my friends, I would. The only thing you and your *crew* are willing to sacrifice, Markeski, are the souls of people who aren't ready to die. You're prepared to give the living over to the psychons to save your own ass. So what are *you* really fighting for?"

Markeski's face twisted with rage. As Rhett watched, his eyes blackened and his pupils lightened. Urcena was taking over, and even if Markeski and the other syllektors weren't armed, Rhett knew what she was capable of. They all did.

But after a moment, Markeski relaxed; his face slackened and his eyes went back to normal. When Rhett glanced back at the truck, Urcena was gone. The streetlight had quit flickering, too.

"You might think I'm a traitor," Markeski said. "You might even think I'm a coward. And maybe I am. Maybe this isn't the path that's right. But it's the only path that guarantees us a future. Think about that before you start a war."

He put his hands up again, sidestepping out of the circle that Rhett's group had formed around him. The other two syllektors backed off, too, and when Markeski walked past them, heading back the way they had come, they followed. Markeski didn't look back.

When they were gone, everybody let out a breath.

Theo squatted down, putting his hands over his face. Mak rushed to him and put her arms around his massive shoulders as best she could.

"I could feel her," Theo said through his fingers. "I could feel her looking for a way back inside my head. But . . . I . . . I knew she was there this time. I knew how to keep her out. Oh God, she was right there, though. She was so damn close."

"It's okay," Mak said, running a hand through his hair, which, Rhett now noticed, was streaked with a little bit of white that hadn't been there before. "She's gone."

"I don't get it," Jon said.

"What?" Basil asked.

"Why didn't they just ghost us? She could have taken us all out with just her little finger. Why didn't she?"

"Because she's waiting to see what happens," Rhett responded after a second. "She *wants* a war. She wants us to fight so that she can destroy us. They think we're building an army."

"Which means they don't know about the Navigator?" Jon asked. "Or they haven't figured it out yet?"

Mak stood. Theo did, too, looking at least partially relieved.

"Exactly," Mak said. "They don't know what we're really trying to do. She won't waste her conduit on a fight with us. Not again. They're just going to wait and see what we come up with."

"Or just send in the psychons to do their dirty work," Basil grumbled.

"Or that."

They stood around the campsite, collecting their focus, gathering their resolve. Rhett could feel it in the air—the uncertainty, the lingering doubt that maybe they'd all signed up for an inevitable ghosting. But he knew what waited beyond a ruined heart. He refused to go back there, and he sure as hell wasn't going to let any of his friends end up there, either.

For all the years that Rhett had lived in New York—basically his entire life—he'd only ever set foot in Grand Central Terminal a handful of times. And every time he'd been there, part of him never wanted to leave.

The whole place seemed to have this weird golden glow about it. Even at such an early hour, the place was streaming with people, moving in lines across the enormous terminal like blood cells. The high ceilings, which Rhett always forgot were green, hummed with the noise that floated up from the floor. And the clock in the center of the room was the beacon around which the chaos somehow became organized.

Rhett and the others, now fully armed, stood staring at the clock. They had left the truck back on Park Avenue and carried with them what they could, which wasn't much more than their weapons and what they could fit into a messenger bag that Jon used to store the spirit radio. In any other case, they may have been tackled by a horde of security officers for all the dangerous metal they wielded. Luckily, they remained unnoticed by the travelers moving around them.

"There," Mak said, pointing at one of the screens that was affixed to the information booth below the clock. Above the screen was the word DEPARTURES. "Track 12."

They made their way down into the belly of the station, following the signs that directed them to their platform. It was all strangely normal, as if they were just regular passengers trying to catch their train back home. In a way, they were.

Once they reached their platform, there was nothing to do but wait.

Basil found a bench and collapsed there. Theo and Mak stood as stoic as ever, with their arms crossed and their lips pursed together into tight, worried lines. Jon stood against one of the steel support beams and clanged the shortened version of his staff against it methodically. They were all on guard after Markeski crashed their campsite. If he (and Urcena) knew where Rhett and the others had been that easily, they knew where they were now. If they kept moving forward, an attack was imminent.

And yet they had no other choice *but* to move forward.

Everyone was on edge, but no one more so than Basil, who was visibly sweating, bouncing his knee, wringing his hands together. He stared straight ahead at the other platform on the opposite side of the tracks. There was nobody over there.

Rhett caught Jon's eye. Jon cocked his head in Basil's direction and pinched his eyebrows together in a silent question. Rhett shrugged— he didn't know what Basil's problem was. He couldn't tell if it was the Ash messing with him, or something else.

Before either Rhett or Jon could ask, Theo leaned toward Basil and said, "You all right, bud?"

Basil glanced his way briefly, then nodded in big, exaggerated bobs of his head, sweat dripping off his face and plopping onto the concrete between his feet.

"Basil . . . you sure?" Rhett asked. He was trying to keep his voice down, trying not to make a big scene and draw Mak's attention to Basil's condition. But out of the corner of his eye, he could see it was already too late. Mak was staring at Basil, her eyes flicking over him, her mind putting the pieces together.

When Mak opened her mouth to speak, Rhett was expecting an accusation, a frustrated realization that Basil was struggling with the Ash and not telling anybody. What she actually said was something else entirely.

"He hates trains. Remember?" Mak said quietly.

"I'm sorry?" Rhett asked, trying to catch up. Jon and Theo gaped at her as well.

"He hates trains," Mak repeated. "He died in a train accident. We went over this."

"Oh," Rhett said, dumbfounded, shocked that Mak was seeing right past the truth. "Yeah."

Mak stepped past him and sat down on the bench beside Basil. She reached out gingerly and rubbed Basil's shoulder. Then she put her entire arm around him and slid closer to his side. They didn't say anything, but Basil appeared to calm down somewhat. His bouncing knee slowed from a panicky twitch to a steady pump, and his eyes gained some focus.

As the train rushed into the station behind him, disturbing the air around them all and filling the platform with the whining screech of

metal, Rhett realized what he should have already guessed: Mak knew that Basil had the Ash. She was too smart not to have noticed his odd behavior. Maybe she even knew that Jon had it, too. Either way, she was keeping it to herself. She was doing the same thing that Rhett was doing—focusing on the mission, on the endgame. This was more than about just Basil and Jon surviving. It was about *all* of the syllektors surviving. So that they could continue to protect the souls of the dead. Basil and Jon understood that. Otherwise they wouldn't have come along, they wouldn't have kept their conditions a secret.

It was a ruinous cycle of lies, told so that the next person in line wouldn't lose their nerve or give up the cause for any one individual. There must have been plenty of other crew members back at the factory who were caught in the same dilemma.

Rhett didn't see an end to it any time soon. These were his friends. Basil was the guy who had brought him on board the *Harbinger* and shown him how to be a syllektor, who came back for him when they could have just left him to haunt and be haunted. They were more than just his best friends—they were his family.

When was it okay to forget about saving the world and just worry about saving the people he cared about?

The train doors opened. Passengers filed past them, lugging bags and babies and books. Some muffled voice somewhere announced that the train was departing for Washington, DC, in fifteen minutes.

Rhett and the others went toward the back of the train and shuffled past an elderly conductor who didn't have anyone waiting to board. The conductor shivered absently as they all moved past him.

When they got on board, they found a mostly empty dining car with wide booths. There was one woman in a corner booth nursing a drink. She couldn't have seen the syllektors step into the car, but she glanced in their direction anyway—in such close quarters it was easy for people to pick up on the subtle energy that the syllektors gave off, the cold chill that they emitted.

Rhett and Jon sat on one side of a booth, Mak and Basil sat on the other, and Theo took a second booth all to himself.

"Don't get comfortable," Jon advised. "The trip to DC won't take very long."

And there they were. Five dead teenagers, all of them dressed in clothes that had been blackened by the afterlife, their only real luggage a collection of insanely vicious weapons and a broken magical lantern, completely unseen by living eyes, riding a train like a bunch of kids heading off to college.

It almost made Rhett laugh. It almost made *all* of them laugh from the looks of it. They glanced awkwardly around at one another, each of them realizing the ridiculousness of their situation at the same time. Even Basil, who was drumming his fingers against the table, had time for one quick smirk.

"So, is train food as bad as airplane food?" Rhett asked Basil, resting his chin in his palm.

"You're hilarious, mate," Basil replied. "A bloody riot."

A few minutes later, the train pulled out of the station and carried them away from the city.

EIGHT

Jon was right: The trip from New York to DC was only a few hours long. And they were all on edge the entire way, even with the sun rising alongside them and the scenery changing from slabs of concrete and panes of glass to snow-crusted trees and mist-shrouded hills, all of it rushing past the windows in blurred smudges. The train cut down the east coast and pulled into Union Station without incident.

After that came the long haul.

The train ride that would take them from Union Station in Washington to another Union Station in Chicago was almost eighteen hours long. Luckily, it was still freezing cold outside and traveling—especially by train—was not high up on many peoples' bucket lists. When the syllektors boarded the train, there weren't very many living people to contend with.

Jon found an entire car full of empty cabins. They were cramped, but they had clean bunks. Anything was better than the ground back at the cemetery.

"Probably wise to settle down for a bit," Basil said, eyeing the open door to one of the cabins with a look of almost mournful longing. "I'll take first watch."

"Nice try," Rhett chimed in. "*I've* got first watch. You guys go chill out for a couple of hours."

The relief that passed over Basil's face was undeniable, and he didn't argue. He slipped into one of the cabins and slid the door shut without another word, leaving Mak behind to stare at the door. The look on *her* face was anything but relieved. Hurt and angry and dismayed, maybe.

Everyone else, including Theo, whose broad shoulders didn't even fit through the tiny door, shuffled off to their bunks with similar looks of exhausted eagerness. Even if Theo and Mak couldn't feel the physical consequences of the last couple days the way that Jon and Basil could, there was a mental toll to the journey that couldn't be denied. Something that a few hours' sleep on a bed of cold, stiff grass wasn't going to soothe.

Jon glanced briefly at Rhett and gave him a quick, sure nod before sliding his door shut. Rhett shifted on his feet uncomfortably for a second, Jon's confidence in him pressing against his mind, squeezing it until it ached with fear. That confidence was unjustified, unproven. Why did Jon have so much faith in the Twice-Born Son, when all it had really amounted to so far was fixing what had already been broken? What they needed right now was someone who could protect everything from being broken in the first place.

Rhett moved to the next car over and plopped down into one of the seats closest to the door, where he could easily turn and stare through to the car where his friends were all now resting. He sat and relished the constant push and pull of the train around him, slowing as it took curves in the tracks and speeding up over straight shots. The world sped past in dancing flickers and the sky hung in steady, unmoving owner-ship of it all, a gentle hand wrapped around a hard, jagged marble. It was *almost* like being on the *Harbinger* again. Almost, but not quite.

Rhett sat and waited, watching the landscape change, feeling the give and take of the train car, shaking and rattling, rocking unsteadily, lulling his mind until he began to relax. And then he relaxed too much.

He fell asleep.

He was back on the *Harbinger*, running through its ever-changing halls. From ancient wood to bolted metal to ornate carpet, the floor transformed beneath him as he ran, panting. He had no idea where he was going or who he was trying to get to. He just knew that he had to get away from where he was right now. Everything was weirdly quiet, unlike the last time he'd been on board the ship, when there were sirens and cannonballs and a giant sea monster wrenching her down into the sea. Now she was still and silent, but somehow the ter-ror was still there.

He ran from it. As fast as his legs would carry him, he ran.

At the end of the corridor, a door waited for him. Just a regular door, flat and wooden with a brass knob. Where would it take him? Maybe it would take him home. Back to a reality where all of this had just been some kind of nightmare, maybe even a coma caused by the accident with his parents. Maybe it led to his friends, to Basil and Mak and Theo. Jon, too. Even Treeny. Except they'd be living in a version of the world where they were all still alive. Together, not scattered across different time periods. They would all be there and be alive. Really alive.

But as he got closer to the door, he realized that it was actually one of two that were down there at the end of the hall. The one next to it looked similar, only it was made from a darker wood, almost black, and the knob was silver instead of brass. Both doors were there, standing side by side, staring at him as if their knobs were mirrored eyeballs, watching, waiting for him to choose.

He knew he couldn't stop running. But he also knew he couldn't pick just one door. He needed them both. He just kept running, waiting for the moment when he'd collide with the doors and be obliterated by whatever it was that was chasing him. He ran, and the sound of something rattling began to catch up with him. A metallic clattering mingled with a long, piercing screech. It was right behind him, and then it was on top of him, and then . . .

Rhett jumped awake to the sound of the train rattling over the tracks. From somewhere nearby, its brakes were squealing. There was also a hand on his shoulder. It was big and meaty and probably could have pulverized his bone with a single squeeze—Theo.

"Yous okay, boss?" Theo asked. He let go of Rhett's shoulder and dropped into one of the seats across the aisle. Rhett was kind of surprised the big guy didn't need all three. "Yous were gettin' a little antsy in your sleep."

"Uh . . . yeah," Rhett said, sitting up, cursing himself for falling asleep after he'd volunteered to take the first watch. "Yeah, I'm okay. Thanks."

"You got it," Theo replied. "Yous want me to take watch? Couldn't sleep anyways."

Rhett was tempted. The idea of a dark room all to himself for a little while sounded like paradise. But he had no interest in the dreams that awaited him.

"You know what, I think I'm good," he said to Theo. "I'll just hang out here. We both can." He gave Theo what he hoped was a comforting grin. Theo looked a little relieved.

They sat for a while, letting the mechanical ticks and hums of the train fill the silence. Both of them watched the trees and hills sweep past through the windows. Rhett wished he had a watch or a clock or something to tell him how long it would be until they reached Chicago. What he would have given to have his smartphone back just for a moment.

Eventually the quiet got to be too much.

"Theo, listen," he started. He was forming the words in his head, picturing the sword as it came down through Theo's chest, when Theo put his hand up. Rhett closed his mouth.

"If you're gonna apologize," Theo said, "don't. Yous did me a favor. Ghosting me was the only thing you coulda done. That . . . thing woulda just kept eating away at me. Besides, yous came back for me. So I say your slate is clean." He leaned across the aisle, staring at Rhett, and said, "Capeesh?" Then he waggled his eyebrows in true Theo fashion.

Rhett chuckled, remembering the first time he'd met Theo aboard the *Harbinger*. Basil and Mak had been arguing and Rhett had gone off on them. He'd used *capeesh* to mock Theo's accent, which, at the time, had not been a great idea. But as usual his temper had gotten the better of him.

Rhett felt lucky to have the big lug on his side again. And he was overwhelmingly relieved to know that Theo didn't hold any grudges for what happened the day the *Harbinger* went down.

Well, maybe there was one grudge, one they all shared against a certain she-thing. But if they accomplished what they had set out to do, they might be able to settle that particular score.

As they nestled back into their seats—both of them a little more relaxed now—Theo said, "Hey, boss, I've been meanin' to ask yous . . ."

Now it was Rhett's turn to put his hand up and stop Theo.

"If you ask me about my hair," Rhett said, "I'll throw you off this train."

Theo rumbled with laughter. "Like to see yous try. But no, I was gonna ask about Treeny."

Rhett's heart sank. He imagined that by now, if he could feel anything of the sort without having to voluntarily activate the sensations in his body, his stomach would have tied itself into an unmanageable ball of knots. But he nodded at Theo to go on.

"I've just been wonderin'," Theo said. "What exactly went down with her?" His face looked small and worried. He looked afraid to hear the answer.

Rhett realized that Theo was like Jon—he hadn't been on the bridge when Treeny ghosted Captain Trier. He hadn't seen her crush Trier's heart in her bare hand and go vanishing into the chaos of the storm. She had been a completely different person in those moments. And of course Rhett knew why. That didn't make any of it okay, though. When Theo had attacked them, he'd been completely under Urcena's control. When Treeny betrayed them, Rhett had been able to see traces of the old Treeny in there, flickering to the surface like flames dancing on top of a pool of oil.

Theo knew what Treeny had done, but he didn't know how.

Rhett told him. He told him about the way Treeny had dug her hand into Captain Trier's chest and removed his heart. In Rhett's memory, she'd been so casual about it, as if she'd been rummaging through the fridge for a container of leftovers. He told Theo about how she turned on them, fighting off Mak and Basil while Rhett tried to hold on to the captain. And he told Theo about the way Captain Trier's body splintered and broke down into those tiny flecks of ash when Treeny crushed his heart in her bare hand.

"Jesus, Mary, and Joseph," Theo breathed. He stared out the window again, shadows from passing trees flickering across his face. When he spoke again, he said, "But it wasn't her."

"It wasn't *all* her," Rhett corrected. "When Urcena took control of you, she took over everything. She and Treeny . . ." He searched for the right words. "They had a bond. Urcena was using her as a conduit, but I think it was more than that. I . . . I think Treeny *wanted* to turn her back on us. And if not on us, then on the afterlife in general."

"What do you mean?"

"I don't think she wanted to be a syllektor anymore, Theo." And as the words fell from his mouth, Rhett realized how much sense they made. He remembered the look of relief on Treeny's face when Basil's scythe pierced her heart. Betraying her friends might have only been a means to an end. Now here they were, trying to undo that end.

"So . . . ," Theo started. "What do yous think is gonna happen when we . . . when *you* bring her back? You think she'll help us?"

Rhett thought about it. The more he did, the less confident he felt about their plan. Especially now. He could try to revive her a thousand times, but that didn't mean she would *want* to be revived. Rhett had learned with Theo that if Treeny didn't want to come back, he couldn't force her to return. And even if she *did* want to be revived and she *did* agree to help them, they were just going to turn around and banish her back to the existence of a ghost anyway. An existence that Rhett knew all too well. How would they all feel about themselves after that? Were they no better than Treeny, then? Full of rage and revenge and bitter cruelty?

He thought about Markeski and his flimsy vision of rebuilding among the living, to continue the work of the syllektors even without the *Harbinger*, which, given the Ash and the psychons and Urcena, wasn't really possible at all.

"I don't know, buddy," Rhett said to Theo, finally answering his question. "I really don't know."

One last leg of the journey.

They passed through Union Station in Chicago without any trouble. At least, none that they could see. If they were being followed or watched by other syllektors, they didn't know it. And psychons certainly weren't stealthy enough to stay hidden.

Rhett and the others kept their guard up nonetheless, peering over their shoulders as they left one train and boarded another. The living people crowding the platforms subconsciously made room for the syllektors to pass, shuffling aside at what might have been a cool breeze or a weird shift in gravity. Once, though, as they came down the stairs to where their last train waited for them, Basil knocked shoulders with a man walking in the opposite direction. The man stopped, looking around for what it was that he'd run into or the person who had so rudely bumped him without apologizing. He looked confused and agitated, and Basil looked horrified.

Luckily, Rhett had been the only one to witness the incident. And when Basil stumbled from the spot, staring at the man who still couldn't see him, Rhett gripped his friend on the shoulder and guided him away.

They were running out of time.

Two hours after that, they were on the train, sitting in empty seats among the other passengers, watching Iowa slip past them in a flat sheet of winter-hardened earth. In the distance, Rhett could see wind turbines turning lazily in the bright morning sun. He watched them, listening to Basil and Mak and Jon and Theo shift uncomfortably in their seats. They were all tired of the journey. They were tired of being crammed into train cars and cooped up with living people who were oblivious to their existence. And Jon and Basil had their own problems.

Rhett was contemplating talking to Mak, confirming what he already suspected—that she knew about the Ash creeping its way up Basil's arm—and picking her brain for a possible solution. He stared at the turbines, which reached up like waving hands, hoping that Mak had some kind of answer, even if it was as simple as getting Basil and Jon back to the *Harbinger* so the souls on board could work their magic, literally. But if Basil was too far gone, would that make a difference? Would—

Something was moving through the dead fields.

Or rather, it was a group of somethings. From where Rhett sat, they looked like black specks, maybe a dozen of them, shifting across the frosted earth. They were fast. Too fast to be animals or people or even cars. The rising sun gave them long shadows and cut their features with strong orange light. They were heading straight for the train, and Rhett didn't have to see their grinning skull faces or the ratty cloaks billowing behind them to know what they were.

"Guys . . . ," he said, standing, gesturing toward the window.

The others looked at him, confused, and then glanced out the window at what he saw.

"Shit," Mak hissed.

They all rose, and Rhett couldn't help but look around at the other passengers on board with them. They had no idea what was coming.

The end of the line wasn't in Omaha after all.

It was here.

"Everybody down!" Mak called, and the five syllektors crouched down in the aisle, staring out the windows, trying to keep an eye on the approaching mass of psychons.

Rhett grabbed the armrest of the seat he'd been sitting in only a few moments before and pushed his back against the seat across the aisle, locking himself in place and ducking his head between his arms, trying to protect everything at the same time. There were no seat belts, so this was as close to secure as he was going to get. He looked down the aisle at the others, who were all trying to do the same thing. Mak and Basil were at the far end, Basil staring at the floor, taking in long, deep breaths. Then there was Theo, squeezing himself into the aisle as best he could.

Rhett caught eyes with Jon. He looked scared. Rhett wanted to reach out for him, wanted to tell him it was all going to be okay, wanted to justify that confidence that Jon so blindly had in him. He wanted, he wanted, he wanted . . . so many things. Things he would never do if he was ducking and hiding.

He stood, gripping the handle of his knuckle blade in its holster. They could jump from the train, meet the psychons before they even touched the train, fight them . . .

But it was already too late.

In the windows, Rhett could see the dark shapes of the psychons rushing through the empty field, their sinewy ropes of muscle stretched taut across their exposed skeletons, cloaks pulled out behind them in rippling curtains of shadow. They raced toward the train at full speed, digging their clawed feet and hands into the dirt. The monsters spread themselves apart slightly, seeming to somehow gain even more speed. A second later, Rhett caught a glimpse of one's horrible face, mostly skull with a few bits of tendon and muscle holding it together. He looked right into its beady little eyes, buried deep in the cavities of its eye sockets, staring out hungrily.

And then the psychons slammed into the side of the train.

There was a sound of shrieking metal, like sheets of steel being ripped in half as if they were only pieces of paper. Everything lurched. The world outside the windows tipped as the train came off the tracks.

There was no gravity. Rhett could see his feet, but they weren't touching the floor. The whole train car seemed to be turning around him. Luggage came spewing out of overhead compartments. Passengers were thrown from their seats, toppling into the windows and the ceiling and other people. Rhett saw his friends holding on to whatever they could, their bodies seeming to float the way Rhett's was.

Outside the windows, the rest of the train was buckling. As their car fell sideways off the tracks, Rhett could see other cars collapsing into themselves like old accordions and folding over onto other cars. One in particular was twisting through the air, flames erupting from its underbelly. It was heavy, and it didn't fall gracefully. It collided with the car Rhett was in, which still hadn't hit the ground, and sent it spinning.

Gravity was back.

Rhett was thrown down into a set of seats, his back crushing against the armrests, and then he rolled again, his momentum carrying him over hard metal and plastic and soft cushions until his back was forced up against something firm. But the firmness didn't last. Whatever it was that he'd landed on gave way almost immediately, shattering into pieces that flipped and glinted around his head as he fell through it.

He'd broken through a window.

The train car, crumpled and coughing up smoke, continued to spin over Rhett as he fell downward. All around him, other cars were rolling and dragging across the ground and flipping up into the air until they were pointing at the sky, ready to tip in one direction or the other. And everything was explosions and screaming and tearing metal. Clouds of black, noxious smoke blotted out the sky, and the beautiful sunny day that had been was lost.

When he hit the ground, Rhett still couldn't get his orientation right. Everything was spinning. And in any given direction train cars were smashing into the ground or falling on top of one another in cries of warping metal and shattering glass. Fire and smoke whirled around and above him, obscuring any clear sight he might have of the destruction.

Out of the smoke over his head, another train car emerged like a torpedo, coming straight down, the door at its front still mostly intact, as if it had never left the tracks at all.

Rhett barely had time to think. He felt for the solidity of the earth beneath him, used it to roll onto his knees. He had no idea what shape his body was in—he couldn't feel any of the pain and wouldn't dare let himself feel it. All he could do was hope that his legs would carry him. He pushed up onto his feet and ran.

There was a foot, maybe less, to spare when the train car came down on its head behind him. The shock wave from the impact nearly threw Rhett off his feet. He chanced a look over his shoulder and watched as the car rippled, the metal creasing and turning into what looked like a giant tin can. Little electrical explosions went off all across its surface and inside it, showering Rhett with glowing sparks.

The car groaned and began to fall. Rhett ran harder, knowing without looking that it was leaning in his direction, threatening to crush him like a cockroach beneath the hard sole of a boot. He could hear the creaking metal and the occasional pop of windows breaking right behind him. He ran, not knowing what was coming ahead, his vision blocked by black, swirling smoke and burning embers. Whining metal sounded right above his head . . .

Rhett leaped.

There was nothing else he could do. He threw himself forward and hoped that it was enough. He hit the ground and rolled. At the same time, the train car smacked into the ground, sending clods of dirt and grass and metallic pieces exploding into the air.

Rhett stayed where he was, with his knees folded under him, his hands covering his head, and his eyes squeezed shut, while soil and ash rained down around him. For a second, he didn't know if he'd been crushed or not. He could still hear the groan of metal and the crackling of fires all over the place, could even still hear more train cars smacking into one another farther down the tracks, the very end of the train finally catching up with the wreckage. But he knew what it was like to be ghosted. He knew that it could all be a brief illusion before the real torment began.

After a few long moments, though, the sounds continued, now mingling with cries for help, the sounds of weeping and moaning and shrieks of pain.

Rhett was still here. He just hoped his friends were, too.

Rhett got slowly to his feet and looked himself over. His arms and legs were covered in pinkish cuts and gashes, lacerations that, had he been alive, would have been bleeding all over the place. But these just trickled. He tested out his legs, made sure they would both hold weight, and pulled up his shirt, where he found a gnarly bruise forming across the right side of his chest and abdomen—clearly the result of a few broken ribs—but nothing he couldn't work with. He reached down to the holster at his thigh; the knuckle blade was still there.

Behind Rhett, the train car that had nearly come down on top of

him was burning and spewing smoke of its own, the whole thing twisted into a shape that wasn't quite right, lying upside down in the grass. But he could hear movement inside. He knew he couldn't just start yelling for Basil or Mak or any of the others—that would draw the psychons, wherever they were, right to him. He'd have to start searching the wreckage.

With the smoke wafting in his face, Rhett went over to the ruined train car. He used one of the still-blinking light fixtures to boost himself up and gripped the handle on the door. It was supposed to slide sideways into the wall of the car. But with the way the car was crimped and bent, the door only slid open halfway. That was plenty. Rhett hauled himself up and into the car, dropping down onto the ceiling just beyond the door. When he looked up, he froze.

The train car was in much better shape on the inside than it was on the outside. A few windows were broken, letting some of the gray smoke in, but Rhett could at least see to the far end of the car, and he could see the way the entire car was warped into a fun house version of itself. On the ceiling—or the floor, as it was now—a handful of lights were still on, some of them flickering in the dimness created by the smoke. The seats were all upside down, a couple rows of them dislodged and hanging precariously. Exposed wires spat glowing white sparks. And the passengers . . . they were all laid out across the ceiling, some of them staring vacantly up at the seats they had been sitting in only a few minutes before, but most of them had their eyes shut, looking almost peaceful. Out of their open mouths, white smoke floated up in languid curls.

Crouching among the passengers were more psychons, waiting hungrily for the souls to rise up.

They didn't seem to notice Rhett as he ducked into the tiny bathroom at his end of the car. They were preoccupied with the souls, stepping around the bodies as they wafted upward, a different kind of smoke. There were three of them, the hoods of their cloaks pulled over their heads and dropping shadows over the horrors of their faces. There was no way Rhett could take on all three, not alone.

He peered out from the little alcove of the bathroom. One of the psychons was only a couple feet away, hulking in the small space. It had a ribbon of white smoke twisted around one of its long, pointed fingers. Rhett knew what happened next: he'd seen it before. The soul began to darken, changing from a pure white to gray to brown and then to black. It thickened, coagulating into a toxic-looking sludge that was nowhere near as weightless and free as the white mist it had been only seconds before. Lowering its face to its cupped hands, where the black muck had pooled, the psychon began to eat, slurping the soul up as if it were hot soup in a bowl.

The others followed suit, devouring one soul after another, feasting on the carnage they had created.

Rhett couldn't just stand here and listen to the wet, phlegmy sounds of the psychons gorging themselves on the souls of the dead. But before he could step out and confront them, he heard another voice, one that somehow brought a smile to his face even under the horrifying circumstances.

"Hey, assholes," Jon said from what sounded like the other side of the train car. And the slurping sounds stopped.

Rhett took his chance.

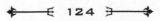

He lunged out from the bathroom, kicked off the opposite wall, and jumped out into the upside-down aisle, unsheathing his knuckle blade as he flew. The nearest psychon had its back turned to him, staring down at the other end of the car, where Jon was waiting, his deadly staff charged and stuttering with tiny bolts of electricity. Rhett took hold of one of the armrests hanging above his head, right behind the oblivious psychon, and drove the four blades of his weapon deep into the side of the monster's head. It didn't even have time to scream; it let out a tiny rumbling whine and then collapsed. Rhett's knuckle blade slipped out of its skull as it fell, coated in black slime.

Down at the end of the car, it was Jon's turn.

The staff moved about him in a blur of metal and energy, spinning like a propeller as if by its own will. But the staff was still attached to Jon's hands, turning with the subtle motion of his wrists. The two remaining psychons watched him, both of them stepping anxiously from foot to foot, not sure what to expect. Rhett had seen what the ends of the staff could do back at his parents' house in Pennsylvania— the monsters had every reason to be anxious.

Rhett let go of the seat he'd been holding on to and dropped back down to the ceiling of the car, careful not to land on any of the passengers' bodies. The sound of his shoes clunking against the metal startled the psychons. They whirled around, their cloaks rustling loudly in the silence.

Jon spun, extending his arm, the staff held tight at the end of it. The metal changed from a spinning propeller around his body to a stiff, powerful length of steel, seeming to uncurl itself as it moved. The electrified staff tore through the air behind the distracted psychons and connected, slamming into the head of one psychon and then the other in a single motion.

A second later, both of the psychons plunked down to the ground, joining the innocent bodies they'd been feeding on.

"Thanks," Rhett said through a sigh.

"Don't mention it," Jon replied, his wrist giving the staff one final turn before bringing the weapon to a halt at his side. The metal retracted into itself and Jon dropped the whole thing into the holster on his back.

"You ever going to tell me how that thing works?" Rhett asked.

"You ever going to stop needing to be rescued?" Jon countered. But he was grinning.

When they looked around, though, they both grew serious in a hurry. Rhett tried to focus on the destroyed train car, keeping his eyes off the death that was littered around their feet. But as he swept his eyes across the seats and windows, Rhett caught sight of the remaining souls, floating lazily in the air, not quite intermingling with the smoke that was blowing in from the fires outside. They hung there, perfect white strands of mist, peaceful and quiet. For the first time since the *Harbinger* went down, Rhett thought he felt the tiniest throb of the push at the back of his mind, that gentle but persistent nudge that always pointed him toward the soul he needed to collect.

He knew that Jon was staring at the souls with him. "What do we do with them?" Rhett asked.

"We don't have much of a choice," Jon said after a pause. "We have to leave them."

The idea of abandoning the souls made Rhett sick. But he knew Jon was right. Even if they did collect these souls, put them in mason jars or water bottles or whatever they could find, there was no way that they could protect them. The souls would have to stay here, drifting within the confines of the train car until someone came and hauled it away, pulverized it and melted it down and turned it into another train car, probably with the souls still trapped within its metal walls. They would ride along the rails with the living passengers, always unsettled, always waiting for some kind of comfort, a resting place that would never come.

"We'll come back for them," Rhett said. The words sounded true, even if he didn't fully believe them himself. "When we finish this, we'll come back and find them and bring them home."

Jon's skeptical look dissolved into one of stubborn surety. He nodded.

"Where are the others?" Rhett asked, dragging his mind back to the present.

"I don't know," Jon said, stepping back the way he'd come. "I got tossed out of the car, separated just like you. They could be anywhere."

"Let's go find them." Anything to get away from the scene here.

They left the way that Jon had come in, through the door at the opposite end of the car, which opened up not onto a grassy field but onto the rest of the wreckage.

Fire and smoke warred with the sunlight, which cut through periodically like brief glimpses of brightness during a storm. All around them, chunks of debris lay within steaming craters. There were huge swaths of grass and dirt that had been carved away, leaving long, hot scars in the earth. To Rhett, it looked more like a spaceship had crash-landed than a train had derailed.

Together, he and Jon moved to start checking the train cars for the others. But before they even made it through the destruction to the next one, they heard the distinct sound of metal clanging against bone.

They followed the sound past one big piece of a train car that had been ripped in half, its outer edge crushed and twisted and looking like angry metal teeth. They ignored the fires and shattered pieces of machinery and more bodies, until they came around one smoldering car leaning against another like a pair of toy blocks, to the actual train tracks themselves.

Basil was there, a scythe in each hand, fending off two psychons at once.

The beasts growled and screeched at him. His overcoat was gone, leaving just the blazer beneath it, Basil spinning his weapons like he always did, as if they were drumsticks and he was going to suddenly break out into blast beats. Scorch marks ran across his face and over his hands, and his clothes were glowing in multiple spots with still-smoking burn holes. He was pale and haggard, his legs trembling, ready to buckle and drop him. His spinning blades were keeping the psychons at a distance, but that wouldn't last long.

One psychon reached for Basil's back, and he ducked, twisting around, gripping his blades firmly. He sliced through the psychon's legs, amputating them at the knee. And before the top part of the monster's body could hit the ground, Basil was slicing with the other scythe, this time cutting through the neck. The psychon fell onto the train tracks in four separate parts.

The remaining psychon took a hesitant step back, its tiny glistening eyes staring out of its bony eye sockets in what could only be fear.

Basil was on top of it before it could run.

He leaped, bringing both scythes together above his head, screaming a battle cry that Rhett had never heard from him. Basil brought the weapons down through the top of the psychon's skull, and as he landed on his feet, the blades sliced all the way through from head to gut. That psychon split in half down the middle and fell on both sides of the tracks at once.

When Basil turned to Rhett and Jon, his scythes were dripping with black blood and his face was splattered with it.

"This is why I don't ride bloody trains," he said. Then he stumbled backward, losing his balance.

Rhett was there, gripping Basil around his middle, trying to hold him up. Instead, they fell together onto one of the only patches of grass that hadn't been scorched by the crash. This close, Rhett could see that the black smears spread across Basil's hands weren't just psychon blood or singe marks—they were the Ash.

Basil opened his mouth as if to say something, but what came out instead was a gurgling, hacking cough. He closed his mouth, opened it. A wet, gasping sound came from the back of his throat.

"Remember . . . ," he choked, "what you promised me." Whatever strength he'd had to bring down the psychons, it was long gone now. The Ash was burning up the last of him right in front of Rhett's eyes.

"He needs a soul," Jon said from over Rhett's shoulder.

Rhett looked back at him, fighting to keep the questioning look off his face. Hadn't it been Jon who said that using souls to treat the

Ash made them no better than psychons? And now he was suggesting that very thing?

"It's the only way to keep him together," Jon went on. "He'll never make it back to the ship this way. Hell, he won't even make it out of Iowa."

"But I thought you said—" Rhett began.

"I know what I said!" Jon was staring hard at the dismembered psychon body just a foot away. One of its fingers curled in a jerky spasm, then went still. When he turned his face back to Rhett, Jon's eyes were full of sorrow. "Monstrous days, right?" he said.

"I won't do it," Basil breathed from his spot cradled in Rhett's arms.

"Nobody gave you a vote," Rhett said. "I promised I wouldn't go out of my way to bring you back. I never promised I wouldn't do everything I could to save you in the first place. Just hang—"

From somewhere amid the roiling smoke, a cry sounded. They all knew the voice right away and spun their heads to look in the direction it was coming from.

"*Is anybody there?*" Mak yelled. "*Guys, we need help!*"

"Stay with Basil," Rhett said to Jon. Immediately, Jon knelt down and pulled Basil out of Rhett's arms and into his own.

"What are you going to do?" he asked as Rhett stood, yanking his knuckle blade back out of its holster.

"I'm going to find Mak," he said. "And hopefully Theo. And then we're getting the fuck out of here."

He ran in the direction of Mak's voice, dodging debris and chunks of torn-up earth. On either side of him, train cars lay broken on their roofs or their sides.

"*Anyone?*" Mak cried again. And now Rhett could hear the strain in her voice, could hear the same metal-on-bone sounds of a fight. They were close. He just needed to—

Glass shattered right in front of him, from the window of a train car on his left that was so filled up with smoke, he couldn't even see inside. As soon as the window was broken, the smoke came pouring out—and so did Theo. His enormous mass came rocketing through the window, pulverizing it, and he rolled across the ground a few times. He had some cuts and bruises that Rhett could see, but mostly he was in one piece.

A pair of psychons came clawing out of the broken window. Behind them, the smoke was clearing out of the train car enough that Rhett could see the shapes of more psychons . . . and Mak. The silhouette of her machete stood out in the haze, like a deadly extension of her arm. But the shapes she was fighting weren't the shapes of psychons— they were too humanlike. They were carrying weapons of their own, swords and knives.

Mak was fighting syllektors.

Outside the car, Theo was getting to his feet, shaking off the tumble through the window. He bounced on his feet a little, one hand curled into a fist, the other holding on to the replacement ax that they'd brought along for him. It was nowhere near what his old battle-ax was—this thing was just a regular wood-chopping ax—but the blade was sharp and it looked light in Theo's meaty hand.

The first psychon lunged for Theo, and Rhett took the chance to do something he'd never tried before. He broke into a run. After a few steps he brought the knuckle blade up over his head . . . then threw it. He gave it as much strength as he could and watched the weapon fly through the air, blades first, whistling right into the face of the second psychon. All four blades dug into its grotesque skull with a sound like a ceramic dish breaking on the floor. The psychon fell back and lay still.

Meanwhile, Theo dispatched the psychon that had attacked him with a simple swing of his ax. It was no syllektor weapon, but it did the trick, gutting the creature through its middle, spraying hot black ooze everywhere.

Theo looked at Rhett, who was bending to yank his knuckle blade out of the psychon's face, and nodded. Then they both climbed up into the train car that Theo had come from, where the sounds of Mak fighting the other syllektors had gone quiet.

When they got inside, they found Mak and two other guys locked in a standoff. Mak had her machete in one hand and a long bowie knife in the other, the ends held at the necks of the other two syllektors. Markeski's syllektors.

"Next time maybe stop for coffee on your way," Mak said over her shoulder. She didn't take her eyes off the guys whose heads she was just centimeters from slicing off. "Take you long enough?"

"Did it take me long enough after I was literally thrown from a derailing train?" Rhett asked. Mak rolled her eyes.

"It's you," one of the guys said. He was the one with the machete under his chin, staring over it at Rhett. There was a tangle of dark curly hair on his head, and whorls of black Ash snaked down his exposed forearms to his wrists, like tattoo sleeves.

"Shut up, Gage," Mak said, jabbing the end of the blade into the soft skin of the syllektor's throat. "Looks like you're pretty sick. What are the chances that I cut your head off and you don't just ghost right here?"

But the guy—Gage—ignored Mak. He lowered an angry stare at Rhett.

"We wouldn't have to do this if it weren't for you," he said. "We lost *everything*—"

"Yous would be wise to close your mouth right about now," Theo said, stepping between Gage and Rhett. Gage's eyes widened slightly at Theo's mass. And for the first time, the guy that Gage was with, the one with the bowie knife at his throat, noticed Theo's presence. He looked the big guy up and down, his eyes wide and unbelieving.

"Theo?" he said.

Theo slowly took his eyes off Gage and turned toward the other guy. His own eyes widened in recognition.

"Mikey?" he said. "What the hell are yous doing running with Markeski's crew? I thought yous was one of the good ones." The wholehearted sound of reproach in Theo's voice almost made Rhett laugh out loud.

"I-I-I thought you were a goner . . . ," Mikey said. "I watched you . . ." He turned his gaze toward Rhett. "I watched *him* ghost you."

"Can everybody please shut the hell up?" Mak said. She pushed against Gage's and Mikey's necks with her weapons until they stepped back a few paces. "You two are traitors. Plain and simple. We don't have the time or the manpower to take you prisoner. But you *will* have to answer to the captain. The *real* captain."

"Mak, there won't *be* a captain for them to answer to if we don't wrap this up. Like now," Rhett murmured.

"What? What happened?" Mak turned her head toward him without moving her arms even a millimeter. She had heard the concern in Rhett's voice. He looked at her.

"Basil's in bad shape," he said. The image of Basil shivering in Jon's arms, the Ash creeping up his neck, floated across his vision. He couldn't bring himself to say the words, but he didn't need to. All he had to do was shake his head, and Mak understood.

"Theo," she said. "I need you to keep these two under control for me. Now."

"Gladly, boss," Theo said. He stepped up behind Gage and Mikey and grabbed them by their collars. Gage kicked and choked against the pressure of the collar around his neck. Mikey simply stood there, a look of shame on his face.

Mak turned to leap out of the car the way that Rhett had come in, but he caught her by the elbow before she could.

"He needs a soul," he whispered. "He said he won't take it, but . . ."

"Oh, he'll take it," she growled. "Figure out what to do with these two idiots." Then she jumped out into a world of smoke and ruin and disappeared.

Rhett looked around. This car looked mostly intact, despite the fire crackling at the far end and the broken window and the litter of clothes and luggage everywhere. And the seats were all empty, either because they hadn't been occupied or because the people who had occupied them had already fled the car. Every seat. Empty.

Except for two.

He heard it first, what they hadn't been able to hear before because everybody was talking. Then the push was there, for real this time, not just some figment of his hopeful, overworked mind. It thumped in his head. It thumped in his heart. Theo gave him a curious look as his attention was drawn in that direction, down a few rows of seats. He could hear the crying.

He shuffled down the aisle. The lights overhead were flickering, and at the far end of the car, the fire was only getting worse. He could feel the others' eyes on him. Gage struggled against Theo's grip, but the big guy held on to him. And when Gage saw where Rhett was heading, he quit struggling. All three of them could only stare now.

When Rhett stepped up to the row of seats that the push had been guiding him to, he found a little girl and a man. The girl was only five or six. She had on jeans and a pair of sneakers and a baseball hat turned backward on her head. A set of light brown bangs fell out from under the hat into her eyes. She was also wearing a turquoise sweater that was a little long in the sleeves, which she kept using to wipe her running nose as she cried. The tears streamed across her cheeks and dripped from her chin.

The man was in his thirties. He had a little scruff across his chin and his glasses sat askew on his nose. He was leaning against the window, where a spiderweb of cracks had formed around his head. There was blood all over the side of his face, matted in his hair. His eyes were closed and he wasn't moving.

The girl nudged the man's arm, and then she shook it with both hands, with as much strength as her little arms had in them.

"Daddy," she said, her voice pleading. "Daddy, we have to go. The fire's gonna get us. Come *on*, Daddy."

Rhett stood there, feeling the thrum of the push, watching the girl try to get her dad to wake up. To her, they were all alone on this train car with the spilled luggage and the growing fire. She didn't see any psychons or syllektors. All she saw was her father, quiet and not moving and covered in something that she might have understood was blood. But she didn't understand that he was dying.

From behind him, Rhett heard Gage's voice, thin and choked from the squeeze of Theo's grip.

"What's he going to do?" he said. "He's going to take that soul for your captain, isn't he—" Theo cut him off by lifting him completely off his feet.

Rhett sat down in the empty third seat in the row, putting the girl between himself and her dad. Now the push was like a manic hammering inside him, thudding until he felt it in every part of his body. The man's heartbeat, losing strength but persistent nonetheless, interlocked with Rhett's, and suddenly it was one heartbeat. *Whump-whump. Whump-whump.*

Rhett reached out and grabbed the man's hand. His eyes were shut, so he didn't look at Rhett, but Rhett saw them moving around beneath the man's eyelids, searching, trying to find a way back to his little girl.

"*Daddy,*" she whimpered between them.

"Come back to her," Rhett said. His voice was quiet but firm. "This isn't your time. She needs you. This is not your day to die. This is not the end."

All along the window, where the cracks encircled the man's head, little tendrils of purple electricity danced. They jabbed and jittered, connecting strands of the man's hair, lancing between his glasses and the metal frame of the window.

"Wake up," Rhett said to the man. "Wake up and get her out of here."

And then he did.

The man's eyes shot open and he heaved in a sharp breath, gasping for air as if he'd been submerged in water and was finally breaking the surface. The girl jumped at the sound of it but immediately threw her arms around the man's neck.

Maybe she knew after all, Rhett thought.

He got up and went back to Theo as the man and his daughter held on to each other. The fire had spread across the entire end of the train car now, and it popped angrily.

The girl gasped. "Daddy, the fire!"

"It's okay, sweetie," the man said, looking at her with eyes that seemed confused and relieved and frightened all at the same time. He swept his eyes around the train car one last time, as if searching for someone else that might have been there. When he saw no one, he said, "Let's go. C'mon."

They stood, hand in hand, and ran out of the car through the one door that wasn't engulfed in flames. When they were out of sight, Rhett finally relaxed.

"You're a miracle," Mikey said. Rhett turned to him. He and Theo and Gage were all silhouetted by the dancing firelight behind them. Slowly, Theo lowered Mikey until his feet were firmly on the ground. "That was . . . a miracle. Straight up."

Rhett looked at Gage, still dangling a few inches off the floor, clutching at his throat, trying to get a full breath of air.

"Put him down, too," Rhett said to Theo. And Theo did so without hesitation. When the tension around his neck was finally released, Gage pulled in a long, shuddering gasp. Rhett looked at him and said: "Go back to Markeski and tell him what you saw. Don't you dare lie. You know what the truth is now, so don't try to hide from it. Tell Markeski, tell any syllektor who will listen to you what happened here. And then get out while you still can." He turned to Mikey. "Got it?"

As Rhett spoke, Theo had come back around and stood beside him, leaving Gage and Mikey alone. They were harmless now, Rhett knew. He also knew that they would do what he told them to do. He could see it in their eyes.

"You really are the Twice-Born Son," Mikey whispered. He looked amazed and fearful. Gage mostly looked frightened.

Rhett opened his mouth to respond, with what, he had no idea, but he never got the chance.

The wall behind the flames, which had been slowly building to an inferno, exploded inward with a shriek of metal. The unmistakable shape of a psychon leaped out of the fire and landed right behind the two syllektors, rocking the entire car with its weight. It drove its clawed fingers into both of their backs. The claws erupted out of their chests, coated in a thin sheen of blood and bits of flesh. Gage looked more perplexed than startled or afraid. He cocked his head, as if trying to solve some kind of problem. Mikey looked down with absolute horror at the slick red claw that jutted from his midsection.

A second later, both men crumbled into dust.

"*No!*" Rhett and Theo screamed together. They were down the aisle before the last fluttering specks of the syllektors' remains could touch the floor. Rhett pulled his knuckle blade from its holster and hacked into the psychon's chest with it. Theo was beside him, slamming the curved edge of his ax into bone and muscle. One blow right after another, until the psychon was nothing but an array of mismatched limbs on the floor.

When they were done, they both stepped back, realizing at the same time that they were standing in Gage and Mikey's ashes, piles of dark dust that now lay mingled with the black ooze of the psychon's innards.

"We have to go," Rhett said, staring down at the ashes. He had an urge to bend down and scoop them up. But what would he do with them after that? Hold on to them until they were back aboard the *Harbinger*, where they could scatter them in the waters of the river? No. That was a ritual of the living. Syllektors were already dead, and being ghosted was just a continuation of that death. Another step down into the grave. All they could do now was move on.

So they did.

Back outside, the chaos of the train wreck was no less frantic. From somewhere far off, Rhett could hear sirens wailing. And in the windows of some of the more mangled train cars, the white, fluttering smoke of dead souls churned, looking for a way out.

He led Theo back to where he had left Basil and Jon and found the two of them in the exact spot they'd been when he'd gone to help Mak.

Basil was sprawled in Jon's lap, his limbs quietly spasming, his breathing harsh and labored.

"Where's Mak?" Rhett asked Jon.

From behind the veil of acrid smoke, something exploded. A fireball punched into the sky and lit the destruction with a quickly fading orange glow. They all turned in that direction and watched the explosion turn into a new column of deep black smoke. All of them except for Basil, who continued to lie with his eyes shut, his body wracked with shivers and dripping sweat.

"She went to get a—" Jon started.

"Hold him down," Mak snapped, emerging from between two crumpled train cars. She stormed up the slight hill to where Basil lay on the tracks. As soon as he heard her voice, Basil began to squirm.

"No," he choked out. "No, I won't do it!" He flailed with as much strength as he had, and for the moment, Rhett, Jon, and Theo only stood and watched. "I won't be . . . one of those things. *Don't make me do it!*"

"I said hold him *down!*" Mak yelled. She stepped between Rhett and Theo, crouching down in front of Basil. Jon gripped his arms as he tried to push off the ground. Mak straddled Basil's legs, digging her knees hard into the gravel under the train tracks and holding him there. She leaned in, gripping both sides of his face in her hands.

"Please," Basil whispered. "Please, don't." A tear blackened with ash rolled down his cheek. He stared at her with eyes that were finally awake, finally aware, but were filled with a desperate sadness. He knew he was going to lose this battle, captain or not.

"I won't let it take you," Mak said. And she pressed her lips to his. There was a tiny gap between her mouth and Basil's, and in it Rhett could see the white mist of a soul rushing from her lungs into his.

When the soul was transferred, Mak sat back. Basil took a deep, strong breath. The tension in his limbs went away, and he lay limp against Jon for a moment. His eyes were open, still fully conscious. His face was a strange mixture of relief and rage. But he didn't say a word.

"He can't hold on to it for too long," Jon said quietly.

"I know," Mak replied.

"If he keeps it and the soul binds itself to him . . ."

"Jon, I said I know," Mak snapped.

"No, Mak, you don't," Jon shot back. He gripped Mak's arm and forced her to look at him. "If he keeps that soul for longer than a few hours, the line between Basil and whoever that soul belongs to will start to dissolve." Jon gave Basil another concerned glance. "He could lose himself entirely."

Mak yanked her arm back. "Then we'll make sure that doesn't happen."

Jon leaned back and nodded, the look of concern on his face only growing more severe.

Rhett didn't know what either of them was talking about; he had never heard anything about souls binding themselves to syllektors before. But he'd have to wait until later to ask, because as he watched, the strokes of black Ash that had etched themselves into Basil's arms and neck began to recede. The patches slipped back beneath the surface of his skin, leaving it clean and smooth and healthy-looking. As healthy-looking as a dead person's skin could look, anyway.

There was a dense silence that fell among the five of them. Nobody moved.

"Guys," Rhett said after a while. "We should go."

One by one, they collected themselves. Mak, Basil, and Jon got to their feet, clumsily trying to avoid touching one another more than they already had been. Basil glowered at nothing in particular. He wouldn't make eye contact with anybody, not even Rhett.

"Jon?" Mak asked suddenly. "What happened to the radio?" She clutched the lantern that was still hooked to her belt with the force of a child holding on to their favorite toy. But she was looking Jon up and down, inventorying what he had on him.

Jon fiddled with his hands. "Last time I saw it," he said, "it was in pieces."

Mak's shoulders slumped, her head dropped.

"Let's just get out of this hellhole," she said.

"Agreed." It was Basil speaking, but it didn't sound like Basil's voice at all, so hard and bitter.

The captain of the *Harbinger* stormed past his crew, and they followed him.

NINE

They stood at the top of a low hill not far from the place where the train lay scattered in smoldering pieces, surrounded by fire trucks spraying tall arcs of water into the flames. The sun glared off the polished red sides of the trucks, making it look like a summer day even though the air was still cold and the grass in which the syllektors stood was limp and brown. The wind turbines were still standing beyond the wreckage, waving contently, oblivious to the tragedy.

Rhett, Basil, Mak, Theo, and Jon watched the police cars and the ambulances arrive, watched the body bags emerge one by one, slick and black and heavy. They could all feel Basil's anger. It hung between them like heavy ropes, a weight they might be doomed to carry for as long as they continued to exist.

There was also the loss of Jon's spirit radio to think about. They could get to the town where Treeny had lived. They could even get to her house. But without the radio, how were they supposed to find the exact place her ghost was haunting? And without Treeny, they wouldn't be able to locate the Navigator. And without, and without, and without . . .

Rhett shook his head and closed his eyes, heaving in a deep breath of air that his lungs didn't need. He had known before agreeing to this plan that there would be plenty of opportunity for failure. Each next step relied on the one that came before it, like a line of dominoes waiting to fall. The first domino, the one that was supposed to bring them to Treeny's ghost, had not fallen, leaving the rest of them at a standstill.

But that didn't mean Rhett and the others couldn't just reach out and push the next one over themselves.

"So now what?" Basil asked. "Is this the part where you lot try to convince me to go back? To give up?" He'd gotten a bit of his strength back, but he still looked sick and frail. His eyes were ringed with deep purple bruises. The soul was sustaining him, but that was all it was doing.

"Now we keep going," Rhett said, glancing in Mak's direction. She hadn't said much since they'd regrouped and gotten away from the crash. But she met Rhett's gaze now and gave him a stiff little nod.

"How are we supposed to get hold of Treeny's ghost without the radio?" Jon asked.

"The best we can do is go to where Treeny lived and hope that we can find her," Rhett replied. "Mak already said that was the most likely place for Treeny to be."

"What if she's not there?" Theo said. His arms were folded across his massive chest as he stared down at the scattered ruins of the train.

"Then . . . we keep looking, I guess," Rhett said. "We keep looking until there's nowhere left to look. And if that doesn't work, then we try to find the Navigator ourselves. No matter what happens, we keep going. Because the longer we wait, the more living people who die and the more souls that are lost." He gestured down at the train, still smoking and blackening. "This is our fault. This war is between the dead and the dead alone. But the living are suffering because of it. We can't allow that to keep happening."

His words hung heavy among them. The silence that followed was even heavier. After a while, though, Mak finally spoke up.

"He's right," she said, breaking the quiet, turning to face them all. "The psychons aren't going to stop coming after us. Neither are Markeski's syllektors. And they sure as hell aren't going to stop attacking the living. We could go knocking on Urcena's door right now and surrender, and she'd still ghost us. The only one she'd spare is Rhett, and that's only because she can use him to do even more damage with the souls on board the *Harbinger*."

"What the hell," Basil said. "I'm doomed anyway. Let's get this shitshow on the road while we still can." There was just a touch of the usual humor in his voice, faint but recognizable.

"Yeah, I'm not quite as optimistic as the captain here," Jon said, cocking a thumb at Basil. "But I'm still in. I'm in until the end. Whatever that is."

"Okay then," Mak said. "Good. Now we just need to find a way to Nebraska. Any ideas?"

"Uh, I have one," Theo said, raising his hand as if he were a student in a classroom. But his eyes were fixed on something down near the wreckage of the train.

When they all followed his gaze and found what he was looking at, Basil groaned.

"You guys are killing me," he said. Then: "Pun intended."

The police cruiser bucked and jerked as Mak drove it alongside the train tracks, giving it as much gas as she could, the sirens blaring on the roof. Basil sat in the passenger seat beside her, and in the back, Rhett, Jon, and Theo held on to whatever they could.

Through the back windows, Rhett watched the broken pieces of the train, now just giving off thin veils of smoke as they receded toward the horizon. He couldn't even see any of the first responders, none of whom had gone chasing after the cruiser when the syllektors drove off with it; they had been too absorbed with trying to find survivors among the wreckage.

Mak kept driving, the train tracks whizzing past beside them until they converged with State Route 63. She swerved the cruiser off the grassy field and onto the solid pavement of the road, causing the three boys in the back to all slam against each other.

The ride smoothed out once they got onto the actual road, though. Basil found a map in the glove box and plotted their route with it, proving to be a much better navigator than he was a driver—not that Mak was much better. They went north on 63 until they split off onto Route 163. They passed through Des Moines, glimpsing the city only in the time it took them to bypass traffic on the shoulder of the road, sirens yelling the whole way. Before they left Des Moines, they stopped off and siphoned the gas out of a few cars that were parked in a sales

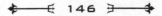

lot, then switched roads and got onto Interstate 80, which, according to Basil, would take them right into Omaha. From there, the little town of Wycoma, where Treeny had lived, was only a few miles away.

A few miles until they would know if they had even the smallest chance of succeeding. A few miles until they might come face-to-face with the person who helped cause this mess they were in. Only a few miles until their own fates and the fates of the rest of the crew were decided, one way or another.

They watched the time—and the road—tick by.

PART

THREE

TEN

Wycoma sat at the far reaches of Omaha's smaller suburbs. In fact, Rhett wasn't sure it could even be considered part of the city at all. It reminded him a little of the town they'd visited in Arizona—Turnstile—where he'd witnessed the gathering of a soul for the first time. Except Wycoma wasn't surrounded by desert and mountains; it was surrounded by the wintered-over remains of cornfields. They were wide and barren, the soil a dull brown color and the broken remnants of cornstalks scattered across the ground and sticking up like snapped bones. The harvest was long gone, and all that remained were the empty fields, waiting for the next season to come around so they could be tilled, fertilized, and regrown.

The town itself was like any other, this one a bit more populated and a bit more economically sound than Turnstile had been. The main street was full of thriving small businesses with quirky names. They were built into old houses that crowded against the street and wrapped around a pretty circle that had a fountain sitting at its center. Tall arcs of water shot out of it and turned the afternoon sun into dapples of light that swam across the surrounding buildings.

Rhett thought it was a gorgeous town, one that would be a wonderful place for a kid to grow up. This was also the kind of place where secrets weren't really secrets, where that hushed little whisper ran through the town like a current of water, carrying all the dark, hidden parts of people's lives with it. It had now been several years since Treeny had died, but Rhett tried to imagine the gossip that would have passed through Wycoma as a result. It made him glad that he'd been living in New York when he died.

There was a parking garage just off the main drag. Mak pulled the police cruiser into it, waiting for the wooden arm to raise so they could pass. Thankfully everything was automated, which meant there was no one around to spot a rather beat-up-looking cop car driving itself into an empty space. Mak switched the engine off and left the keys hanging in the ignition.

"Someone's going to be really weirded out when they find this here," she said, opening her door and collecting her machete and the lantern, which had been sitting on the console between her and Basil for the entire journey. "But at least we're leaving it in one piece."

The five syllektors abandoned the cruiser and made their way out of the parking garage on foot. The sun sat low in the sky and cast a deep orange glow across the entire town. Windows shone with captured fire. It was amazing, Rhett thought, that it had only been a couple of days since they left the rest of the crew back in Pennsylvania. They were no longer there, of course. And thank goodness for that, because if Markeski and his group of syllektors had been able to track Rhett and the others down, they must have been able to locate the mill.

They could only hope that the crew got out of there before Markeski showed up.

"Okay, Captain Winthrop," Mak joked, gesturing to Basil, who was still holding on to the map from the police cruiser's glove box. "Lead the way."

Basil shot her a withering look but consulted the map anyway. He shook it out, trying to smooth the wrinkles from hundreds of folds and refolds. Rhett wondered if anybody walking by would see a map just floating there by itself—he'd never fully figured out the mechanics of the syllektors' visibility to the living and maybe never would. After a moment, Basil pointed down the street to their left.

"This way," he said. And then: "God, I miss the days when we had the push to lead us around."

They followed Basil's lead until they had almost completely left the town behind. Now there was just the road and the brittle cornfields and the uneven shape of Wycoma getting smaller and more distant behind them.

"You sure this is the right way, boss?" Theo asked. He was looking around anxiously, ax gripped tightly in his hand. Rhett understood. They were out in the open, surrounded by nothing but a bunch of dried-up, empty fields—if more psychons showed up and wanted a fight, there would be nowhere to hide, nowhere to potentially get an advantage. It would just be the psychons and the syllektors out here on an old road, pummeling one another into oblivion.

"Yes," Basil said simply, and kept walking.

The sun was close to the horizon now. Pretty soon it would be dark and they'd really be screwed. Rhett wanted to say something, to suggest maybe holing up in the car overnight and trying again in the morning. But before he could even try, Mak pointed down the road.

"There," she said.

Rhett could see the shapes of a decent-size farmhouse and barn, sitting just off the road with a vast expanse of land stretching out behind them.

"That's it?" Rhett asked. "That's her house?"

"Well, it used to be," Mak replied. "Even if her family doesn't live there anymore, her ghost might still be haunting the place."

"Never thought I'd be crossing my fingers and hoping to find a ghost," Rhett said, "but here we are."

Mak grinned at him.

The group continued down the road, hurrying now with the house in sight, as if it might be some kind of mirage that would vanish as soon as they got to it. But the nearer they got, the more defined the house and barn looked.

The barn was in rough shape, sagging to one side, paint peeling off in random clumps. It might have once been red but was now a graying shade of brown. There wasn't a single tree or bush around either building, just patchy dead grass that cut off where the fields started.

In only slightly better shape, the house was two stories tall with an enormous wraparound porch and dark blue shutters that looked like they might have been recently painted. The lights were on in the house, a few windows glowing brightly from within. And there was

only a single car in the short driveway, an old Grand Am with chipped paint and a few rust spots.

When they were close enough, Rhett could read a name on the side of the mailbox that must have been painted there years before: UNDER-MAN. Treeny's last name.

They stood in a line in front of the yard, unseen and unheard.

"Now what?" Basil asked in a whisper.

"I don't know," Mak replied softly.

"Why are we whispering?" Basil said.

Just then, the front door opened, startling all of them. Behind the screen, the shape of a man stood in the doorway. He was backing up, pushing the screen door open with his rear end. When it was open and the man swung around, Rhett could see that he was carrying a plate of food in one hand and a steaming coffee mug in the other. The man himself was old, bordering on elderly. His back was hunched and his shoulders sagged. He wore a faded pair of jeans that were too big for his withering frame and a plaid button-down shirt that was the same way, the extra fabric flapping under his arms and at his sides. His face was small and wrinkled, and his hair was gray. But between the glasses he wore and the freckles that were now mixing with liver spots across his cheeks, the resemblance was undeniable. Rhett heard Mak gasp at his side as she saw it, too.

This man could have been Treeny's grandfather, but given how long it had been since she died, he was undeniably her father.

They watched him carry his dinner across the porch to the side of the house, where there were a pair of rocking chairs and a little table between them. He set his plate and mug on the table, then lowered himself into one of the chairs with a great sigh. Rhett thought the man would wait, that someone else must have been coming to join him since there was an extra chair there. But no one did. The man took up his fork and started eating, watching the sun as it dipped below the horizon.

"Okay, no really," Jon said. "Now what?"

"We talk to him," Rhett said. They all turned, blinking, to look at him.

Jon gaped. "We . . . what now?"

"How do we even do that?" Theo asked.

"I don't know," Rhett replied. He turned to Mak and Basil. "You guys have any ideas? I know we can do it. Captain Trier told me that we're able to manifest ourselves if we need to. I think this qualifies."

Mak was still staring at Rhett as if he had grown an extra set of eyeballs just above the ones he already had.

"Well . . . yeah. I guess," she said. "But . . . it's hard. And . . . *why?*"

"Because we don't have time to waste. I don't have any interest in putzing around here until we just happen to find Treeny's ghost. She could be here or she could be anywhere in town. We have no idea where exactly she died or what place would have had any special meaning to her. *He* does." Rhett crossed his arms and nodded his head toward Treeny's father, who was oblivious to the five dead teenagers having a conversation in front of his house.

The rest of them slowly turned their gazes in the same direction, staring at Treeny's dad with a mixture of pity and reluctance. Rhett knew what they were thinking. The poor guy had lost his daughter however many years ago, and it looked like he didn't have anyone else left. How was he going to react to these five strangers showing up out of nowhere and drudging up her death?

Rhett didn't know, but he knew they had to try.

"Okay," he said. "How do we do this?"

Mak sighed and shook her hands out, as if they had gone numb and she was trying to get the feeling back into them. She took a step back, giving herself some space from the rest of them.

"You remember what it was like when you realized you had control over your senses?" she asked.

"Yes," Rhett replied.

"It's like that. But you have to completely give yourself over to that feeling." She looked down at her own arms and legs, at the scrapes and bruises that had been put there by the train crash. She glanced at the others' various injuries as well. "And it's going to hurt," she added.

Basil, Jon, and Theo spread themselves out. Theo was bouncing from one foot to the other. Jon was cracking his knuckles. Basil was . . . not looking great. But there was a confidence in his eyes, a newfound rigor against the trials of the Ash that Rhett hadn't seen up until now. Maybe it was the soul doing its work, or maybe it was something else. Rhett didn't know or care—he was just glad to have a little bit of the old Basil back.

Rhett watched the others stretching and dancing on their feet for a moment until he realized that they were trying to limber themselves up in preparation for being able to feel all the pain and exhaustion that their bodies had endured the last few days. He followed suit, shaking his hands and stretching the muscles in his arms and legs, rolling his head down and then back, none of which he could feel. Yet.

"All right, mate," Basil said. "The trick is to not let up when you switch your senses on. Do whatever it is you do mentally to accomplish that. But keep going with it. Follow that feeling until you're as close to feeling what it was like to be alive again as you can get."

Mak was nodding in agreement.

"Okay," Rhett said. "I think I can do that." If it was anything like learning how to sense the push, he *knew* he could do it. But he was nervous just the same.

All five of them closed their eyes, standing in a rough circle in the front yard. They took deep breaths. And then Rhett heard Theo groan and Jon yelp, as if he'd been hit by something. He heard Basil's breath become shaky and labored beside him. Mak made a low moaning sound deep in the back of her throat. They had switched their senses on, and the pain was coming through.

Rhett did the same, forcing the nerves in his body to spark and begin sending signals back to his brain again. And as soon as he did, the wave of agony that fell over him was almost unbearable. He could feel the hot, steady ache in his right side where his ribs had broken, could feel the cuts and bumps all over his body. There was a twinge in his bad ankle. Below the pain was the exhaustion, a blanket of it that covered every limb and muscle and bone, pushing down on him, threatening to push him into the ground and never let him up again.

But instead of stopping there, Rhett did as Basil had said; he followed that feeling. He focused on the pain in his ankle, the one that he had not only broken as a kid but that had been mauled by a psychon in San Francisco. He remembered what that ankle felt like when he was alive, when he would spend too much time walking or running. Long school days were the worst. By the time he'd get off the bus and make his way up to his parents' apartment, the ankle would be throbbing. It was throbbing now, and he tried to hold on to that, tried to let the ache permeate through his entire body. The exhaustion, the pain, the heartache. It was all there, suffocating him from the inside. He could feel the chill that hung in the air, could feel it deepening as the sun took its warmth with it to the other side of the planet. Every part of him pulsated with the sensations of a living, breathing body.

The others hadn't moved at all, which meant they were still concentrating as well. This really was hard. More so because Mak had been right: It did hurt. A *lot*.

Rhett pushed his senses down to the ends of his toes and into the tips of his fingers. He pushed, and pushed, and pushed . . .

. . . until the hairs on his arms and the back of his neck stood up, bristling from the cold breeze coming off the vacant field. An enormous chill ran through him, almost more like a spasm that made his whole body twitch and shake for a second. He could hear the others going through the same thing, one after the other. And if a living person happened to be driving by at that moment, they would have seen four young men and one young woman appear out of nowhere.

Rhett opened his eyes. "Did it work?"

Mak squatted down, hands on the sides of her head, eyes still shut. "Yep," she said. "Definitely worked."

Jon was leaning against the mailbox, holding a hand tightly against his abdomen, wincing.

Rhett went to him, favoring his bad ankle as he walked, and put a hand on the younger guy's shoulder.

"You all right?" he asked.

"Yeah, sure," Jon replied, half laughing and half groaning. "Nothing like traveling halfway across the country, getting thrown out of a train, and being attacked by soul-eating monsters on a regular basis to really make a guy feel just peachy. I'm living my best life here. Can't you tell?"

And despite everything, Rhett actually felt laughter bubbling up inside him, cutting through the pain if only for a brief second.

Theo seemed to be doing okay, but he definitely looked paler than usual. Basil, on the other hand, looked worse than ever. He was sitting in the grass, hunched over, arms limp at his sides.

"Basil?" Rhett said, leaving Jon at the mailbox. Slowly, nervously, fearing that something awful was already happening. "Basil? Talk to me, man."

And then Basil jerked his head up, looking around at all of them with wild, bloodshot eyes. There was a strange grin on his face, caught somewhere between humorous and drunken.

"Hello there," he said. He didn't *sound* drunk. In fact, he sounded more with it than Rhett had heard him since their first real conversation in his office back at the factory. He sounded surprised, though, as if he'd just unexpectedly run into Rhett on the street.

Mak was there, standing beside Rhett, her own ailments apparently forgotten.

"Basil," she said softly. "Sweetheart."

Basil's eyes found hers and then that weird grin turned into a broad, genuine smile. There was a pain in his eyes, though, and Rhett could tell that the fog was clearing. Whatever strange effect the process of manifesting himself had had on Basil, it was already beginning to wear off.

Rhett put out a hand, and Basil took it, allowing himself to be helped up.

"Sorry, mate," Basil said. "That was . . . odd."

There was no time to react before Mak was leaning in, grabbing Rhett by the elbow.

"The soul," she whispered. "He's had it for too long. Showing ourselves probably isn't helping. It's binding itself to him. If we don't make this fast, it could take him over completely."

Rhett's eyes widened.

"I . . . *Why* is that a thing?" he said, trying to keep his voice restrained. He was about to suggest that maybe Basil stay behind and go back to his normal state while the rest of them went ahead, when another voice called out to them.

"'Scuse me!" the voice said. It was coming from the porch. The five of them turned to Treeny's father as he spoke again. "Can I help you?"

Everybody froze.

Treeny's father stared down at them, hands resting on the railing that went around the porch. What a sight they must have been, all of them dressed in dark clothes, armed with dangerous-looking weapons, and none of them appearing to be over twenty years old.

What are we supposed to say? Rhett thought. *Are we supposed to tell the truth? Because if so, then we are about to have a lot of convincing to do.*

Then Basil stepped forward.

"Hello, sir!" he said, putting a hand up in a friendly wave. His British accent was gone, replaced by a voice that was distinctly American but not the mocking, jocklike accent that Basil put on when he was trying to be funny. This voice sounded as if the person it belonged to had never once set foot in Europe. "Are you Mr. Underman?"

Treeny's dad gave Basil a cautious look but returned the wave and said, "I am. Most people just call me Whit, though. Who's asking?"

"My name's . . . Jake, sir. These are my friends. Are you Treeny's dad?"

The name seemed to send a little jolt through the man. His face grew dark and his eyes narrowed just the slightest.

"I was," he said simply.

"We, uh, we were friends of Treeny's," Basil went on in his new voice. Rhett watched as Basil casually slipped both hands into the pockets of his pants, a gesture that Rhett had never once seen from him. "From school. Before she died."

Whit ran an inspecting eye over all of them. "You all look a little young to have known my Treeny. It's been a long while since she passed. Almost fifteen years."

"Well, you see, sir, we were actually pretty young when we knew your daughter." Basil was on a roll. Rhett had a pretty good idea where it was all coming from, and it made him anxious with worry. "She was part of a mentoring program at the elementary school. They used to send some of the middle schoolers over to read to us once a month. Treeny was one of the nicest ones. One of the smartest, too."

Jon scoffed, probably at the idea of Treeny being nice, and Rhett jabbed an elbow into his side.

On the porch, a little smile was breaking out on Whit's face.

"That sounds like my Treeny," he said. "Don't recall any mentoring program, but it was so long ago now. She had so many programs and things that she was part of, it was hard to keep track of 'em." He let out a tiny laugh.

Basil laughed with him, nodding, as if they were old friends reminiscing about the good ol' days. "Well, sir, Treeny was a big inspiration to us as kids, and we owe her a lot. We're all in high school now, over at Millard West, and we're working on a project about the most influential people in our lives. We were hoping we might be able to ask you some questions about Treeny so we can include her in the project."

Whit cocked his head to the side, looking like he was trying to decide whether he wanted to believe Basil or not. He glanced at the rest of them. Rhett could see out of the corner of his eye that Jon, Mak, and Theo were all nodding anxiously, and he felt a goofy, uncomfortable grin form on his own face.

The moment stretched out, and Rhett became certain that Whit was going to decline and send them away, which would put them back at square one, back to having to do all this on their own and hope that it worked out.

But then Whit straightened up, a broad smile lighting up his face and crinkling his features even more.

"I'd be happy to," he said. "Come on up. I'll put on some more coffee."

The tension relaxed, and Rhett felt the knot in the pit of his stomach loosen. It was weird to really feel things again, even if it was only temporary. Which was another concern—he didn't know how long they would be able to stay like this. They could be sitting with Whit and vanish right in front of his eyes, reverting back to their normal syllektor state without warning. They were going all-in again, hoping that this latest bet wasn't the one that broke them.

"You know," Whit said as Rhett and the others approached the porch steps. "Not to judge, but you all look a bit . . . out of sorts. Or maybe it's just a fashion choice or something? What's the word the kids used when Treeny was in school?" He had a hand to his lips, pondering his own question.

"Grungy?" Rhett offered.

"Derelict?" Jon tried.

"Orphaned?" Mak added.

Whit snapped his fingers and pointed up at the porch roof.

"Emo," he said.

Jon snorted and Rhett elbowed him again.

"Treeny was my little girl."

They were on the porch, the sun flashing its last tiny sliver at them. Whit was seated in one rocking chair, Basil in the other. The rest of them stood, bracing themselves against the chill that the evening air brought with it. They weren't used to being able to feel the cold if they didn't want to, but as long as they were manifesting themselves to talk to Whit, they had no other choice. Whit had brought out mugs of coffee for them all, though, and they held on to them with both hands, letting the steam warm their faces.

"She was my whole life, her and her mother," Whit continued. He had a fresh cup of coffee himself, but it sat on the little table, untouched, as he spoke and stared out at the sun and the shadows that spilled across the barren cornfield, seeping between the broken stalks together but never quite mixing, like oil and water.

"What happened to your wife?" Rhett asked before he could stop himself. He was curious, thinking about his parents and what might have happened to them if he had been the only one to die in the car accident that night.

The edges of Whit's mouth twitched. "After Treeny died, my wife wasn't the same person. Treeny and I were close, but she and Genevieve—my wife—were best friends. They did everything together. Genny's the reason Treeny was so smart. She taught her so much." His eyes were more distant than ever, and now they looked bright and wet. "Never really understood what Genny saw in a goon like me," he whispered.

Rhett and the others watched Whit, waiting. The only sound was a lone crow that had landed out on one of the dried-up stalks, pecking at it. After a moment, Whit laughed.

"Never answered your question, did I?" he asked Rhett, who could only hold on to his coffee and stare. Whit went on without any prompting. "As I said, my wife changed after Treeny passed. She'd always had this optimism, this hope. You could always see it there in her eyes.

I used to call it her little spark. But after Treeny . . . Genny just couldn't quite get her spark back. She blamed me, of course. *I* blamed me, so I couldn't well blame *her* for blaming me, could I?" He paused, but not long enough for any of them to answer his question. "No. No, I couldn't. So when she said she was leaving, I . . . I didn't have the heart to try and stop her."

The crow unfurled its dark wings and lifted into the air, like a living shadow.

Basil finally broke the silence, his voice still carrying its newfound American accent.

"If you don't mind me asking, sir," he said, "we never really found out what happened to Treeny. Not exactly. We were kids when she died, so our parents didn't give us the whole story."

Rhett continued to marvel at Basil, his strange understanding of how to approach the conversation with Whit, his ability to twist the truth into something useful. What he said wasn't exactly a lie—he really didn't know how Treeny had died, and judging by the curious looks on their faces, neither did Mak, Jon, or Theo.

They waited while Whit collected his thoughts.

"Treeny was smart," Whit said, absently scratching his chin. "But she was . . . different. Quiet. Happy, mind you. But quiet. She played around on the computers at school. Spent all her time at the library. There were always stacks of books in her room. I never really understood where it came from. Her shyness, I mean. Genny and I were always pretty sociable. Treeny was . . . not. To say the least."

There was a general air of agreement that passed over Rhett and the others. In the time that Rhett had known Treeny, the most she had ever spoken was when she was mostly possessed by a demon. The memory of it sent a shiver through him.

"Which is why it's hard to believe she was ever part of any program to read to little kids," Whit went on, and the five syllektors stiffened. "All the clubs and activities she ever did were the ones where she didn't have to interact too much with other people. But I suppose dealing with grade school kids is a lot different than dealing with kids your own age. Especially for Treeny. Middle school was rough on her. So rough, in fact, I'm certain it killed her."

They all relaxed as Whit steered the conversation away from the made-up program that Basil had come up with, and Mak spoke this time.

"What do you mean?" she asked.

"What I mean is kids are brutal when they want to be. Especially in those in-between years with puberty and whatnot. I've gone out to middle schools over the years and talked to kids about Treeny's story. I've seen firsthand what their personalities are like. It's one of the scariest things I've ever laid eyes on."

"So . . . she was murdered?" Basil asked cautiously.

Whit waved a hand at him. "No, no. Nothing like that. What happened to Treeny was an accident, pure and simple. But the accident never would have happened if she hadn't been so miserable from school."

"What exactly *did* happen, sir?" Mak asked. Her voice was low, barely there. Rhett could hear it wavering from the cold. The sun had completely fallen below the horizon, blanketing the fields in darkness. They were talking now by the soft glow of the porch light.

"She fell down our well," Whit said. It was so blunt that Rhett almost wasn't sure he'd heard him right. "The one over there, on the other side of the barn." Whit was pointing toward the far side of the sunken barn, where there was a narrow patch of yard, like an alley, between where the barn ended and the cornfield started. It was drowning in darkness right now, but Rhett could almost imagine what the well looked like.

Everybody else looked caught off guard. Even Mak, who had her arms wrapped tightly around herself, shivering, was staring at Whit with wide, uncertain eyes.

"H-how?" Mak said.

Now Whit got that faraway look in his eyes again, gazing up at the blackened hulk of the barn.

"She was out here reading one of her books. I could see her from my bedroom window. I think I was up there folding laundry or something. She was reading, but I could tell she was struggling to focus on it. Normally when she reads, she gets nice and cozy somewhere, squeezes herself into the tiniest possible space, and can just sit there for hours. I watched her go through ten books one Labor Day weekend, and I swear to you it was like she didn't move from the couch at all the entire time." He choked out something that might have been laughter or might have been a sob. Maybe it was both. "Anyway, that day she just wasn't into it. I could see it even from the second floor. She'd been having a lot of trouble that week. Kids at school wouldn't let up on her. And she was being pretty hard on herself about her grades, as usual. I . . . I think it all just kind of stacked up. I watched her wander around the yard, keeping an eye on her in between folding my drawers.

"She went over to the well and . . . and she set her book down on one of the stones. It was a library book. I remember because they . . . pulled it out of there along with her." He scratched at the armrest of his chair. "*The Grapes of Wrath*," he said. "I tried to read it myself after she died, but golly is that Steinbeck fellow a bore. Treeny didn't think so, though. Treeny loved his books. She read everything of his. She . . ."

Whit's voice broke, and his lower jaw shook. Rhett had heard enough to know where he might find Treeny's ghost, but he waited for Treeny's father to finish his story. The others did, too. It was the least they could do for the old man, who had once been younger and stronger but who was aged unfairly by tragedy and years spent alone, dwelling on all the things that could have been.

"She wasn't paying attention," Whit continued after he'd gotten a little more control of himself. "I think she might even have been crying. I don't know for sure. I wasn't paying attention, either. I was busy with the laundry. I should have gone down there. I should have talked to her. That wasn't really my thing, though. That was Genny's thing. She was always so much better at getting through to Treeny than I was. But she wasn't home. She was out at some Tupperware party or something. I . . . I don't know if things would have been different if she'd been here, but . . ."

Whit blinked away tears before going on. "The book slipped. It fell into the well. Treeny leaned over the edge to try and save it. But the well is old. Really, really old. And even with how tiny Treeny was, she leaned just a little too far, and the stones came apart. The wall broke and she fell in. I didn't even see it happen. One minute I saw her standing there, then I looked down to fold my Lynyrd Skynyrd T-shirt and when I looked back up again, all I saw were her legs getting swallowed up by that damned hole. It was that fast." He wasn't even trying to hold back the tears now. They traced the wrinkles of his face, getting caught in the scruff of his whitening beard. "Lately, I swear I can see her standing out there. By the well. She just stares at me for a split second. And then she's gone. What I'd give to just hear her voice one more time. I . . . I'll never stop wishing that I'd just gone and talked to her that day. My poor little girl . . ."

The night filled up with the sound of Whit sobbing into his hands. *How many times has he done this over the years?* Rhett wondered. *How many days does the constant reliving of what happened to Treeny weigh so heavy on his heart?*

For the first time since he'd died, Rhett was glad that his parents had suffered the same fate as him. At least this way they wouldn't have to try and continue on without their only child, possibly letting their marriage fall apart, letting their lives fall apart. Whit had let his entire life become defined by the single most tragic mistake he'd ever made. And Rhett had no doubt that his parents, as courageous and strong as they were, would have done the same thing.

"I'm sorry, kids," Whit said eventually. His tears had run out and he was back to staring blankly into the darkness that lay untouched by the dim porch light. "I think we might have to table this conversation for today. It's getting late, anyway. I'm sorry I sort of monopolized the conversation. You're welcome to come back another day if you'd like."

"That won't be necessary, sir," Mak said, pushing off the railing that she'd been leaning against. Her face was sad and her cheeks were red from the biting cold. "I think we have enough information. Thank you. Thank you for sharing that with us." She looked genuinely grateful.

"You're welcome," Whit said. He was eyeing them all strangely, though, as they stood up and got themselves together, like he was truly seeing them for the first time. "How did you all get here, anyway?" he asked. "Did you come in a car?"

"No," Rhett replied, looking hard into the man's eyes.

Mak crouched down in front of Whit then and took both of his hands into hers. As soon as she did, Rhett watched goose bumps form along Whit's forearms.

"Listen to me," Mak said gently. "Treeny is a good person. She's done a lot of good things. She's strong. And she was in a good place after she died. A place surrounded by people who were her friends, people who cared about her deeply. She got lost somewhere along the way. But I promise you we're going to do everything in our power to find her." Mak squeezed his hands one more time before letting them go.

"I . . . I don't . . . ," Whit stammered. But before he could get much more out, Rhett and the others stood before him. Basil was hunched over, obviously in pain, but Mak had an arm around his shoulders. She glanced over at Rhett and nodded.

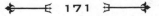

And just like that, Rhett let it all go. He pulled back and let his senses fall away, and the strange relief of feeling the cold fade from his bones was something he hadn't expected. Jon actually let out a sigh as he did the same thing. Theo, Basil, and Mak all followed, and to Whit, it would have looked like the five kids who had shown up at his doorstep unexpectedly to ask about his daughter's death had vanished into nothingness, disappearing right in front of him.

His eyes darted around as he lost sight of them, his mouth a wide, gaping O.

"Wait," he breathed. "Wait. *Wait!* Come back! *Come back!*" He was still sitting in his rocking chair, but he was gripping the armrests until his knuckles were an empty white. And even though he couldn't see them, to the syllektors it was as if he were yelling right at their faces.

Rhett looked over, trying to make sure that Basil was doing okay, but he saw Mak first, closing her eyes and turning her head away.

"Can we get off this damn porch now, please?" she said.

ELEVEN

Rhett stepped off the porch, and he felt weightless. The drain that manifesting himself had put on his body was gone. No feeling in his limbs, no pain, no cold. It was just the nothingness that he remembered washing over his body on the night he died, and he never thought he'd be so grateful for it.

The others stepped onto the grass behind him. Basil stumbled a few times, looking as if he'd forgotten how to walk. His eyes were wide and fearful, and he looked lost; Rhett was afraid of what that could mean. They all stood there for a moment, with the black shape of the barn looming nearby, and behind that, the well.

Whit called out again, begging for them to come back, to show themselves again. But then he went quiet, sitting back in his rocking chair, surrounded by six cups of cold coffee, probably feeling like all those years of being alone had finally broken him. Rhett hoped that Whit would go inside soon—he didn't like the idea of having the old man nearby when he (hopefully) revived Treeny.

And the well was where she was, Rhett was sure of it now. The question was whether Treeny would *want* to be revived.

He felt the heartbeat then, the persistent thumping that passed not just through his head but through every part of him. He moved toward it, leaving the others where they stood, crossing in front of the barn.

"Oh, we're doing this *now*?" Jon asked, his voice a hoarse imitation of what it normally was.

Mak helped guide Basil after Rhett, and Jon and Theo followed. The crumbled, ancient-looking well sat in the narrow stretch of grass between the barn and the fields, made of stacked stones that were misshapen and ill-fitting to one another. There was a section missing from one side, and the stones around that area seemed to sink inward. The whole thing looked like it was barely holding together.

Rhett wondered absently why it had never been filled in. There was a modern water pump plugged into the ground nearby, and surely the house had to have indoor plumbing that tapped into the water source. So why was this old relic still here? Why had it been allowed to remain after killing a young girl?

But the questions were stifled by the insistence of the heartbeat, pounding heavier and heavier as Rhett stepped closer to the well. As he did, the moon drifted behind the dark outline of the barn, and he was enveloped in blackness.

"Rhett," Mak whispered from behind him. "Rhett, be careful."

He could feel the others positioning themselves at his back, as if he were here gathering a soul instead of resurrecting a ghost. He heard the smooth metallic sound of weapons being drawn. They were preparing for a fight, and who could blame them? The last time they saw

Treeny, she'd ghosted Captain Trier and kicked the crap out of Mak and Basil.

Rhett stepped up to the well, the heartbeat louder than ever now, vibrating through him like a bass drum. He was standing right in front of the gap in the stones, the missing chunk where Treeny had fallen through. He leaned over it and peered down into the perfect blackness of the hole.

For a brief second, he was sure that there was a set of eyes down there, black with pinpricks of white for pupils, staring back up at him. But then he blinked, and the image was gone. The heartbeat that Rhett felt inside him wavered, hesitated, and then came back at full strength, slamming into him and causing him to stumble back a couple steps.

Treeny wanted to come back. She wanted to be revived. Desperately. And there was no way of knowing why. Was it because she was trapped haunting this place where she had felt so much misery in her life? Or was it because a part of her was still tethered to Urcena? If it was the latter, reviving her would only bring Urcena right to them again. And with her the psychons, Markeski, and all the syllektors who had betrayed the *Harbinger.* An army would fall upon them, and they wouldn't stand a chance.

"What's happening?" Basil whispered to one of the others, probably Mak. He sounded drunk again, and he was still missing his own accent. "What's he doing?"

If there was a response, Rhett didn't hear it. He shook his head, clearing his thoughts, and stepped forward to place a hand on one of the well stones. Everything was consumed by the sound and the feeling of the heart beating beyond the veil of the afterlife's version of death. Mentally, he was pushing through that veil, splitting it open, allowing what was on the other side to come forward.

"Treeny," he said. "We're here. We're here for you. It's time to come back now. We need your help."

As soon as the words left his mouth, Rhett no longer felt the heartbeat. It simply vanished, like a stereo being switched off. All the energy that had been humming through him was gone. There were only the quiet ticks and whistles of a solemn winter night and the nervous shuffling of his friends behind him.

Then a plume of dark smoke erupted from inside the well. It shot into the air like a geyser, and Rhett staggered away from it. Theo caught him before he could fall over.

The smoke roiled and churned, spilling over the rocky sides of the well, vomiting out of the missing section, a moving, living storm cloud with flickers of purple electricity coursing through it.

Right in front of that broken hole in the well, arms and legs formed, followed by a torso and then the head of a person facing away from Rhett and the others, staring at the well. The smoke poured into the body, filling it up, defining its features even more. Fingers emerged, and hair. And as the last of the smoke funneled into the body, it gained its colors—dark jeans and a dark blouse, pale, lanky arms spotted with freckles, bright red hair that was now streaked with a single patch of white, like a racing stripe.

Treeny stood looking down into the darkness of the well, her hands dangling at her sides. She was standing in the black shadow of the barn. Rhett couldn't tell what she was thinking. He couldn't tell if she had any Urcena left in her.

When she turned around, though, her glasses glinting in the moonlight, her eyes were normal, big and round and fearful, brimming with tears. Her movements were slow as she finally faced them, and her face was full of pain.

"I'm so sorry," she whispered before falling to her hands and knees on the ground.

Nobody ran to help her. Nobody moved except for Basil, who jerked and took a single step back. Rhett didn't dare look over at him, didn't dare take his eyes off Treeny. She stayed like that for a long time, on all fours, head hung, as if she were carrying an enormous object on her back that she just couldn't lift.

Rhett fought the urge to at least help her to her feet. Out of the corner of his eye, he saw Theo twitch, almost stepping forward. Theo had been like a big brother to Treeny; if anyone would want to help her, it would be him. He stood his ground, though, and they waited for Treeny to get up on her own.

She clambered to her feet, using the uneven rock wall of the well for support. The streak of white hair fell in front of her eyes, and she stared at it with a curious look for a second before pushing herself all the way up. She stood in front of them, trying to bring her shoulders up so that she would be standing as tall as she could. But she looked smaller than Rhett remembered.

They were all quiet for a long time. Rhett, Jon, Basil, Mak, and Theo stood across from Treeny, all of them with their weapons drawn.

Except for Rhett, who only had his hand hovering near his hip, where the knuckle blade rested in its holster.

Treeny took a single shaky step forward. The rest of them took one step back. Treeny nodded, as if she understood, but behind her glasses there was nothing but defeat. That single step had brought her out of the darkness and into the moonlight, though, and her eyes drifted over to the house, to the porch, where Whit still sat, oblivious to what was taking place just a few yards away.

"Is that . . . ?" Treeny started, her eyes wide.

"Yes," Mak said sharply. Then she softened, but only a bit. "He told us where to find you."

Treeny turned her head but not her eyes—she kept those locked on her father, who must have looked so old and diminished to her. "He . . . what? You *talked* to him?"

"We had to," Rhett said. They were all still staring at Treeny like she was a wild animal ready to pounce at the first sign of danger. "We don't have a lot of time."

She wrenched her gaze away from her father, turning her whole body to face her former friends. The light from the moon pooled in the lenses of her glasses, obscuring her eyes, but Rhett could see the anger coursing through her. Her fingers shook at her sides. Rhett tensed, allowing his hand to drop to the handle of his blade.

"How dare you?" Treeny said. Her voice was low and bitter and almost childlike, but there was no trace of the she-thing. "How dare *all* of you? Who said you could invade my life like this? Who gave you permission to *interrogate* my father? Why . . . why couldn't you just let me be?" But she didn't mean it. Rhett knew that even if none of the others did. He had felt her desire to be revived.

"*You* gave us permission, Treeny," Basil said. He was standing straight, a scythe in each hand, and Rhett was glad to hear the British accent again, even if it looked as if Basil was using every ounce of his strength to stay in control. "You let this happen when you decided to betray us." There was a rage in his eyes that Rhett had never seen before. Something about seeing Treeny again must have jolted Basil back into the driver's seat of his own body. But for how long?

"I didn't . . . ," Treeny tried, but the words fell apart before she could get them out. Her shoulders fell. "You don't get it."

Theo stepped forward then, ax still in hand. Treeny didn't flinch away. She gave him a small, sad smile, clearly happy to see him.

"I do," Theo said. "I get it."

Treeny looked confused for a moment, but then shocked understanding swept across her features. Her eyes drifted up to the streak of white in Theo's hair, the one that matched her own.

"No," she said.

Theo was nodding before the word was all the way out of her mouth. "She got me, too. For a little bit, anyways. I did . . . horrible things. But these guys came back for me. They needed me. And they need yous, too, Treen. We all do."

"If they need me so much, why are they looking at me like I'm something that has a bunch of sharp teeth?" She stepped to the side so she could see Rhett and the others around Theo's broad arms. "She's not coming back," she said. "She can try, but I know how she got in now. And I know how to keep her out. I will *never* not be in control of myself again."

Finally, everybody relaxed. Everybody except for Basil.

As Mak, Jon, and Theo sheathed their weapons, Basil stared around at them, looking shocked and almost angry.

"What the bloody hell is everyone doing?" he said. "Have you all forgotten the plan?"

Over Basil's shoulder, Rhett saw Jon pause with his arm still over his shoulder, his deadly staff still in hand. He glanced between the back of Basil's head and Rhett. Rhett focused hard on Jon and gave a minute shake of his head. Jon dropped his hand away from the weapon.

"Basil," Mak warned. "You're not yourself."

"Do you all not remember what she did?" Basil cried. "Were you not there for that? Did you not see her rip Captain Trier's heart right out of his bloody chest?"

Rhett glanced at Treeny, who was watching them all uncertainly, fear in her eyes. She took one hesitant step back, her gaze locked on the curved blades of Basil's scythes.

"Basil!" Rhett nearly shouted, stepping toward his friend. "Captain Winthrop!"

That finally got Basil's attention. He turned to Rhett, a little of the anger in him becoming diluted by guilt.

"This is not how this is going to go down," Rhett said. His voice was hard and unwavering. "Do you understand me?"

Basil glared at Rhett, silently challenging him. Rhett could see Basil's struggle to stay focused, his eyes locking and unlocking.

"Last I checked, mate," Basil said, "you answer to me."

"Not for this, I don't," Rhett shot back. "This was never your call to make. If we go through with this, then we're no better than the demon that forced us to come here in the first place."

"So that's what I am to you now?" Basil said, his eyes thinning to narrow slits. "I'm a demon because I ghosted Treeny once? I'm a psychon because I feed on souls to keep my strength? I'm just a bloody fucking monster, right? *Right?*"

"*Will everybody shut up?*" Treeny cried.

Silence fell upon them, and everybody turned their attention to Treeny. Even after what she did, Rhett still thought of Treeny as the quiet young girl with the big brain. What he was realizing now was that she was only ever that quiet because she was being smothered by the thing that had taken over her mind.

"You can stop talking about me like I'm not standing right here," she said, quieter this time. "I'm smart enough to figure out what's going on. Theo said you need me. But he didn't mean you needed *me*. You just need information that you think I have. And once you get it, you're just going to ghost me again to protect yourselves. Right? Does that about sum it up?"

Rhett and the others looked guiltily at one another. Around them, the empty fields seemed to spread out wider than ever, the darkness and the moonlight making everything look like it was cast in silver. Rhett wanted nothing more than to run away into that shining world and disappear forever.

"Treeny, no—" Mak started, but Treeny cut her off.

"It's fine," she said, turning her face away from them. "It's really okay. I understand. You guys have a plan to stop Urcena. And I'm a liability."

There was no good response to that. They all kept quiet.

Treeny stood up straight again, a look of strange compliance falling over her.

"What do you need to know?" she said.

For the third time since Rhett had returned from haunting the halls of his very first home, he listened to the plan they had concocted. It sounded more desperate now than it had the last two times it was recited, but Treeny stood patiently listening, with her arms folded and a fist tucked under her chin.

When Mak was finished, they all glanced at the house, where the porch was now dark and empty. At some point, Whit had given up and gone inside.

They stood in silence for a while after that, while Treeny pondered the unspoken question that had been attached to the end of Mak's words. *How do we find the Navigator?* Treeny stared up at the moon, arms still wrapped around herself. To Rhett, it felt like a long time passed. An hour. Maybe two. But when Treeny turned back to face them and finally say something, the moon was still in roughly the same spot it had been.

"You know this is a bad idea, right?" Treeny asked, sweeping her eyes across the five syllektors, four of whom had once considered her a friend, family even. They all nodded in response. "And that even if you get a chance to talk to the Navigator, and she *does* open a doorway back to the river, there's no guarantee that Rhett will be able to resurrect the *Harbinger*, even with how strong his ability has gotten?"

They all nodded at that, too. Then Basil, still fighting against the soul that was keeping the Ash at bay, said, "Wait . . . *she?*"

Treeny wouldn't look at him, wouldn't look at the shining metal blades that he still held at his sides, but she responded to him.

"You *would* assume the Navigator is a guy," she said with a little smirk.

"We get that this whole thing is pretty far-fetched, Treeny," Rhett said, crossing his arms. "But it's all we've got. So if you know where the Navigator is, tell us how to find hi—er . . . her. Please."

Treeny looked at Rhett seriously. She opened her mouth to speak, but no words came out, only laughter. She was giggling, gripping her stomach, hunched over, leaning against the warped wall of the barn for support.

The sound was unnerving. She'd laughed that way the night the *Harbinger* went down, and Rhett wasn't sure he'd ever truly forget the sound.

"Sorry," she said, as if reading their minds. She put up a placating hand. "I promise I'm not possessed by a power-crazed demon this time," she went on. "I just can't believe that this is what you're resorting to. A bunch of what-if scenarios, all of which will most likely result in the end of the living world as we know it."

"We've been over all that," Mak said, irritation creeping into the edges of her tone. "We understand the odds, Treeny. We're not looking for your approval. We just need to know if you can help us."

The laughter died, and Treeny was back to looking serious and contemplative. She was twirling the white strand of her hair around her finger.

"What does it matter?" she said after a pause. "If I say yes, you ghost me. If I say no, you ghost me. Either way, I don't get to stick around to see if this ridiculous plan works. So why should I even bother?"

Sadness and desperation, it seemed, had been replaced by anger. Rhett shot a frustrated glance in Basil's direction, but Basil was already looking down at his shoes, shame hanging on his features. If he'd waited just a few more minutes, Treeny would have talked without knowing anything about what they were planning on doing to her.

But Rhett was glad that she knew. He was glad that they didn't have to trick her into helping them. He couldn't blame her for wanting at least some kind of consolation prize for her efforts. And after she got it, he knew she would return to haunting the well behind her family's home without a fight. Rhett knew all this, even if ghosting her no longer felt like the right thing to do. In fact, it never had.

"We'll let you talk to your dad," Rhett said. The words were out of his mouth before he even knew he was going to say them. Everyone except for Jon stared at him, shocked. Jon was only nodding, clearly understanding it was the only thing they had that they could give to Treeny.

Treeny stared at Rhett, as if trying to decide whether he was being genuine. Rhett silently willed his friends to keep their mouths shut, especially Basil, who had already used his I'm-the-captain card once tonight.

After another long, tense pause, Treeny said, "Okay."

Rhett relaxed, and so did the others.

"Okay," Jon echoed through a sigh. "Now, we need to know two things. What is Urcena planning to do once she has her hands on Rhett, and how do we find the Navigator?"

Treeny chuckled again, and once more Rhett was struck by how much more confident this version of the young girl was. She had been smart and sullen and shy before. But now she was smart and strong willed, almost cocky. She was no longer a part of the force that had been their team. Now she was a force of her own. And Rhett knew deep down that Treeny had been telling the truth: There was no way Urcena would ever get control of her again.

"What's so funny?" Basil asked.

"Nothing really," Treeny said, barely stifling more laughter. "It's just that you aren't going to find the Navigator."

"Wait . . . what? Why?" Mak asked.

"Because," Treeny replied, "the Navigator finds you."

"Ooooookay," Jon said through a sarcastic laugh. "Maybe we should focus on one thing at a time here."

"Agreed," Rhett said. "Let's start with Urcena. Then we'll worry about the Navigator."

Treeny's face grew dark. She knitted her eyebrows together, blinking rapidly. She was either confused or trying to hold back tears, maybe both. Behind her, the big Nebraska sky loomed.

"She didn't let me in a lot," Treeny finally said. Her voice had regained that quiet, compressed quality that Rhett remembered from the *Harbinger*. "When she did, it was . . . terrifying. Everything about her is like something out of a horror movie—"

"We put that together for ourselves, darling," Basil interrupted. "We don't need her biography. We just need to know what she's got planned for Rhett if she gets hold of him."

Treeny glanced in Rhett's direction. The shadows in her eyes were deeper than ever, fearful.

"You have no idea how much you're capable of," she whispered. She looked away. "During those rare times when she left me alone, I did as much research as I could. I was trying to . . . I don't know. Understand her, I guess. Figure her out."

"And what did you find?" Mak asked.

"The same as I always found in the ship's library. Legends mostly. Myths. Half truths. Embellishments. Stories of biblical proportions that seemed so outlandish, even for the afterlife. She'd mentioned Twice-Borns so many times that it was like a bad song stuck in my head, even when she wasn't there."

"Treeny," Rhett prodded, trying to be gentle. "We don't have a lot of time."

"I know, I know," she replied anxiously. "I'm sorry. I'll get to the point." She made eye contact with Rhett again. "She's been watching you since you were born. Plaguing you. Waiting for you to die so she could get closer to you. And when you wouldn't die on your own, she helped you along."

"The car accident," Mak murmured.

Treeny nodded. "And even then, she couldn't just take you. All the legends about Twice-Borns say that their power has to be given up willingly. There are stories of Twice-Borns and demons marrying each other and ruling over entire worlds together, stories of Twice-Borns

being consumed by demons and the resulting tainted power destroying the demon from the inside out. Stories of Twice-Borns who couldn't handle the power, who were tempted by the demons to give it up, and the demons causing cataclysmic damage."

"I still don't understand. What does a demon want with the power to revive the dead? How much damage can that realistically cause?" Rhett asked.

"Not a lot," Treeny replied. "But reviving the dead isn't the only power that Twice-Borns have been known to have."

Her words swallowed the sound around the well. Rhett could only stare at her.

It was Jon who asked the question. "What else can they do?"

"They can do the opposite of reviving the dead." Treeny's eyes lowered again. "They can *cause* death."

"Jesus," Basil whispered.

"So that's what she wants," Mak said, her hands on her hips. "She doesn't give a shit about psychons or syllektors or the souls on board the *Harbinger*. None of it. She wants Rhett's power because with it . . . she could wipe out life on Earth as we know it."

Treeny didn't respond. Nobody did. Rhett felt his hand reach up and cover his mouth. *Find your power*, Urcena had said what felt like eons ago now, on the Golden Gate Bridge. *And then I will come for it.* She hadn't been talking about Rhett's power of revival. If what Treeny said was true—and why wouldn't it be?—then Urcena was waiting on something far, far worse.

"That's all I know," Treeny said after a while. "I'm sorry I don't know more, but . . . she wasn't exactly interested in chitchatting."

"It's okay," Mak said. Then, after a nervous glance in Rhett's direction: "Let's just move on for now, okay? If we can get back to the *Harbinger*, if Rhett can resurrect her, then we might be able to bait Urcena into a trap. She caught us off guard the first time, but that's not going to happen again. Let's talk about the Navigator."

"According to the information that was kept in the *Harbinger*'s library," Treeny said, her voice a whole different tone than it had been moments before, "the Navigator doesn't exist in any one fixed spot. After all, she *is* a traveler, meant to sail her boat across the river with the souls of the dead aboard."

"I thought the Navigator was retired," Basil said, looking to Mak for confirmation. She only shrugged.

"She is. So to speak," Treeny replied. She had stepped back over to the well and was peering down inside it, but not to the bottom. She was looking around at the inside wall, ducking her head close to the stones that lined the upper edge. "But that doesn't mean she isn't going to keep moving. Who knows what kinds of worlds she's seen?"

"Okay . . . ," Rhett started. His head was still back with the last topic of discussion, but he was doing his best to shake it off and keep up with this one. "I'm still lost on how you know the Navigator is a woman."

Treeny rolled her eyes and absently pushed her glasses back up on her nose, still searching along the inside wall of the well.

"Greek histories and myths always made Charon—their interpretation of the Navigator—out to be a man," she said. "But all the evi-

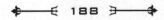

dence aboard the *Harbinger* suggested that she's a woman. And her name isn't Charon."

"So then what *is* her name?" Jon asked. There was a hint of frustration in his voice.

"No idea," Treeny replied with a shrug. "Aha!" She darted over to one side of the well's circular wall and began dismantling the stones there, one by one, carefully setting them down in the grass. After a moment, Theo went over to help her, silently leaning his ax against the side of the barn and grabbing a stone from her hands before she could set it down. She looked surprised at first, then gave him a grateful smile.

"I think we're missing the point here," Mak interjected. "All we need to do is talk to the Navigator, whatever gender they are, whatever their name is, and get them to relight the lantern. For the love of all things holy, how the hell do we *do* it, Treeny?"

Treeny had her hand inside one of the stones that she had uncovered, digging around in a hole that had formed naturally in its center. When she pulled her hand back out, she was holding something that winked in the moonlight. Satisfied, she held it up so Rhett and the others could see what it was—a large, round silver coin.

"With this," she said.

Rhett understood immediately. Or at least he thought he did. In the Greek myths he'd read as a kid, the deceased had to pay their way across the River Styx with a coin. The price for a ticket to get on the *Harbinger* had apparently been reduced to nothing, but the Navigator was clearly still kind of cheap.

"Don't we need a . . . you know, a dead person for that to work?" Rhett asked. It appeared that he was the only one who had figured out what Treeny was getting at; the other four were all still looking at the coin with their eyebrows scrunched together.

"Nope," Treeny said. "It just needs to be put into the mouth of someone who's already dead. Which, luckily, we already are."

"*There's* something none of us ever thought we'd say," Jon said. He took off his red hat and ran a hand through the short-cropped tangle of hair underneath it.

There was a metallic *thwing* as Treeny flipped the silver coin into the night air and then caught it deftly in her opposite hand.

"So who's doing this thing?" she asked.

"Does it matter?" Basil said.

Treeny nodded. "It does. The Navigator, from what I've read, isn't much of a talker. She only appears to the soul that is summoning her with payment. And even then, it might be difficult to get her to stick around. Whoever does this is going to have to keep her attention long enough to get the lantern lit *and* get her to open a doorway back to the afterlife." She admired the coin in her hand. "This is my lucky coin. It's the only one I've got. That means it has to count."

There was a thoughtful silence among them. Rhett gazed out past the bent and brittle cornstalks to the horizon. He tried to remember what the horizon had looked like from his cabin aboard the *Harbinger* and realized that he barely could. The image that came to mind was a faded, stuttering picture of gray tones and deep shadows, like a strip of damaged film reel. It was funny that he longed to be in that dismal world, the place he'd rejected at first. Somewhere in that world,

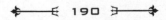

his parents' souls were waiting. And he'd made a silent vow to save them. No matter what.

"I'll do it," he said. "If she's anything like Urcena, she'll recognize my power. And hopefully that'll get her attention. Besides, that power is the reason we're in this mess. It might as well do us some good for once."

Nobody tried to protest. But none of them looked happy about it, either. After a while, Treeny spoke up again.

"The Navigator is nothing like Urcena," she said, and flicked the coin at Rhett. It flipped through the air and landed in his palm. "She's way more dangerous."

The barn doors groaned in protest as Rhett yanked on one of them and Theo pulled at the other. They opened with a cackling growl, and the wide doorway spewed out a swirl of dried hay and dust. Inside the barn, darkness reigned, cut only by a few slivers of moonlight that peeked through the cracks in the walls. A hayloft in the back looked like the throat within a huge, gaping mouth.

Rhett stood in front of the barn, coin in one hand, lantern in the other, suddenly afraid of being swallowed.

The others stood nearby, watching him. Their worried faces looked particularly tired in the dwindling silver light. It was getting closer and closer to dawn, and for some reason Rhett was sure that this wouldn't work in the daytime. And another day wasted was another day that Urcena had to attack the living to feed her psychon army, or to use Markeski's syllektors to help them do it, or to realize that Rhett and the others weren't actually building an army at all but searching for a way to bring the *Harbinger* back from the grave. Another day wasted was another day closer to the extinction of the syllektors entirely.

"Remember," Treeny said. "She's going to come to you thinking that you're a soul trying to pay for passage to another realm."

"Wait . . . that's a thing?" Basil asked, slurring his words slightly. Mak shushed him.

"When she realizes that you're not," Treeny went on, "she's probably going to be . . . upset."

"Upset enough to want to destroy me?" Rhett asked.

Treeny paused, then said, "Worse."

"Awesome." He hesitated, then went on. "I'm going in here so the rest of you will be protected if something goes wrong. Do me a solid and stick to that plan? I don't want anyone coming in after me, even if it sounds like I'm being vaporized. Got it?"

"Do *us* a solid and come back out of there in one piece, okay?" Jon said. He looked anxious, chewing on his lower lip.

Rhett could only nod. He was about to step forward into the barn when Basil's voice stopped him.

"Honestly, mate, I still don't really know what's going on," he called. "Just make sure you come out of there with your head on straight. I'd hate to have to tell people that my best friend got disintegrated by our predecessor." The faintest trace of the old Basil, the *real* Basil, hung in his voice for the first time since the train wreck. It was a wonderful sound.

Rhett laughed even as he caught sight of the black tendrils that were once again curling up Basil's neck. "If that's your way of apologizing, I'll take it," he said. "You better make sure that *you're* here when I get back."

Basil nodded with a knowing smirk, leaning against Mak for support. She held on to him but turned her face away. Rhett was certain that he saw tears in her eyes.

He gripped the lantern, holding on to its weight like an anchor, and stepped toward the barn. As he approached, he reached up with his other hand and slipped the silver coin into his mouth. Even with his senses tamped down again, he could taste the metal on his tongue, replacing the icy flavor of the night air with something heavy and harsh, something that reminded him of blood.

He stepped through the open doorway and into the barn, leaving the moon and the night behind for full-on darkness. It washed over him like a sudden rain shower—quick and organized and unrelenting—and as it did he thought of his death, of the car crash that killed him and his parents and ultimately led him to the *Harbinger*, right where Urcena had wanted him. He thought of those moments immediately after the crash, sitting in the road, staring at his own lifeless body as it hung inside his mom's Volkswagen.

He focused on the way he'd felt then, confused and afraid, his mind crowded with emotions and his body shouting in pain. He'd waited for some kind of transference to happen, a crossing-over. But it never came. Instead, what he'd needed was a guide, someone to lead him from this world, the living world, to the afterlife. That's when Basil had arrived. Basil had been Rhett's ferryman to the underworld of death. Now he needed another one.

The coin was still gripped in Rhett's mouth as he stepped fully into the shadows of the barn, and once he was in the middle of the space, he stopped, eyes closed, focusing on the thoughts that rang out in his head like tornado sirens. He called out with his mind. He *beckoned* with it, hoping deep down that it was working.

After only a few seconds, it did.

The barn doors swung shut with a hollow *crack*. Rhett was alone in the dark, and he refused to open his eyes, refused to be distracted. He held on to the gross metallic taste in his mouth and continued to send out his mental sonar. But he already knew that his call was being answered.

The Navigator really was out there, and she was coming for him.

He could hear water sloshing, and not a small amount of it. The sound was like wet leather sliding across a board—it was the sound of a tide lapping onto a beach.

Rhett opened his eyes and still saw only black emptiness at the back of the barn. Beneath the extra cover of the hayloft, the darkness was impenetrable. But within the shadows, he could just make out the winking of something bright. Actually, it was *two* somethings: eyes, staring at him from the dark, moving closer. They shifted fluidly across the plane of shadows as if carried by black clouds. It was only after his eyes began to adjust that Rhett saw that the eyes were attached to a tall, narrow body, with lanky arms that gripped a long pole and used it to guide something out of the emptiness.

A boat.

The Navigator came sailing across a tide of shadows on an old rowboat, her eyes wide and piercing, somehow creating their own light. Rhett could still hear the water sloshing against the sides of her boat, but he couldn't see it. The woman and her vessel were mostly made out of darkness, with the exception of the few sprinkles of moonlight that danced across them as they got closer. She stood in the boat, a half a person taller than Rhett, staring down at him, and with both hands, used the ferryman's pole to guide herself across the unseen body of water to where Rhett stood.

He could only look up at her, his mind stuttering and his mouth full of silver.

The woman halted the boat only a few inches from Rhett's feet, and then she crouched down, using the ferryman's pole for support. This close, Rhett could see the blue fire that lit the insides of her irises. It danced and flickered and cast a small amount of light on the pole in her hand. Rhett glanced at it and saw it was bone-white and carved to look like hundreds of skeletons entangled in one another. Limbs wrapped around limbs in anguished embraces, some of them reaching up toward the top, some of them clawing over others. They were just skeletons frozen in place, but Rhett had the feeling that maybe the pole hadn't been *carved* that way at all.

When he returned his gaze to hers, she was staring into him with her burning eyes.

"You," she said, her voice a long, heavy groan that reverberated across the old wooden beams of the barn, "are already dead." Each word was strung out like a thrumming bass note, her voice dense with the eons of her age.

Rhett opened his mouth to speak but realized too late that the coin was still in his mouth. He tried to form the words *I know* and nearly swallowed the damn thing. As he spat it out, he watched the Navigator stand and begin to nudge the boat away, back into the dark sea that it had come from. Rhett didn't think. He reached out and took a hold of the boat, keeping it in place. The Navigator turned her head and stared down at Rhett's hand. The movement was slow and sinister and full of shocked rage.

"Do you wish to know true death, boy?" she said. Her voice filled up the space as if it were being amplified.

"I've already known true death," Rhett responded, forcing himself to hold her gaze. "And I've beaten it."

It was the tiniest movement, but Rhett was sure that he saw her eyes widen just a fraction. She turned back to face him and then she began to guide the boat slowly around Rhett. Her eyes never left his, her movements sure, precise, and honed by centuries of practice.

When she had circled around to the other side of the barn, the Navigator finally glanced away, looking briefly over her shoulder at the shut doors. This far from the blackness at the throat of the barn, Rhett could see more of her face, her drawn-out features, long and withered but still somehow pointed and strong. There was a tuft of fluttering hair on her head, but that was the only other thing Rhett could make out. Everything else was still wrapped up in the dark.

"You are syllektors," the Navigator said, looking back at Rhett. "You and the ones who wait for you."

"Yes," Rhett said. "The crew of the *Harbinger*."

At that, the Navigator let out a rusted croak that could have been a laugh or could have been a grunt. Either way, she didn't smile.

"The *Harbinger*," she said, her tone mocking. "A waste of my time, to be sure. What a crew you are. To something that was so easily brought to ruin by a single demon." She made the same throaty noise again, and Rhett heard crackling in the barn's sagging roof.

"We were betrayed," Rhett pushed back. "It wasn't our fault. We're trying t—"

"Trying to what? Trying to resuscitate what does not live?" She crouched down again so that she was eye level with Rhett. The blue flames circled around within her irises. "The *Harbinger* is merely a vessel, boy. A *thing* that carries cargo on its back. A *thing* that cannot be rebuilt by sheer willpower. Not even by a Twice-Born Son." Her fiery eyes shimmered knowingly.

"It can. I can do it. I can rebuild the ship. And with it, we can regroup. Come back stronger, defend ourselves." Rhett hesitated, his voice confident, his mind anything but. He held the flameless lantern up for the Navigator to see. "But I can't find it. Not without this. And not without a way back to the river. We . . . *I* need your help."

The Navigator regarded him with something that might have been pity. She stood for a second time, her eyes seeing into Rhett in a way that he could actually *feel*, like a snake squirming around in his brain. She probed, and again her eyes widened just a hair, just enough for Rhett to know she saw something that maybe didn't scare her but that at least surprised her.

"People like you," she said finally. "They are dangerously powerful. Life has always had a counterpart. And it leaves nothing in its wake but dust. Dust and silence. That thing is in you, too, boy. Beware of it."

Rhett could only stare at her. She actually smirked, and her whole face contorted with her lips, an ugly ripple across her features.

She went on. "There was a girl I knew once. Like you. Twice-Born. She was stronger than anything I'd ever witnessed. Stronger than the devil-wench you're dealing with now, to be sure." She quirked a haggard eyebrow at him. "Maybe not stronger than you, though. We will have to wait and see."

"What . . . what happened to her?" Rhett asked, finding his voice again.

A shadow fluttered across the Navigator's face, her eyes searching the barn wall for something that wasn't there. When she spoke, her voice hummed with anger. "She allowed herself to be broken. As you and your friends have."

Rhett straightened. He looked past the ancient woman at the barn doors behind her. Beyond them, his friends were waiting. They had all come so far with so little to hope for and were willing to go farther.

"We're not broken," Rhett said, defiance flooding his voice. "Not yet."

The Navigator continued to stare down at him for a long time. Rhett could hear the invisible tide rippling across the invisible beach. What he could only hear, he was sure the Navigator could see. To her, there were sand and stars and an ocean that led to anywhere. And Rhett suddenly took pity on this woman who had nothing to survive for. She wandered alone, existed alone, and would eventually disappear into oblivion alone. Whether she decided to help him or not, Rhett knew that his end of the deal would always be the better one.

A moment later, though, the fire in the Navigator's eyes brightened, and she turned her gaze onto the lantern Rhett held. She lifted one gnarled hand, curling it slowly into a fist. When she opened her hand again, a flame ignited within the black metal casing of the lantern. It sputtered and danced for a second and then became still, the tip of the flame circling slowly, trying to find a direction to point in.

"Once you have returned to the other side, the flame will guide you to your ship," the Navigator said. There was a strange mixture of pride and irritation in her voice now. "Leave this place. Close the doors. When they open again, you will be returned to the river."

With that, she began to push her boat back around to where she had originally come from, lifting and dropping her ferryman's pole.

Rhett was still staring at the lantern, wonderstruck, startled and delighted to see the orange fire burning inside it again. He spun around to watch the Navigator go.

"Th-thank you," he stammered. "Thank you."

The Navigator stopped suddenly, the pole thunking against something below the surface of . . . whatever it was that she was floating on. She turned the boat around so that she was looking at Rhett again from a few feet away. Her blue-flamed eyes were almost enraged with impatience now.

"My payment," she said slowly.

"Oh . . . right," Rhett replied. He knelt down and picked the silver coin off the floor. When he stood again, the Navigator's eyes were only an inch from his. She was suddenly so close that Rhett could hear the dragging rattle of her breath. He stifled a shout. Carefully, he held the coin out to her. "Here."

She tilted the pole in the direction of Rhett's hand, and as she did, a few of the skeletons that were wrapped around the outside of it came to life. They clawed and reached for the coin until Rhett finally understood and handed it to them. They gripped it in their tiny, bony fingers and hefted it inward. Rhett watched with his mouth hanging open as the coin sank into the pole, pulled below its surface by the skeletons.

Standing up straight, the Navigator pushed the boat backward, away from Rhett, sailing back into the darkness.

"I have one more question," Rhett called before he could stop himself.

"Speak quickly, boy," the Navigator said. She was moving farther and farther away, getting smaller and less distinct in the black shadows, but she didn't have to yell. Her voice carried.

"What's your name?"

There was a pause, and Rhett didn't think she was going to answer. But then she did.

"My name is Ními," she said. Her voice hummed through the brittle beams, lingering even as its source began to vanish.

Rhett watched the Navigator—Ními—guide her boat back into the darkness, her black figure merging with the other shadows at the back of the barn before disappearing entirely.

TWELVE

Outside, the sun was beginning to show itself along the horizon. When Rhett pushed the barn doors open in a daze, he was startled by the soft pink glow that permeated the sky. How had an entire night slipped by?

The others were all sitting around the yard, spread out as if they were taking a break from training, weapons scattered around them like forgotten toys. All of them except for Mak, who was pacing back and forth, steadily carving a line in the grass with her feet.

When they saw him, they all stopped fidgeting, stopped glancing anxiously around, stopped even the unconscious act of breathing, which they hadn't needed to do to begin with. They stopped . . . until Rhett held the lantern aloft, showing off its newly lit flame.

Jon was the first on his feet and the first to cross the yard to where Rhett stood just outside the barn. He leaned in and stared at the pointed flame burning inside the glass casing of the lantern, marveling at it.

"Dude, I could kiss you right now," he said.

Rhett chuckled. "I'm not sure your boyfriend would like that too much."

"What boyfriend?" Jon asked, and winked.

Rhett laughed again, and they settled on a fist bump. The laughter felt good in his throat, like a cool drink of water, washing out the metallic taste of the coin.

Theo, Treeny, and Mak came over. Basil was sitting with his back against the well, head tilted back. He wasn't looking good.

Slowly, Mak took hold of the lantern in both hands and slipped it out of Rhett's. She stared through the glass at the single flame that continued to draw circles with its tip. It had no direction right now, but it would soon.

Rhett turned and carefully pushed the barn doors closed, giving them each one more nudge to make sure they were firmly sealed—or at least as firmly sealed as they could be. The old wood creaked, and it reminded Rhett of the steam room aboard the *Harbinger*. Hopefully, if the Navigator was to be believed, all they would have to do was open these doors one last time and they would be on their way back there.

"How was that?" Treeny asked with a strange smile.

"Uh . . . unsettling," Rhett said. "It was unsettling. To say the least."

"Well, you can't say I didn't warn you."

Rhett grinned. "You're right. Thank you, Treeny. And I'm sorry about your lucky coin. She . . . took it."

Treeny waved him off. "I figured as much. It was about time I put it to good use anyway." Her smile wavered. She stepped back, letting Theo and Mak close the circle around Rhett. He looked past them even as Theo smacked him on the shoulder.

"Congratulations on not being ghosted a second time, boss," he said with a slanted grin.

He watched Treeny turn away and head to the porch, then up the steps and inside. Nobody else seemed to notice her slip away.

"So what now?" Theo asked. "We gettin' back to business?"

Rhett nodded.

"Yes," he said, then pointed back to the barn. "When we open those doors, we'll have a way back to the river. And once we're back there, the lantern will guide us back to the *Harbinger*."

"We hope," Basil called from his spot on the ground. His skin had an odd translucent look to it, and the crusted black tendrils had found their way almost all the way up his neck now, bending up under his chin. His eyes were bleary and distant, lulling around in his head like oiled marbles.

The Ash that plagued Basil was worse than ever. Not to mention there was a soul inside him that was no longer fending the disease off but starting to take control of his body. And as he watched his friend suffer, Rhett couldn't help but worry about the other crew members back at the factory who had been struggling with the Ash themselves. How many had already been turned to dust by it?

Rhett shot Mak a glance, but she only shook her head. Her eyes dropped as she did, finding the lantern light again.

"Maybe when we get closer to the *Harbinger*," she murmured, "he'll improve. But . . . I don't know . . . I . . . ." Her voice broke and she turned her face away.

Rhett gripped her shoulder gently.

"He will," he said. "He has to."

She turned and walked back toward the road, letting the lantern swing at her side. Rhett let her go, and he also let go of that tiny flicker of hope he'd offered her. They hadn't gotten this far with optimism. Mak knew that better than any of them. True hope was in the realistic idea that they could *do* something about their problems. The Ash that was slowly destroying Basil—and had already destroyed many of their crewmates—was a problem they could do nothing about.

"What was it like?" Jon asked. "In there, I mean. What was . . . *she* like?"

"Treeny was right about one thing," Rhett replied. "The Navigator isn't much of a talker."

A little while later, they all reassembled near the barn. All of them except for Treeny, who was still inside the house.

Basil was up on his feet again, with Mak under one of his shoulders to help keep him upright. He caught Rhett's eye and grinned lazily. Rhett tried to smile back, but he knew it would have been forced, unnatural. He just nodded instead.

"That's a long conversation," Basil said, tilting his head toward the house.

The sun had come all the way up from below the horizon now, and the house sat glowing in the warm orange light. The whole world was shining around them, soaking up the morning sun and casting it back, luminous and lively. It looked nothing like the place that had been all cold and shadows just a few hours ago.

"We don't even know if she's really talking to him," Mak said.

"It doesn't matter," Rhett cut in. "We promised she could have some time with him. Let her have it."

"We don't have much longer to wait, though, mate," Basil said. He was shrugging and cringing, trying to approach the subject a little more gingerly this time around. "She's a loose end."

Almost as if she'd been given a cue, Treeny came walking out the back door then, the screen door smacking noisily against its frame and her feet thumping against each step of the porch with a heavy finality. She crossed the yard and stood in front of Rhett and the others, arms wrapped around her middle as if she were holding her tablet again. She looked so much like the Treeny that Rhett had met that first day he boarded the ship. Her eyes were on the ground, unwilling to meet anybody else's.

"I'm ready," she murmured.

When the words left her mouth, Theo stepped back a couple of feet and turned his back on the whole scene. Rhett glanced that way and caught the behemoth's shoulders heaving with huge breaths.

Beside him, Rhett could feel Jon tensing up.

Mak let go of Basil as he pulled himself up, flattening out his blazer with one hand and slipping a scythe out of its sheath with the other. He took in a deep breath of his own and let it out slowly, and as he did his eyes seemed to gain focus, his grip tightened on the handle of his weapon.

Basil stepped forward and stood in front of Treeny, glaring at her, clenching and unclenching his fist around the grip of the scythe. He said nothing as he brought the tip of the long, curved blade up and leveled it at Treeny's chest.

This was it. The public execution they'd all been dreaming of and dreading since the moment Treeny dove her hand into Captain Trier's chest.

A stillness fell over all of them. There wasn't a breath or a whisper as Basil's fingers tightened around the handle of the scythe.

And then Basil exhaled and stumbled back, letting his arm—and the weapon that it held—drop to his side. Mak was there to catch him before he could fall.

Treeny opened her eyes and looked around almost in a panic, unbelieving.

"I've seen enough of my friends' ashes," Basil said, his voice a bitter growl. "You're not the one who deserves this blade."

There was a knot in Rhett's head that he hadn't even known was there until it released itself, and all the tension it had created tapered off. He relaxed, and he felt Jon do the same.

Theo turned around with the same unbelieving look on his face that Treeny had, and when Mak helped Basil back over to the barn, Theo barreled over to Treeny and wrapped her up in a hug that looked as if it should have broken her back. She hugged him back, laughing and crying, the tears sparkling in the early sunlight. They each had a strange bit of white in their hair, and they both looked tired. So tired. But they also looked free.

Rhett turned around to face the barn doors, still sealed shut. Mak and Basil stood off to the side, holding on to each other, but they were watching Rhett, waiting. He found Basil's eyes and nodded approvingly. The newest captain of the *Harbinger* had made the right choice after all, which meant that they had all been right to trust him this entire time. Rhett felt stupid for ever doubting it.

He stepped up to the barn doors, and he could feel everyone's eyes on him. Treeny and Theo had quit celebrating and were staring along with Mak, Basil, and Jon, the question hanging silent and weighty between them: *Is this going to work?*

It better, Rhett thought.

He gripped the doors by their rusted handles and shook them a little, testing their weight, then threw them both open in one fluid pull.

The sound of the ocean greeted them.

Where before there had only been dust and damp and darkness, there was now a long, craggy shoreline made of harsh outcroppings and daggerlike pieces of rock. It stretched away from the Nebraska grass and curved until it was out of sight. Alongside it, the gray ocean waves smashed into the rock, sending foamy white sprays high into the air. The chopping water spread out beyond the shore, running away to the dim line of the horizon. Above everything, the clouds hung low and bleak, roiling with enough ferocity to match the ocean.

Except it wasn't an ocean. Rhett knew that. It was a river, as dark and brooding as one would expect a river in the afterlife to be. And they were looking at it through the open doorway of an old barn that stood amid the bright sunshine of a cool morning in the middle of America. The sun didn't even come close to penetrating the doorway. It was like staring at a giant TV screen that had been built into the side of the barn.

The syllektors looked around at one another, and Rhett noticed a look of odd relief on Basil's face. The Ash had been caused by pro-longed distance from the souls that powered the *Harbinger*; maybe it wasn't so foolish to believe that reuniting Basil with the ship would help cure it after all. Or maybe Basil was just happy to see the river again.

Rhett didn't wait. He started walking. The others followed, all of them stepping through the oversize doorway together, their feet moving from the soft grass of Treeny's father's lawn to the hard, uneven rocks of the shore. When they were all through, the doorway broke down, disintegrating into a swarm of tiny particles that blew away like dust in a heavy wind. They had returned to the river.

They were almost home.

The "shoreline" turned out to be a narrow strip of rock that extended out from something bigger. When Rhett turned around—just in time to see the last flecks of the doorway they'd come through float away—his eyes widened and his mouth fell open.

"G-guys?" he called over the clatter of the waves. "Where the hell are we?"

Mak and Basil were the first to turn, followed by the other three.

"Shit," Mak cursed under her breath. And then, louder: "This is the wreckyard."

Bulging out, up, and away from the little outcropping that the syllektors had landed on was a huge, rocky island. The land itself was everything Rhett had come to expect from the afterlife: dark and jagged and reaching like enormous fingers. But scattered across the island in almost geographic formations were hundreds upon hundreds of shipwrecks.

There were centuries-old wooden boats that lay flayed across ragged spans of rock, their slats spread apart like decaying rib cages. There were long, pointed schooners rotting among the stones, their masts brittle and snapped. There were lobster boats and yachts and Navy destroyers and sleek fiberglass sport boats, all of them rotted and broken, covered in barnacles and tangled in black seaweed. They created a kind of mountain, dotted with fogged-over portholes and jutting with masts that still held on to the rags of old sails.

Near the peak of this horrible piece of land Rhett spotted the rounded shape of a submarine, balanced across the edges of several other boats. He could make out the protruding shape of the conning tower and, printed along its side, the word *Minerve*. A strong enough wind could have sent the sub rolling down the pyramid of shipwrecks right to where the syllektors stood.

Rhett had the sudden urge to back away from the place and never return. He glanced over and found Jon watching the waves slosh against the rocky shoreline with wide, unnerved eyes. Jon gulped once, loudly.

"We have to go," Mak said, as if she'd read Rhett's mind. "Now. The psychons scour this place all the time for new scrap to add to their ship."

"Lovely spot for the Navigator to drop us, huh?" Basil said. He was standing with his arms wrapped around himself and the collar of his blazer turned up to block the sprays of water coming off the rocks, but he was standing on his own two feet while Mak examined the lantern.

"Look," she said, her eyes focusing on the flame burning behind the lantern's glass. Instead of turning in constant circles, the flame's point was now locked in a specific direction, leaning away from the wreck-littered island.

"Okay," Rhett said, his voice brimming with confidence again. "The Navigator must have put us here because she knew we'd need a boat. If we can find something that still floats, we can follow the lantern."

Theo immediately broke away from the group and began rummaging through the debris at the base of the mountain, flinging whole wooden beams out of the way as if they were no heavier than pool noodles.

"And what if the lantern isn't leading us back to the *Harbinger*?" Treeny asked. She was staring at the flame, biting her thumbnail.

"Where else would it be leading us?" Mak asked. For some reason she turned to Rhett. He couldn't find any accusation in her eyes, but the fear of betrayal was still there. He had a feeling that it always would be. For all of them.

At least until Urcena was destroyed.

"There's nowhere else it would be taking us," Rhett said, answering Mak's question. "The lantern was a part of the *Harbinger*. It guided the crew for who knows how long before Urcena came along and separated them. It's taking us back to the ship. It has to be." He looked at Treeny, who had winced at the sound of Urcena's name but was now staring back. She nodded.

Rhett turned, expecting to see Jon scaling the side of the mountain made of ruined sea vessels. Instead, Jon was frozen in place.

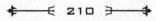

He was staring out at the water, at the churning clouds and frothing waves. A few miles out, a dark mass obscured the sky, one that was just as pointed and misshapen as the wreckyard. Except this shape was one Rhett recognized.

It was the psychons' ship. The *Cyclops*.

"We have to move," Rhett said. "We have to move now."

"What? Wh—" Mak started, but the words died in her mouth as she looked up and saw the silhouette of the *Cyclops* bobbing along the horizon. "Ah fuck," she muttered.

"Hey, boss!" Theo called. "What about this?"

He was gesturing to a long aluminum fishing boat at his feet. It looked newish and mostly intact, with an outboard motor attached to the back end. It was definitely not something designed for six people, but it was the most intact-looking boat that Rhett could see among the scrap.

"That's gonna be tight," Jon said, glancing at the boat and then glancing nervously at the frothing water.

"It's all we've got," Rhett said, moving to help Theo pull the boat out from under some other debris. Mak and Treeny joined him, and the four of them began shifting hunks of other wrecks and yanking on the boat, trying to free it from where it was buried.

Jon and Basil stood by, watching the growing shape of the *Cyclops*. Neither of them seemed bothered by the Ash now. Their concern was with the ship that would be crawling with psychons and its quickening approach. If they caught sight of the syllektors on the wreckyard, they'd come at them full speed ahead.

A moment later, Basil and Jon were with the others, working desperately to pull the boat free.

"*Seriously?*" Basil cried, yanking at the boat until the cords in his neck stood out. "Why won't this bloody thing come loose?"

They rocked it and cleared out more space around it, but it wouldn't come free. The motor was caught on something, Rhett realized. Something massive that was concealed by the other pieces of ruined ships piled on top of it. Something they'd never be able to move.

"We have to find something else," he said. "This thing isn't coming out."

"It's too late," Treeny said, pointing. "Look."

The *Cyclops* was in full view now, dark and looming, the disarray of old ships that had been stuck together to create the strange raftlike design now completely visible. It looked like a giant, floating sea urchin. There were maybe a handful of lights on in some of the portholes, and as it got closer, Rhett could hear a soft, hollow jingle from the skeletons that had been strung up around the ship's hull.

It was *already* coming at them full speed ahead, cutting through the waves like a meteor through the atmosphere . . . and it wasn't slowing down.

Theo, Jon, and Basil were still pounding away at the hunk of metal pinning the boat's motor down. Mak had given up and was watching the psychons' ship as it drew closer and closer, seeming to get even faster along the way. There was a strange, perplexed look on her face.

Rhett remembered seeing the *Harbinger* for the first time, watching

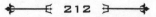

as it sliced its way toward him. That had been slow, graceful. What the *Cyclops* was doing now was barreling down on the island like a fist swinging toward a punching bag. It was going to crash right into the rocks.

"*Get out of the way!*" Rhett yelled. He dropped down off the starboard side of an old sailboat to where Jon was kicking the aluminum fishing boat, still trying to get it free. Rhett grabbed his arm and turned him so he could see what was happening. Jon's eyes widened in the shadow of the hulking ship.

Theo and Basil leaped over the little boat and everybody clambered away, pulling themselves up and over and around the wrecks to get back to the narrow outcropping that they'd arrived on.

Rhett could hear the *Cyclops* now, groaning and creaking, steam billowing out of its many clustered smokestacks, the water sloshing against its hull. And then he could hear it grinding against the rocks beneath the surface of the water. Wooden parts of its exterior crackled, while metal parts shrieked.

The syllektors jumped away from the wreckyard and onto the rocks just as the *Cyclops* smashed into the island.

Everything seemed to shift beneath Rhett's feet, and he stumbled forward—along with the others—nearly falling on his face. He stopped and turned. The sound of the crash blocked out even the chaotic noise of the river: wood splintering, glass shattering, metal screeching. The *Cyclops* seemed to fold over onto itself, debris exploding outward in a shower of oak, iron, and rust.

The mountain of shipwrecks jolted under the force of the impact, unsettling every part of it. Some of the wrecks fell in on top of the

Cyclops immediately, breaking away and rolling into it, one wreck colliding with another. Other parts of the pyramid began to collapse inward, rotted wood finally giving way under pressure, as if being ripped apart by an earthquake or a volcanic eruption.

Rhett and the others watched, helpless, as the island fell apart. Some of the debris tumbled in their direction, missing them by inches. All they could do was duck down in a huddle and wait for the worst to be over.

But when Rhett chanced a look up, trying to see if anything was coming their way, he saw the submarine *Minerve*. It had dislodged from its already precarious spot at the top of the mountain and was rolling down it, skittering over the tops of the imploding shipwrecks, smashing through whatever got in its way.

"RUN!" Rhett screamed, and yanked on the two people he had under his arms—Jon and Theo. Everybody else saw what he was seeing and ran with him toward the end of the outcropping, tripping over loose rocks. Behind them, the submarine crunched into jagged stone and bounced after them even faster, its metal hull making a bonging sound like a bell.

They reached the end of the outcropping, running side by side, and jumped into the only place they had to go: the water.

As Rhett's head went below the surface, he looked up and saw the black mass of the submarine roll off the edge of the craggy shoreline and spin through the air above them. It hit the water only a few feet in front of where the syllektors had and sent a churning white wave right into them. Rhett lost grip of any sense of direction. He simply rolled with the undercurrent, surrounded by bubbles and the constant roaring of the water.

And then he stopped, slamming into something hard. A crimson cloud appeared in the water around him, swirling lazily. He imagined that if he'd had his senses tuned in, there would be enormous pain blooming from . . . somewhere. Instead, all he could see was the blood, curling around his head, blotting out his vision even more.

He realized he was holding his breath. He inhaled, letting the water pour into his lungs and bubble up into the back of his throat. His body jerked responsively, rejecting the unwanted fluid. Whatever it was that he was pinned against, he smacked into it a few more times while his body spasmed, sending more curtains of blood folding through the water.

Despite being impervious to the pain, Rhett was afraid that his body wouldn't be able to hold it together much longer. It might fail him, and he could get sucked away from the island by the current, watching helplessly as his useless body was flung farther and farther away from where he needed to be, from his friends.

A moment later, though, the thin veil of blood that floated around him began to dissolve, and the torrent of bubbles and dust that was kicked up by the submarine hitting the water began to settle. He could see somewhat clearly again.

In front of him, a brief stretch of sand and rock wrapped around the island. Beyond that, there was nothing, just a steep drop-off into utter blackness. The island itself was jutting up like a stone finger. Where it came from, Rhett had no clue—there was no way to see the bottom. What he *did* see was the *Minerve* again, sinking down into the wide-open pit of darkness, its black metal hull beginning to blend in with the lightless water below. It groaned and whined as it sank, like some kind of strange whale.

He was about to try to swim back to the surface, but then he spotted something in the murk. Something wearing a beat-up red baseball cap.

Jon was floating out in the never-ending chasm, kicking and flailing not far from where the submarine was plummeting downward. And he wasn't floating—he was sinking. Rhett remembered the way he had looked at the water when they'd first landed on the island. He'd been afraid of it. Now he was panicking.

Rhett pulled his feet up and planted them on the rock that he had been shoved against, and then he kicked off, pushing through the current with all he had. He pointed himself toward the place where Jon was sinking. When his momentum wore off, Rhett swam, kicking his legs and sweeping his arms, trying to move as fast as he could. Jon's face came into view as Rhett got closer. His eyes were wide, searching around frantically. His mouth gulped in water.

Jon was sinking faster than Rhett could swim. He was out over the chasm now, the vast field of black stretching away from the island for as far as he could see. Jon was flapping his arms and kicking out with his feet, trying to slow his descent. But the current was plunging down off the island's sandbar, pulling them both under now. Even if Rhett could get hold of Jon, he wasn't sure he'd be able to get them both back to the surface.

He reached, preparing to be swept down into the abyss.

Something dropped down beside him. He only caught a glimpse

of it at first, but when he squinted at it, he could see it was a thin metal cable with a hook on the end. Rhett looked up, following the cable up with his eyes to the vague shape of a boat floating on the surface above them.

He reached out and grabbed the cable. Beneath him, Jon was still panicking. Rhett tried to get his attention. He yelled but only managed to produce a gargling sound and a stream of bubbles. He shook the cable, swinging it slowly through the water, hoping to sweep it right into Jon.

The cable was still being lowered into the water, but when Rhett pulled on it, trying to get near Jon, it stopped. He managed to pull it right into Jon's path, and it slid across his side as he sank. He looked at it, confused, and then looked up, spotting Rhett. Rhett gestured for Jon to hold on, and they each wrapped the cable around their hands and arms.

Rhett gave one almighty tug on the cable, and a second later it was being pulled back up to the surface, with him and Jon attached to it.

The water got less murky as they neared the surface, and the outline of the boat became more distinct. It was big and rusty but obviously still intact. He broke the surface and found Basil and Theo leaning over the back of the boat. Theo reached out with one of his barrel-size arms and pulled Rhett up.

He hit the deck in a splatter of water, on his hands and knees. A few seconds after that, Jon sloshed down next to him, lying on his back and staring up at the open gray sky, his eyes enormous and frightened.

The boat's engine rumbled below them, but there was a second, smaller motor running somewhere. Rhett looked around and saw the cable that had saved them being slurped back up into a winch. When the hook at the end of the cable knocked against the device, Basil switched it off.

"Handy, eh?" he said, cocking an eyebrow at Rhett.

Rhett opened his mouth, intending to say, *What the fuck?* What he said instead was, "*Glug bub glurg,*" around a mouthful of regurgitated water. He coughed it up onto the deck of the boat, his body heaving from the effort. Beside him, Jon was on his side, doing the same.

It took a little while, but eventually Rhett was able to collect himself. Slowly, he got to his feet.

The boat was some kind of exploratory vessel. It was short and wide, the winch and a crane hanging over the back end. The bridge was up on a raised platform near the bow, and within it, Mak was operating the boat with Treeny beside her.

Next to Rhett on the floor, Jon groaned. Rhett knelt down, got an arm under Jon's elbow, and helped him to his feet.

"Are you okay?" Rhett asked.

"No," Jon said after a pause. "That sucked." He took his hat in his hands and wrung it out, splashing more water down onto the deck of the boat.

Rhett grinned. "Seriously."

"Thank you, though. For coming after me." Jon continued to stare at the soaked red hat in his hands, holding it the way he might have held a dying pet. "I thought maybe you were going to leave me behind."

"Never," Rhett replied, running a hand through his sopping hair. "You're part of the team. Whether you like it or not."

He leaned in to get a fist bump from Jon, but before he could make it, something exploded nearby.

They all looked up to see the *Cyclops*—or what remained of it—engulfed in flames. Something inside it had begun to burn, and the flames were quickly spreading not just across the ship but across the entire island. The syllektors' boat floated nearby as the wreckyard burned.

Mak and Treeny came down from the bridge and stood with the others, watching the fire, the brightest thing in the dark world of the afterlife.

"Is the lantern okay?" Rhett asked Mak.

"Yeah," she replied faintly, her eyes still locked on the crumbling remains of the *Cyclops*. There was a troubled look on her face.

"What's wrong?"

After a few seconds, she said, "Listen. What do you hear?"

Rhett did as she said, and all he could hear was the crackling of the fire and the occasional rumbling from one of the shipwrecks breaking down. He told her as much.

"Exactly," she said. She nodded at the *Cyclops*. "If there were any psychons on that thing, wouldn't we hear them? Wouldn't we see them jumping ship? Wouldn't they be coming after us?"

Rhett stared at the embroiled ship, slowly disintegrating under the heat of the flames. There were no screeches to be heard.

"There wasn't a single psychon on board when it crashed," Mak said, completing her thought.

"Then where are they?" Rhett asked.

But none of them had an answer.

THIRTEEN

They steered their little boat away from the wreckyard, cutting through waters that looked as if *they* were on fire, blazing white from the light of the flames that had completely overrun the island. Whatever shipwrecks had been there would be reduced to rubble and ash in just a few hours.

Rhett wasn't watching the fire that had grown wild and reckless, though. He was watching the fire that was small and contained and was serving a purpose: the lantern's flame. Its point leaned, and Mak put the boat in that direction. Occasionally, the flame would shift slightly, and Mak would correct the boat so they stayed on course.

They were on their way. To what, nobody knew. But as the hours wore on, and the droning of the boat's engine became more and more like some kind of torture device, Rhett knew they were getting close.

He could hear the faintest flicker of a heartbeat somewhere in the back of his mind, and it was getting louder.

The river stretched out around them for as far as he could see. The low, bubbling clouds competed with the water, trying to figure out which one was more restless. Above them, thunder rumbled and the clouds lit up with flickers of blue and white. The water smacked its waves into the side of the boat, rocking it, but in a way that was almost soothing, as if the river were trying to welcome them back.

Rhett was mildly terrified that the boat wouldn't hold together. The whole thing seemed to jerk and jostle in a way that was not soothing at all. Parts of it rattled and knocked and whined. They would be lucky if they made it to their destination before the whole thing simply gave up and fell apart beneath them.

Then another thought occurred to Rhett.

"How much gas does this thing have?" he called up to Mak.

She consulted one of the dials on the control panel in front of her, then leaned back and said, "None!"

Rhett didn't know what that meant, and he decided not to speculate.

They carried on for what must have been an entire day. Treeny and Theo hung out at the back of the boat, not talking, just watching the water spew out from underneath the stern. Mak kept her place up on the bridge. Rhett and Jon sat on the hard deck, their heads leaned back against the metal sides, trying to ignore the mind-numbing hum of the engine. Across from them, Basil leaned against the side of the boat, actually standing on his own and looking far better than he had back at the farm in Nebraska. In fact, when Rhett peered at Basil's neck, he could make out only faint remains of the ashy tendrils that had been curling their way up toward his face. Basil had his arms crossed in front of him, looking almost as cheeky and sarcastic as the day Rhett first met him.

"What're you gawking at, mate?" Basil asked. He had caught Rhett staring.

"Nothing," Rhett said quickly, turning away. But an undeniable smile had forced its way onto his face. When he glanced back at Basil, he was smiling, too.

The cure for the Ash was what they had expected it to be all along. The *Harbinger* was the cure, and the closer they got to it, the better Basil looked. And Jon might as well have not had the Ash at all; there wasn't a trace of it on him anymore.

It was all good news, but Rhett still needed to take care of something.

He stood and crossed the deck to where Basil was and waited for Basil to look him in the eye. It took a few seconds, but finally he did.

"I think you're done with that soul now, bud," Rhett said gently. Basil's cheeks twitched in a way that could have been a grimace or could have been a wince.

"Things got pretty weird back there, huh?" Basil said. "I can still feel it. The connection to the soul, I mean. Now that we're back and I'm already getting stronger, it's . . . it's not as potent. But I can still feel it."

"I know," Rhett said. "Which is why I need you to give it to me. Let me carry it for a while."

Jon was behind Rhett then, standing with his hands shoved down into his pockets.

"And when he can't carry it anymore, I'll take it," he said.

"We all will," Mak said. She had come down from the bridge and

was standing with her arms folded next to Jon. Loose strands of her hair whipped around her face in the wind.

From the end of the boat, Theo and Treeny were watching, and they both nodded their agreement.

Basil looked around at each of them and then settled on Rhett again.

"I'm . . . I'm afraid, mate," he said. "I'm afraid of what will happen if I let it go."

"I know," Rhett replied. "I am, too. But we have to get that soul back to the *Harbinger*. You can't keep using it. We'll all take turns carrying it if we have to, and we'll make sure that it gets back safe. It's our job, remember?"

Basil wrung his hands together, watching them anxiously. For a moment, Rhett didn't think that he was going to give up the soul. *And who can blame him?* Rhett thought. They had forced the soul on him in the first place—now they were forcing him to let it go. It needed to be carried, like a newborn to its first home, with all the gentleness and protection it deserved. Basil knew that as much as any of them.

Which is why he finally closed his eyes, pulled in a deep breath, and let it out in a rush of whistling air. At first, there were only thin wisps of white smoke that seemed to almost be fighting against the current coming from Basil's lungs, trying to push their way back into him. But then it relented and allowed itself to be released. It came spewing from the back of Basil's throat and twirled into a fist-size mass of dense mist. Tracing along some of the curls of smoke were tendrils of something black and venomous. As Rhett watched, though, the black stuff crusted over and flaked away, like dead skin. The soul was left unmarked, unaffected by the wind, floating among them.

"We don't even know who they were," Basil said. "Not really, anyway." There was a touch of sadness in his voice, but his eyes looked as if he'd just woken up from a long, long sleep.

"We never do," Rhett said. And then he leaned in, pursing his lips as if for a kiss, and felt the cool rush as he pulled the soul into his own body. It went willingly enough. When it was done, Rhett stood and said, "Okay. Now you guys really have to save my ass if anything goes wrong."

They all laughed together. Maybe for the last time.

The boat carried them far and fast. There was no trouble, no psychons, no demons, no anything. It was the sky, the water, and the syllektors in their crappy little boat, buzzing along like a tiny fruit fly across an endless expanse. A new day had just been breaking when they crossed the threshold back into the afterlife, but now there was no way to tell for sure if it was the same day or a new one. Time passed, that was all Rhett knew.

He carried the soul for a while, hours longer than he would have if they had been gathering it the normal way. Under those circumstances, a syllektor was only made to carry a soul for an hour, maybe two—long enough to get from the site of the death and back to the steam room. Rhett held on to this soul for as long as he could. He held on to it until he started to feel uncomfortable, until he started to feel as if he wasn't alone in his own head. When that sensation began to creep into his thoughts, he let Mak take the soul.

They kept going, the water sawing at their boat with jagged waves. Until they hit something.

Whatever it was, it was dense and metal. The boat hit it going full speed and was lifted out of the water by the impact, riding over the top of the object like a skateboard grinding across a rail. The metal scraped across the bottom of the boat, sending a few sparks shooting up on either side. Mak tumbled out of the bridge and landed hard on the deck below. Basil, Treeny, and Theo were nearly thrown overboard. Rhett and Jon just held on from where they sat on the deck, feeling the boat buck and wobble beneath them.

A moment later, the boat slid off the object and dropped back down into the water with a splash. The engine was still running, but Basil ran up and switched it off before it could carry them too far away from what they had hit.

"What in the bloody blazes was that?" he said once the boat was quiet, hurrying back down to where Mak still lay on the deck. He knelt down beside her. "Are you all right, love?"

Rhett watched as Basil took Mak's hand, maybe without even thinking about it, and held it to his chest. She smiled up at him.

"Yeah," she said quietly. "I'm okay."

Basil helped Mak up, and everyone went to the back of the boat. Theo and Treeny were already there, staring down into the water.

Rhett didn't know what he expected to see. Maybe a piece of the *Harbinger*'s hull. Maybe it would be the glass cube full of souls, just floating there, waiting patiently for them like a present beneath a Christmas tree. Whatever he thought, it was a hope that was too good to believe in. And that's why he was only mildly surprised when he reached the back of the boat and saw an enormous iron anchor floating in the water.

It was just the anchor, floating perfectly flat on the surface, like a person relaxing in a pool. The thing was at least as big as the boat that the syllektors had hit it with, and there was a chain attached to it, with links that were nearly as big as Rhett himself. The chain went down into the depths of the river, disappearing into the blackness below.

Rhett looked around at the others and found them all staring at the anchor with a kind of reverence. It seemed that he was the only one who didn't understand what this was or where it came from.

"What is it?" he asked.

"It's the *Harbinger*'s anchor," Treeny said.

Basil stepped away, heading back up to the bridge.

"Why is it . . . floating?" Rhett said.

"She must have left it behind," Mak said softly. Her voice was just below a whisper, but Rhett caught it.

"Who? Who left it behind?"

"The *Harbinger*. She left it here so we could find her," Mak replied, nodding to herself, almost trying to make the words sound believable to her own ears.

Basil came back down and rejoined the others. He was carrying the lantern in his hand, holding it up, watching the flame.

"Look," he said.

Rhett and the others pulled their attention away from the anchor and peered at the lantern. Jon and Treeny both gasped, and Rhett had to hold in his own startled response.

The flame that burned within the lantern had flipped, its point now aimed straight down, connecting with the wick, its bulb floating in the air above it.

"Is everything else about to turn upside down?" Rhett asked. "Because I don't think I'm prepared for that."

"It's telling us where to go." The voice belonged to Theo, and everyone looked at him, blinking. He swept a glance around at everyone. "Don't yous see? We have to follow it down to the bottom. Our ship's down there somewhere."

Jon took a frightened step backward, and everyone else looked back at the anchor, bobbing with the waves, seeming to almost beckon them toward it.

"He's right," Treeny said. "The anchor's chain must still be attached to the *Harbinger*. If we follow it, we'll find the ship."

"Guess we're going for another swim," Basil said, beginning to do some exaggerated stretches.

Rhett was glad to see him feeling so good, but he could have punched Basil in the face right then. He noticed Jon, too, staring at the water that had already come dangerously close to pulling him under.

"You all right?" Rhett asked.

Jon's eyes were darting around wildly, and when he realized it, he shut them. He squeezed his eyelids together, breathing in deep. When he opened his eyes again, he looked more like himself.

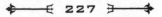

"Yeah," he said. "We have to do what we have to do."

Rhett nodded. But he gave the choppy sea his own anxious glance.

Mak attached the lantern to her belt again, its upside-down flame burning brightly. She was going to go first so that the others could follow the light.

Rhett wanted to ask why the lantern's flame wouldn't go out when it hit the water—a fact of which Treeny had been very sure—but given what they'd had to go through to get that fire relit, he figured it was a stupid question.

They checked their weapons, making sure that everyone still had what they needed. Rhett was relieved to find his knuckle blade still resting in its holster on his thigh. He had a bit of a reputation for losing it. Jon adjusted his staff in its sheath over his shoulder, and the others resecured their blades. Basil pulled his scythes out and did his trademark drumstick spin with them. Treeny was the only one without a weapon, but she was aglow with confidence, ready to dive in, literally, when everyone else was.

"Okay," Basil said. "Everyone keep hold of the anchor chain, and everyone stay close to Mak. She's got the only light we have. I'll go last and keep an eye on everybody."

Mak went in first, jumping into the water hands-first in a perfect, graceful dive. Theo went next, doing a cannonball that created a splash approximately the size of a small nuclear detonation. Then it was Treeny.

Jon and Rhett approached the back of the boat together, and Jon was bouncing on the balls of his feet, psyching himself up.

"Don't suppose you're willing to save my ass twice in one day," he said, watching the water. There wasn't any humor in his voice.

"Well . . . if I have to," Rhett replied, and nudged Jon with his elbow. He grinned, and Jon managed a tiny chuckle. "Just make sure that thing doesn't switch on and turn us all into fried calamari," Rhett went on, nodding at the staff sticking up behind Jon's back.

At that, Jon actually laughed. His body relaxed, and a second later he was launching himself off the back of the boat. Rhett followed.

The water was freezing. Not that Rhett could feel it, but he could tell by the way that the others' lips were turning blue. He let the water engulf him, plunging below the surface before floating back to the top.

They waited on Basil, who had climbed back up to the bridge of the boat. He switched the engine back on and put the thing at full throttle. The boat sprayed a torrent of water at Rhett and the others. They pushed away from it, sputtering, and grabbed hold of the anchor.

For a second, Rhett had a frightening, irrational suspicion that Basil was taking the boat and leaving them. But then he spotted Basil sprinting back across the deck, essentially running in place as the boat pulled away from where it had been floating. Basil reached the stern and leaped into the water, doing a far less graceful dive than Mak's. He hit the water and the boat careened away, a literal ghost ship now.

Everybody stared at Basil as if he had lost his mind.

"What?" he said. "We don't need it anymore. If somebody unpleasant happens to come this way, we don't want them to know we've been here, do we?"

"And what if there's nothing at the end of this chain and we have to come back up?" Mak asked, fury roaring in her eyes. "What then, Mission Impossible?"

"I . . . uh . . . oh." Basil looked back at the boat as it raced farther and farther away. "Shit."

"It's fine," Rhett butted in. He felt weird having this conversation while they all floated in the water, like they were regular teens having a pool party. "All this means is that we *have* to find something down there. Even if we don't see it right away." He looked around at the others. His friends, his family. "Together," he said.

And they all nodded.

"I'd say take a deep breath, but . . . ," Mak said, shrugging. Her hair clung to her face, making it look almost windswept. "Here we go." And then she blew out, releasing all the air from her lungs, and—

"Wait!" Basil cried. He was paddling over to the other end of the anchor, where Mak was still holding on. She was staring at him, confused. But before she could say anything to scold him, Basil had pushed between the others and was floating right in front of her. He didn't hesitate, just wrapped one arm around her waist and slipped his other hand behind her neck. She looked surprised at first, but then she relaxed and let herself fall into him.

They kissed, floating in the unending river, as if they were alone there. There was something powerful in it, something that wiped away all the tension and hurt feelings and regret. It was instant and remarkable.

When Basil pulled back, he said, "I want you to know that this is all I've ever needed. Whatever's waiting for us down there, it doesn't

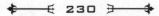

stand a chance as long as I have you with me. I'm sorry that I made this even more miserable than it already was. I never should have pushed you away."

Mak smiled at him, brushing a few droplets of water from his check with her thumb.

"I was so angry when I died," she said. "I feel like that anger never left me. I didn't make it easy for you, either. But from the moment I set foot on the *Harbinger*, you've made my nightmare a miracle, even when it seemed like I hated your guts." She shrugged, smiling a rare, goofy smile.

They kissed again, the tiny punctuation on the end of their embrace, and finally let each other go.

Mak shook her head, refocusing, and then let out her breath and allowed her body to sink below the surface.

Even through the chopping waves and the dimness of the water, Rhett could see the glow of the lantern illuminating Mak and the enormous anchor chain beside her. She grabbed it, using it to pull herself downward.

"Here we go," Theo echoed, his accent making *here* sound like *hee-ya*. And then he was gone, dropping under the water with just a single plop.

Treeny followed, taking her glasses off and stuffing them into one of her pockets, then pushing off the impossibly huge anchor and flipping over, kicking her way below the surface like she was a trained diver.

Rhett tipped a wink at Jon. "Don't get lost."

He smirked. "After you."

Then Rhett closed his eyes, fighting the instinct to take a deep breath, and sank into the water.

When he opened his eyes again, it was like he was in a completely different world. Back at the wreckyard, he hadn't had time to really appreciate the vastness of the chasm below the river's surface. But now, with the anchor chain as reference, he could see just how unending it really was. There were no creatures, no fish, no masses of rock or coral. It was just water and darkness, stretching far and away. Soft light rippled across the surface, sending faint dapples across the chain and his friends down below. But the deeper they went, the fainter the light got. Soon, the lantern would be the only source of light they'd have to see by, which would make finding anything at the bottom extremely difficult.

Rhett took hold of one of the iron chain's links, which were big enough that he could have swam through them if he wanted to, and began to haul himself down, following the bottoms of Treeny's sneakers, kicking steadily in front of him.

He realized that he still had his mouth closed, and his lungs were empty. The idea of essentially drowning himself again gave him the shivers, but it would be easier to make it down to the bottom if he did. So he opened his mouth and gently unclenched his throat, letting the water in. It spilled into his lungs, and again his body tried to reject it, coughing and twitching and panicking without his consent. After a second, though, his chest stilled, and he quit breathing. Already, he felt heavier. It felt as if he could just let go of the chain and sink leisurely to the bottom without any effort at all. And he'd never been more glad to have his senses blocked than he was right then, knowing that his body was probably crying out in anguish from all the trauma he'd put it through.

The all-consuming black of the chasm began to overtake them, but before it could, Rhett glanced back to make sure that Jon and Basil were following him.

Jon was there, just several inches from the tips of Rhett's shoes, his hat no longer on his head but stuffed into one of his back pockets. He gave Rhett a quick thumbs-up. Basil was right behind him, his face looking strangely bloated and squashed from the force of the water pushing against it. Rhett wanted to laugh but couldn't.

Behind Basil, the surface of the water was beginning to be swallowed by the murky depths. Rhett could see the gray, roiling sky, but it was broken into shards, shuddering above him like an optical illusion. It was strange that he was so afraid to leave that terrible sky behind when he'd been so afraid of it to begin with. But here he was.

The syllektors sank. They pulled themselves ever downward, with the flickering firelight inside the lantern shining outward like a tiny star in the gargantuan emptiness of space. Mak carried that star, and the others followed it.

Rhett had no idea how far down they were. And even if Treeny did know, he couldn't ask her. They followed the chain in silence, without even a bubble trail to keep them company.

Occasionally, Rhett would let his gaze stray from Treeny's shoes and glance around, hoping to see something familiar. After what must have been a couple of hours, he *did* see something familiar. But it was something that nearly made him lurch back in horror.

Even in the oblivion of the deep water, the shape of it was dark enough to stand out. He remembered the curl of its tentacles as they smashed into the *Harbinger*. He remembered the rows of teeth that lined its gigantic mouth. The reaching, creeping circles of legs that took the place of suction cups along its limbs.

Before them, and almost encircling them, was the looming shadow of the kymaker.

Except it wasn't moving. What Rhett remembered as a writhing, raging sea monster was now simply floating there, its motionless tentacles twisting away from it, a couple of them suspended around the anchor chain, as if it had been guarding the spot where the *Harbinger* sank.

It was very clearly dead, hanging lifeless in the water. Its corpse was almost bigger than the living monster had been, now bloated and waterlogged. That didn't make it any less terrifying.

The syllektors glanced at one another, silently trying to determine if it was safe to pass this close to the beast. There was still the slim possibility that it could just be playing dead, waiting for someone to try and pass so it could snap to life and pull them into its toothy maw.

After a brief moment of contemplation, though, Mak kept going. Rhett could hear her voice in his head saying, *We don't have any other choice.* And she would be right. It was either risk demise by sea monster or go all the way back to the surface, where they had no boat and no way back to anywhere.

They went on, following the anchor chain and passing only a couple of yards from the lurking shapes of the kymaker's tentacles. Rhett tried to imagine how miniscule they probably looked in front of the massive body of the monster and was again astounded by how tiny they were compared to this world. Sometimes that thought was more frightening than death itself had been.

The monster never attacked. It just kept on floating, killed either by its original ambush on the *Harbinger* or by something else afterward. *Is Urcena powerful enough to murder a creature of this size?* Rhett wondered. Could she have taken her rage out on the kymaker when her attack on the ship proved fruitless and Rhett slipped through her fingers? Probably. Likely, in fact. The monster had failed the demon, and so the demon had ended the monster.

They left the dead kymaker behind and continued to sink down through leagues and leagues of water. The lantern stayed lit, but after a while it was only bright enough to illuminate a small swath of the darkness around them, including the anchor chain, which now seemed to stretch forever in both directions. Rhett recalled the moment that now felt like an eternity ago, on the day the *Harbinger* was dragged down into the river, when he and Basil and Mak had been fleeing the psychons, running down through the secret passageway to the furnace room. That stairwell had felt like this—bottomless, boundless, endlessly dark. It was like a strange sort of limbo, running both from and toward danger, feeling eternally caught in between.

But that stairwell had ended, and so did the river.

After another handful of hours, the lantern light finally illuminated something other than murky water and the rusted iron of the anchor chain. The glow fell upon the flat, sandy bottom of the river, perfectly smooth except for where the chain connected to it. There, a sort of crater had formed around the spot where the chain disappeared into the sand. It was embedded, with only half a link protruding from the river bottom. Aside from that, there was nothing. Only more sand and water in every direction.

Mak pulled herself to the very bottom and pressed her hand against the sand. It gave way and enveloped her fingers. There was no ship hiding just beneath the surface. In fact, there was no reason to believe that there was a ship at all. The anchor and its chain could have broken off the ship and drifted miles away from where she actually sank.

Rhett glanced around at the others and was met with the same look of near-panicked disappointment that he knew he was wearing himself. This was the end of the line. The last domino that wouldn't tip over.

But Mak kept digging. She buried her hand all the way into the river bottom and scooped some of the sand out. She tried to fling it over her shoulder, but of course it immediately turned into a cloud that drifted lazily away. By the thin light of the lantern, she kept digging, and eventually Basil swam down beside her and began to help.

What else was there to do but hope?

Rhett and Jon sank down and planted their feet in the sand around the crater. They began to dig, too. Theo and Treeny were right behind them. Then all six of them were pulling their hands through the sand around the chain, sending dense clouds of the stuff floating up into the water. They dug and dug until they had deepened the crater by almost two feet and revealed almost all of the rest of the chain link that was buried there. Their bodies moved slowly against the pressure of the deep. They were beaten and exhausted and resurrected from ghostdom and recovering from the Ash and literally drowned, full of water so that they could find their way here. The

lantern's flame still pointed downward at this spot, still flickering brightly even amid the sand and dirt swirling around it.

If the *Harbinger*, their home, was anywhere, it was right here.

And then Rhett stuck his hand in the dirt once more, meaning to pull another load of sand out, and something broke through. It wasn't black metal or wood or even glass.

It was sunshine.

Rhett pulled his hand away, half expecting some kind of explosion. But what stabbed through the sand wasn't fire or electricity. It was pure, brilliant sunlight, a single ray of it that shot out of the hole in the sand and up like a laser beam.

They all looked at one another, mouths dangling open. And then they were all digging again, heaving more sand away and uncovering more sunlight. Rhett tried to peer into it, but it was too bright to look at. The light shimmered in a pool within the crater they had formed, and as it grew, Rhett realized that it wasn't a pool of light itself but the surface of some other pool of water. Beyond that surface was a clear sky, lit with a hot white sun.

Frantic now, they pulled as much sand out of the crater as they could, widening the surface of the other pool, and revealing not just the light itself but also the fact that the anchor chain went down (*up?*) and out of the pool into . . . somewhere else.

When the pool was as wide as they were going to get it, Rhett looked over at Jon in time to see him preparing to dive into it. He must have been desperate to get out of the water, but they had no way of knowing what was on the other side of that warbling surface. Rhett grabbed Jon's elbow and held him back, giving him a concerned look. Jon gestured around himself—at the water, at the chain, at the deepness of the river—and then made a slashing motion across his throat.

Rhett understood, and he let Jon go.

In one smooth motion, Jon slipped down into the too-bright pool and vanished through it.

Rhett, Mak, Basil, Treeny, and Theo waited, all of them staring into the light, waiting for some kind of signal. An instant later, they got it in the form of Jon's hand poking back up out of the pool, waving at them to come after him.

Without hesitation, Rhett waved his hands through the water, pulling himself up into a weightless standing position. He took a step forward and allowed himself to fall through the surface of the water, into the intense light.

He fell downward for a moment . . . and then gravity shifted, and he was falling *up*ward. He came shooting up out of the pool of water, sopping wet, and flipped once before smacking face-first into a pile of dry white sand. It took a second for the world to quit spinning, but when it did, he pulled himself up onto his hands and knees, coughing up the water that had invaded his lungs, and peered around.

Even without his senses, he could tell that it was excruciatingly hot. The white sand was everywhere, piled up into dunes that were more like small mountains, and the heat radiated off it in liquid shimmers. The sun was directly above, a bright burning hole in the sky, crushing its heat into the world. This desert, Rhett quickly realized, was as vast and limitless as the river from which he'd just escaped. It

spanned the entirety of his vision in every direction, hot and brilliant and deadly.

"Hell of a jump," Jon said from behind him. Rhett turned to find him lying back in the sand, propped up on his hands as if he were sunbathing. There was a giant grin on his face, and his red hat had returned to his head, flipped around backward so that he could get the sun full in his face.

"Where are we?" Rhett asked, pulling himself to his feet and trying to brush off some of the sand that was caked to him.

"No clue. I'm just glad to be out of the damn water."

A set of hands was reaching up out of the pool, waving around, looking for something to grab hold of. Rhett and Jon stepped over. Each took a hand and pulled. Treeny came up out of the water, her eyes wide, her mouth spitting up all the water that her lungs had taken on. When they were clear, she took in the surroundings.

"What the . . . ," she said.

They helped Mak through, and then Theo pulled himself through, because not even the strength of four of them was enough to lift his weight. Finally, Basil climbed up and out, dripping and coughing.

"I feel like this is a step in the wrong direction," he said when he'd gotten himself together. "Anybody else feel like this whole setting is a little counterintuitive?"

"Look," Theo said, pointing at the sand around their feet.

Partially buried there, coming out of the pool of water and stretching up one of the massive sand dunes, was the anchor chain. It was coated in sand and barely visible, but it was there.

"I guess we keep following it," Mak said. She was looking down at the lantern, at the flame that had now righted itself. The point was aiming in the same direction as the chain.

They didn't have to go far.

The dune was a struggle, an unstable mound of sand that collapsed under their feet and sent tiny avalanches down behind them. They clawed their way up it, hauling themselves over the sand until they were practically covered in it.

When they finally, frantically reached the top of the dune, they each let out a gasp or a cry. Rhett couldn't tell if they were in surprise or delight or horror. It didn't matter.

Strewn across the desert, broken into ragged hunks of metal and debris, was the *Harbinger*.

FOURTEEN

They stood staring for as long as they could, until Mak finally turned her head away, eyes squeezed shut.

"We have to go down there," Rhett said quietly. "We have to find the cube. And at least one functioning doorway back to the living world."

Gradually, they all came out of their daze, squinting against the sun, and nodded. They stumbled down the other side of the dune. Sand billowed up into their faces as they practically rolled down it, holding on to the anchor chain, which was pulled taut from the top of the dune to somewhere within the wreckage.

It looked even worse when they reached the bottom.

Debris was scattered everywhere—twisted beams, pieces of furniture, hunks of wood. There were chunks of entire rooms, broken open and half-buried in the sand, looking like ancient set pieces for some movie that was never filmed. The *Harbinger* itself was cracked apart like an egg, with whole sections of it standing like buildings that had had their facades scraped off, revealing all the individual floors and rooms behind them. Ragged slabs of metal and snapped wooden beams hung from everything, sagging downward, coated in rust and sand. Colors were faded by the harsh sun, portholes shattered or popped out like bottle caps. As they walked into the heart of the destruction, all of it towering over them on both sides, it felt even more like walking through some forgotten city of the apocalypse.

"Look at it," Jon said, brushing his hand across a rust-covered chunk of metal. "It looks so . . . *old* all of a sudden."

"Yes," Treeny replied. Her voice was distant, focused on something else. "It looks like it's been here for decades, not just a few years."

"How can that be?" Basil asked.

"Time must work differently here," Treeny said simply.

"I still want to know where *here* is," Rhett heard himself saying. He was staring up at a torn-open piece of the wreck, at all the decks layered on top of one another like sections of a cake. He could see into them, to halls that he had walked through and rooms that he had been in, could see all the sand and dirt that had accumulated there.

He was still staring when he took another step forward and something beneath his foot cracked. A larger something rattled almost musically in front of him, and he nearly fell over the top of it. He stumbled back, almost losing his footing, and saw what it was: the chandelier, the one from the ornate room that Basil had taken him through on his very first journey through the *Harbinger*'s halls.

Magnificent, isn't it? Basil had said.

Now it lay in the sand like a wad of discarded stars, still twinkling in the sunlight, but in a sad kind of way. A forgotten way. Basil took one look at it before storming forward, kicking white puffs of sand out behind him.

"God, this sucks." Mak sighed.

Rhett stared at the chandelier, unwilling to let himself be pulled away from it. It had been so pristine and so perfect that first time he'd seen it, hanging there like an arrow of light.

"This is the dazzling landscape of your dreams," Rhett muttered.

"Huh?" Mak stared at him, concern growing in her eyes.

"Nothing," he replied. He shook his head, clearing out the muddled thoughts. "Let's keep going."

There was more to the wreckage, of course; the *Harbinger* was a ship the size of a small city. And broken apart like this, it felt like a *big* city. There were parts and pieces scattered all over, as far out as a couple of miles, it seemed. Out near the edge of the debris field, Rhett spotted the shape of a crumpled smokestack, the only one that would have made it this far, considering its twin had been dropped into the kymaker's hungry mouth. It stood on its end, bent and sinking in on itself, like a cigarette butt stuck into a sea of ash.

Rhett wanted to lie down right here and bury his face in the hot sand among the destruction that his power had brought upon their ship. The power that was supposed to bring the ship back from the dead. But he had no idea how he was going to fix this.

"We need to find the column," Mak said, her voice straining against the emotion that was ready to burst forward. "If we can get our bearings with that, then we can find the steam room, or at least the cube, and the doors."

"What about the lantern?" Rhett suggested.

Mak held it up so everyone could see. The flame inside was pointing straight up, flickering absently. "It was only ever meant to get us back to the *Harbinger*," she said. "And it's done that. We have to figure the rest out for ourselves."

"Let's split up," Basil said. "Rhett, Jon, and Theo, you guys go that way." He pointed to their left, at one looming chunk of the ship. "Mak, Treeny, and I will go this way." He pointed to their right, at another.

"I'm not really a fan of this whole Scooby-Doo strategy," Jon said. "I think we should stay together."

"Agreed," Mak added.

"There's six of us here," Basil said. "We don't have a lot of time. The rest of the crew have been at the rendezvous point for who knows how long already. Between the psychons and the Ash, they're sitting ducks until we get in touch with them. The quicker we find the cube and the doors, the quicker we can bring them out of the living world."

"To what?" Treeny interjected. "To *this*?"

"Yes, to this," Basil said. "Look." He rolled up the sleeve of his blazer and shirt, revealing the smooth flesh of his forearm beneath. The black patches of Ash were gone. "The cube is here. I can feel it. And just being this close is enough to get rid of this bloody disease. These aren't the best circumstances, no, but we have to at least help the syllektors that we can. And fast."

"He's right," Rhett said. "We'll cover more ground. We'll split up just until we find the column. Good enough?" He was directing the question at Basil, who nodded. "Okay, let's go."

"Wait," Jon said. Everybody halted, watching as he stepped over to Mak. He put his hand out and wagged his fingers at the sky, as if he was asking her to give him some cash. "Cough it up," he said. "Literally. You've held on to it for too long already."

A look of relieved gratitude fell across Mak's face. Rhett understood. She had kept the soul for even longer than he had. By now she must have been feeling like she was losing control of herself.

She exhaled, and the soul unfurled from inside her throat. It hung between her and Jon, a perfect, milky cloud, until Jon inhaled and let the soul slither down into his chest.

"Thanks," Mak said. The look on her face said she really meant it.

"I'll send you my bill," Jon replied, and winked.

They broke off into the two groups. Rhett glanced back over his shoulder and watched as Basil, Treeny, and Mak walked into the shadow of the wreck, stepping up onto one of the open-ended decks. Then he, Jon, and Theo did the same on their side.

When they came fully into the musty darkness of the deck, Rhett realized they were in the cargo hold, surrounded by upended crates, some of them broken open and spilling out food that was so rotten it had all but disintegrated. Inside the ship, without any lights and without the constant creaks and groans of floating on the water, everything was eerily quiet. The only sound came from Theo's heavy strides along the wooden floor.

"You've been pretty quiet, big guy," Rhett said to Theo. "Everything okay?"

"It just . . . it ain't supposed to be like this, ya know?" Theo said.

"Yeah. I know, buddy."

They wove their way through the maze of fallen crates, seeing only by the scant light that fell in from the jagged opening they'd come through.

"If we're headed the right way," Jon said, "there should be a door right about . . . aha!" He pointed ahead, to a shadowed doorway set into the side of the hold. The door itself was iron and was supposed to be sealed in case the hull was damaged. But it was hanging open, attached by only one hinge. "Depending on what side of the ship we're on, this is either going to take us to the column or to the engine room."

"There isn't an engine room anymore," Rhett said, recalling the encounter they'd had with Urcena and Treeny there, surrounded by the furnaces. Urcena had ripped the room apart when Basil ghosted Treeny.

"Well, where the engine room *should* be, anyway," Jon corrected. He ducked below the crooked door and stepped into the corridor beyond. Rhett followed, with Theo coming up the rear.

Everything on this side of the door was black. There wasn't even a shred of light. They felt their way along the walls, kicking piles of sand and mysterious bits of debris. Every noise echoed loudly back at them. A place that had been so overwhelmed with energy before was now empty and silent. It was creepier than any house a ghosted syllektor could possibly haunt.

They moved through the hall as it turned at ninety-degree angles, winding deeper into the remains of the ship. There were a couple of short sets of stairs and some doors that led to miscellaneous rooms, more cargo holds, mostly. And they navigated all of this in pitch-darkness, ears trained on the tiny sounds they made, also listening for any signal from the others.

Finally, they rounded another corner and found a tiny bit of light waiting for them at the end of the hall. Rhett was able to make out the details of the corridor and recognized it for what it was. He hurried with the other two to the opening at the end, stepping around and over fallen chunks of the walls and ceiling.

The hallway dropped off into a circular chasm, some of which was lined with a spiral staircase: the column, but a barely recognizable version of it. The staircase had fallen in a lot of places, including right in front of where they now stood. The broken pieces were piled at the bottom, only twenty or thirty feet below. The rest of the column reached up above them, open at the top from where the bridge tower had been ripped out, letting a few rays of sunlight fall through. What remained of the staircase looked unstable, ready to break apart at any moment.

Rhett peered upward, trying to see any feasible way to the top. Somewhere among those upper decks, the cube and the room of doors waited.

"We should get the others," Jon said, staring up through the dim, ruined spiral.

"There's no point in getting them if we don't know that what we're looking for is up there," Rhett replied.

"How the hell do we go *up*," Theo said, "without falling *down?*" He was eyeing the bottom of the column, where the broken stairs lay piled up on top of one another, jagged and pointed, ready to pulverize the syllektors should they fall.

Across from where they stood, Rhett saw that at least half the staircase was still intact, and it wound its way up to a length of stairs that were still holding on entirely. If they could get across the fifteen or twenty feet that separated them from that partial staircase, they could make their way higher. Only a handful of decks separated them from the room of doors.

"I have an idea," Jon said, sighing. "But Theo won't like it."

He reached over his shoulder and pulled out his weapon. The staff extended in his hand with an audible *schunk*. It was missing the white curls of electricity jittering up and down its length, but as Jon glanced back at the hallway they'd just come from, then looked the other way at the yawning gap in the column, silently measuring distances, Rhett started to get the idea.

So did Theo.

"Yeah, I'm out," Theo said, eyeing the staff. "I'll double back and find the others, bring 'em back here. Yous two can do whatever batty nonsense yous want."

Rhett nodded. "Okay. Just be quick."

Theo gave him a quick nod and then turned, heading back down the shadowed corridor.

Meanwhile, Jon was poking the end of the steel staff into the warped and scorched metal of the landing. He jabbed the staff downward and leaned into it, testing his weight.

"This ought to be interesting," he muttered, before taking several steps backward. He held the staff with both hands over his shoulder, tightening and retightening his grip on it. "I'll go first, then toss it back for you."

"You sure about this?" Rhett asked, cocking an eyebrow.

"Yeah," Jon said. Then, a second later: "Yeah. Definitely. This is fine. Everything's fine."

Without any other preamble, Jon darted forward. His footsteps thudded against the floor. A long, groaning cry began to rise from the back of his throat. He gained as much speed as he could, rushing past Rhett, who cringed, bringing his shoulders up to his ears, desperately afraid of what was coming next.

Jon brought the staff down hard against the floor. It ground into the already weakened stone of the landing and stuck. He pushed up and out. His whole body rose, feetfirst, and shifted out over the drop to the broken stairs below. Now he was full-on screaming, flailing, the staff still held tight in one hand. He hung in the air for what felt like way too long . . . and then fell. Dropping like a meteorite, he plummeted down to the staircase on the opposite side. He hit the landing with a *whump* that sounded like it knocked the air out of him.

A moment later, Jon stuck out his arm, a thumbs-up hanging on the end of it.

"There is not a chance in hell I'm doing that," Rhett said. He came to the edge of the staircase, his arms folded.

Jon got to his feet, brushing off his clothes. "Well then, I guess you're staying here," he said. Then, in one motion, he shortened the staff, allowing the ends to slide back into themselves, and tossed it over the gap to Rhett, who caught it with a look of irritated humor.

"This is what I get for saving you from the river?" Rhett asked. He found the almost invisible button on the side of the staff to elongate it. When he pressed it, the ends shot out and he had to jerk away before his face was impaled.

"Yeah, well, I *did* kind of help save you from being a ghost forever, so . . ." Jon put his hands out and shrugged.

Groaning, Rhett took a few steps back, set his feet, measured his own distance, trying to mentally calculate how much speed he'd need to make it across. He took the same stance Jon had, with the staff over his shoulder . . . and ran.

He planted the staff into the floor at the end of the landing.

He pushed his body up and out into the empty air.

He felt the staff lose its hold and screech across the ground, taking all of his momentum with it.

He dropped, still desperately holding on to Jon's weapon, arms and legs reaching in every direction for something to grab . . .

Then he felt Jon's hands around his wrist, grasping it. Jon swung his arms with the motion of Rhett's fall, his feet planted at the very edge of the stairs so that if he lost his balance, they would both end up as minced meat at the bottom of the column. But he was using what little momentum Rhett had to swing him like a pendulum. Rhett saw the blunt and immovable shapes of the cracked stairs below, saw the pale blue sky through the top of the column where the bridge used to be . . .

After that he saw pocked gray stone, right up against his face, as he landed ungracefully on the stairway beside Jon. Both of them were on their backs, panting, surrounded by a fog of sand and dust that had been kicked up by their impact.

"Now you owe me one," Jon said, breathless.

"Uh-huh," Rhett replied. He shortened Jon's staff again and flung it at its owner.

"We're gonna do that again on the way back, right?"

"I'd really rather not," Rhett replied.

It took a couple minutes for both of them to get their heads straight again, but once they did, they were able to get to their feet and survey the column from their new vantage point. There was a clear, mostly unbroken path up for several decks. They climbed almost all the way to the next gap before finding what they needed.

"Here," Rhett said. They had reached the deck that belonged to the room of doors. Half a deck up, the staircase ended in a broken ledge and didn't pick back up again for fifty feet or so. Getting up to where the steam room should have been was going to be nearly impossible. But for now, they could make their way to the doors and hope that one of them still worked.

Another short corridor opened up onto what Rhett recognized as the diamond-shaped room, once lined with the doorways that could transport them back and forth to the living world, but it was flooded with sunlight. He and Jon hurried in that direction. They stepped into the place where they had each been hundreds of times. Except there was only half a room waiting for them.

The rest had been ripped away, opening up onto the desert and the rest of the wreckage down below. What had once been a sealed-off room was now more like a balcony, basking in the bright sunshine, its two remaining walls lined with doors that were broken out of their frames or folded into jagged halves or missing entirely, leaving only a faint, rectangular outline on the wall. The place was in shambles, and all of the doors were ruined.

Except for one.

Rhett spotted it immediately, the only door that stood upright, in one piece, made from a dark wood with a shining, silver doorknob. It reminded him of the door from his dream, the one he'd had back on the train from DC to Chicago, and it frightened him instantly.

It shouldn't have frightened him. It should have been a saving grace, the gateway to reunite them with the rest of the crew. But it scared him all the same.

Jon walked toward the door.

"This is the only one that looks intact," he said, his voice laced with sadness. "Let's hope it's got a little juice left in it."

But Rhett didn't want him to touch it. He stood staring at the door, with the ragged drop-off to the desert sand behind him, the sun hitting his back. There was a noise coming from that direction. Someone yelling. Someone *screaming*. He turned and stepped over to the edge, hearing a subtle crackle in the wood beneath his feet. Far down below, at the bottom of the piece of wreckage that Basil, Mak, and Treeny had gone into, he saw those same three people, running, yelling his name and Jon's. Theo was with them, too. They were all screaming.

Then, behind them, Rhett saw more syllektors come pouring out of the wreck, not running after his friends, but running *with* them. It was the rest of the crew. They had made it back already. But how?

Mak was close enough now that she spotted him standing there, watching them from above. She stopped, cupped her hands around her mouth, and screamed, "*Rhett! IT'S A TRAP!*"

He whirled around, but it was too late. Jon already had his hand on the doorknob.

"Jon, wait . . . *no!*"

He turned it. The door creaked open, and on the other side stood Anton Markeski, surrounded by hundreds of psychons.

The rendezvous point had been an out-of-business grocery store in West Virginia. It was chosen because the handful of the crew who had used that particular doorway to get back to the *Harbinger* remembered it as being well away from a large living population, abandoned, left to rot in a clearing of weeds where no one ever went. It was supposed to be off the radar.

Now that same grocery store was filled with slobbering, grinning psychons, their cloaks drawn over their heads, casting shadows across their bone-and-tissue faces. Above them, the rusted carcasses of old fluorescent light fixtures hung silently, and somehow a few of the remaining bulbs were stuttering at random. Markeski headed up the group, his own face grinning manically.

Jon stumbled back from the door, nearly falling into Rhett. He caught him and kept Jon upright before they could both fall off the edge of the wreck. Down below, the rest of the crew gathered, staring up.

"You know," Markeski said from his side of the doorway. "This was really too easy."

He took a step forward, edging closer to the threshold. Rhett glanced at the door itself and knew he wouldn't be fast enough to slam it shut. The psychons would come pouring out before he even got close. Besides, the connection had clearly already been made. Markeski and Urcena—who, Rhett realized with a pang, was not reliant on the doors to move between the worlds—must have led the psychons to the rendezvous point. Then Urcena could have reestablished the connection from this side; easily captured the crew, pinned as they were between her and Markeski and the psychons; and then trapped them inside the desert. Until the moment was right.

Until the one syllektor she really wanted showed up.

"You bastard," Rhett growled.

Markeski shrugged. "I was never all that fond of gathering souls anyway. Overworked and underpaid and all that." He took another step toward the door, and now Rhett spotted a handful of Markeski's syllektors on that side, too. They were part of Markeski's crew, but they didn't look nearly as confident as he did. In fact, they looked petrified, surrounded by towering psychons, the things they had been trained to fight *against*.

But there was a reason that Markeski looked so calm. It flashed briefly in his eyes, but Rhett had seen it so many times now that it barely fazed him anymore. Markeski's eyes shifted, turning black with those tiny points of white. It lasted only a second, but Rhett knew that Urcena was close.

Rhett shuffled his feet backward, Jon close to his side. His heels jutted out over the edge, breaking a few splinters off the floor and sending them falling down to where the crew stood watching.

"Give yourself up, Soul Keeper," Markeski said, his face a twisted, malicious parody of itself. He took another step forward. The toes of his shoes crossed over the threshold from the living world to this one, and when they did, they turned to ash and fell away. Where Markeski's toes had been, there was now a pair of pale bare feet, with dark, purplish veins written across them. Another step, and more of Markeski's body broke apart into spirals of ash. His face was momentarily charred and featureless, and then the ash blew away, revealing the horrid, grinning face of Urcena.

She spoke with her face attached to what remained of Markeski's body, but now it was truly her voice, layered with thousands of others that penetrated Rhett's mind and threatened to snap it in two.

"*Do you think me so foolish to have let you walk away without a purpose?*" she asked, referring to that night in the cemetery. She'd been sitting in the truck then, letting Markeski speak for himself. Now she was destroying her own puppet. "*You're in* my *world now, Soul Keeper. This is where demons are bred. This is where they reign.*"

One last step forward, and the rest of Markeski was annihilated, his limbs and torso scorched into ash in an instant and swept away. That left only Urcena now, her body drenched in perpetual water, dripping onto the floor, her hospital gown heavy and faded across her shoulders. She stared at Rhett and Jon with her tiny white pupils, lost in their sea of black. Her head was cocked to the side, as if asking a question, and her matted hair fell across her face in soaked ropes.

When she smiled, her teeth were grimy and sharp, like a shark's.

"*Now come,*" she said, her voice drilling into Rhett's head. "*Let me break you.*"

The psychons lunged, funneling out of the grocery store and clambering into the remains of the *Harbinger*. They looked strange in the sunlight, almost like animatronic movie props. But the way they moved was terrifyingly real, clawing across the wooden floor and up the walls, like a swarm of insects. They were so close that Rhett could hear the fluttering of their cloaks and the sound of their bony claws gouging into wood.

There was no other direction for Rhett and Jon to go, so Rhett pulled them both backward off the broken edge of the floor. They fell away, watching as the psychons swept up and across the wreckage of the ship, a mass of dark cloth and white bone.

The drop was farther than Rhett expected, and he held on to Jon, hugging him close. In an instant, they smacked into the sand, creating a crater of their own.

They fell nearly at the feet of Mak and Basil. Treeny and Theo were right behind them, along with the rest of the crew.

"We have to move," Mak barked. "Now!"

They pulled Jon and Rhett to their feet, and Jon's mother, Marta, was there to greet them. She wrapped her arms around her son, squeezing him with what looked like all her might. Her shoulder bumped his hat askew.

"I'm so sorry," she was stammering in Jon's ear. "So, so sorry. They were going to ghost us. We didn't know what else . . ."

"Mom," Jon said, grabbing both sides of Marta's face. "It's okay. You did the best you could."

"I hate to break this up," Basil said, "but . . ." He pointed up to the broken hole where Rhett and Jon had been standing only moments ago. The psychons were still scrambling out of it, climbing both up and down the side of the *Harbinger*'s hull. Urcena stood right on the edge, her arms outstretched with her army of psychons racing past her.

"*Your power will be mine!*" she said. "*Your ship will be mine! The souls you so poorly protected will be MINE!*" Urcena leaped from where she stood. She fell through the air, arms held wide as if they might help her catch flight, and landed in a crouch right in front of the crew.

Her impact sent a shock wave rippling out around her that knocked the syllektors backward. Beneath her, the sand hardened, melting into itself and becoming something else entirely: glass. The ripple of her landing had the same effect all around the shipwreck. The sand under the syllektors hardened in an instant, becoming smooth and hard as concrete. It crackled below the surface like ice.

Rhett was up first, pulling whoever was near him onto their feet. The rest of the crew scrambled to get up, slipping across the smooth glass. Some of them were trapped with their arms or legs buried in what had previously been sand. They squirmed and fought to get up, but their limbs were encased.

Psychons came flooding down around where Urcena stood, charging into the crowd of syllektors.

Above everything, dark clouds began to form out of nothing, materializing in the sky and quickly blotting out the sun. The clouds were dense and flat gray, hanging there like a smooth blanket. There was no thunder or lightning, though, and when Rhett expected rain to begin pouring down on top of them, instead there was snow. It drifted down slowly at first but began to pick up speed, changing over from a flurry to a blizzard in just seconds.

The syllektors that tried to run were quickly headed off by packs of psychons. They encircled the crew, blocking them in.

Rhett looked for Basil and Theo, and when he spotted them, he felt another rush of panic.

One of Theo's enormous arms was trapped beneath the glass. Basil was there beside him, picking at the ice around the limb with one of his scythes, chipping away at it without any real progress. Rhett pulled the others together, and they huddled around Theo, staring out at the psychons that surrounded them. The syllektors who had weapons were ready to use them. Those who were unarmed put up their fists, defiance and rage in every face.

"What do we do?" Marta asked.

Jon had pulled his staff from its sheath and gave it a slow turn in his hand, letting it buzz menacingly. Mak had her machete, and Treeny had a dagger that she must have gotten from someone else. Basil was twirling his scythes. And Rhett slipped his knuckle blade from its holster at his side.

"What we couldn't do the first time," he said. "Defend the *Harbinger*."

FIFTEEN

There was a war after all. And it began as most wars do—with bloodshed.

The syllektors and the psychons let loose on one another, clashing across dunes made of glass, surrounded by the broken, towering hunks of wreckage that had once been a single monstrous ship. The sounds of metal and bone and flesh smashing into one another rang out across the desert, and snow fell in huge, clumping flakes that skittered across the glass, making it slippery and nearly impossible to move across.

But the bloodshed came from somewhere else.

Theo was still trapped with his arm buried up to the middle of his bicep in glass. Basil was trying to chip away at it with his scythe, even as psychons and syllektors fought all around him. Theo pressed his free hand to the surface and pulled, his face straining with the effort. It was no use.

"Just cut it off!" he yelled. He closed his eyes and turned his head away, not because he would feel any pain, but probably because he didn't want to see it happen.

There was no time to react. Rhett watched as Basil swung his scythe. It cut cleanly through Theo's arm, disconnecting his shoulder from the rest of the limb.

Syllektors generally didn't bleed all that much, from what Rhett had experienced. But there was still plenty of blood dripping from the place where Theo's arm used to be. The young man himself only stood, reaching over his shoulder with his remaining hand and removing his ax from where it hung. He gripped it tightly and swung it at the first psychon he saw, screaming angrily as he did. The psychon broke apart into two pieces and slumped heavily to the glass beneath it.

Then they were all fighting.

Everywhere Rhett looked, psychons were slashing and lunging. The armed syllektors stood half a chance, but the ones that went against the psychons with just their bare hands only lasted for a few brief moments before finding claws buried in their chests and breaking down into dark swirls of ash. Rhett wanted to help them, to reach for them and fight with them. But he was caught in his own battle, taking on three psychons that had circled around him, swiping with their long claws.

He ran forward and jumped, kicking off one psychon and slamming the knuckle blade into the face of another. The psychon flailed away, grabbing at its face as Rhett yanked his blade out, sweeping his arm around and slicing through the stomach of the second creature. The first one, the one he'd kicked, was right behind him when he landed on his feet. He launched his fist upward, and the blades stabbed into the psychon's head under its chin. The thing went limp instantly,

all of its weight coming down on top of Rhett. But he had removed his blade and was out from under it before he could be crushed.

Not far away, Jon was spinning low, his hat turned backward, his staff singing through the air and catching a cluster of psychons around their ankles. They fell over like a set of bowling pins. His hands seemed to maneuver the staff with a will all their own as Jon turned away from the spasming creatures he'd just dropped and found his next target. Marta was right behind him, mostly protected by her son but punching and kicking at whatever came her way.

The top of Theo's head was visible just above the violence, even through the snow that was coming down. Basil, Mak, and Treeny were lost in the fold somewhere.

Rhett whirled around just as another psychon barreled toward him on all fours, cutting into the solidified ground with its claws. The creature charged at full speed, and Rhett met it with a backhand, secretly enjoying revenge for all the times a psychon had done the same to him. It lost its footing and slammed face-first into the ground at Rhett's feet. Its legs folded over the top of its head. Rhett quickly removed them from its body.

The snow fell harder than ever, and the ground was splattered with streaks of blood and the black sludge that ran through the psychons' veins. Rhett turned on his heels, peering through the chaos, trying to spot Urcena. What he spotted instead was a bluish glow from up above. It was the reason that some of the psychons had gone *up* the wreckage instead of down it.

The cube.

It was nestled into the tattered side of the ship several decks above, where the room of doors was. The remains of the steam room jutted out around it, splintered and unprotected. The cube had been obscured by the brightness of the sun before. But now that the clouds had taken over the sky, its effervescent glow was the only bright thing Rhett could see. It was engulfed in psychons, creeping across its surface, more antlike than ever. Rhett knew there was no way they could get into it, but just seeing it like that, covered in monsters, was enough to send him into a panicked rage.

He heard a roar of anger bubble up in his throat, and as he let it loose, he ran at a psychon that had just knocked a guy flat on his back, ready to deliver the last destructive blow. Rhett used all of his momentum and weight to tackle the psychon. Together they slid across the ground, but before either of them could get up, Rhett was slamming his bladed fist into the beast's face and chest and neck, not looking at where he was hitting, just plunging his knuckle blade into it over and over, furious that he and the ship's crew had been backed into a corner all over again.

Then there were hands on him, pulling him off the psychon.

"Hey! Mate! It's all right! You got it!" Basil was yelling in his ear. He pulled Rhett away. "You got it, mate. I promise. Let it go."

Finally, reluctantly, Rhett did. He pointed up at the glowing shape of the cube. "Look."

"I saw it," Basil replied. They were yelling over the crashing sounds of the battle. "It'll hold together. The creepies can't get into it. Where'd the she-devil go?"

"I don't—" Rhett started, but he was cut off.

"*Is this not enough?*" Urcena's voice boomed. All of them, even some of the psychons, started and put their hands on their heads, trying to block out the violent noise of her speech. *"Will you not surrender even as your friends are destroyed, Soul Keeper?"*

"None of us are surrendering, you meddlesome bitch!" Basil yelled, his hands, still holding their weapons, cupped over his ears.

Urcena chuckled menacingly in their heads. *"Very well."*

Beneath the battle, the hard, smooth ground shifted slightly. Below the surface, there was a crackling noise again, like ice fracturing. On the other side of the wreckage, long cracks formed along the ground, shooting out like strikes of lightning. They interconnected, webbing together, the glass bowing as something pushed up from under the surface. It broke through a second later, a long, armored limb that reached out and scraped frantically across the ground, trying to find purchase. When it did, the rest of it emerged behind the leg, shattering through the glass and sending huge, daggerlike chunks flying. Some of them landed amid the battle, crushing psychons and syllektors alike.

There were seven more legs to go along with the first one, each of them easily as big as any of the pieces of the *Harbinger* that lay scattered around it. The spider heaved itself up and out of the ground, its white-and-gray exoskeleton nearly vanishing against the clouds and behind the snow. It made a wet hissing sound and clicked its giant mandibles together. Eight black orbs on top of its head stared down at the battle that was somehow still going on even as the creature loomed above it.

"Ugh," Basil groaned. "Why does there always have to be a giant bloody monster?"

The spider swept one of its legs into a piece of the ship and sent it rolling across the glass, the impact shattering both. Metal beams and shards of glass rained down across the psychons and syllektors, and the spider jabbed its legs into the ground, dislodging even more. It leaned down and closed its fuzzy, dripping mandibles around several bodies at its feet, not caring whether they were syllektors or psychons. It devoured its bite in a few short seconds.

Now even the psychons were forced to defend themselves against the creature, lashing out at its legs with their claws. The spider lurched up onto its back legs, kicking its free ones through the air defensively as it backed away. When it came back down, the impact was like an earthquake. More pieces of the *Harbinger* broke free and came falling into the battlefield. More glass shattered and cracked.

"This is a massacre," Basil said. "We have to find the others."

But Rhett's attention was focused on the cube and the psychons that swarmed around it. They weren't just trying to break into it; they were nudging it closer and closer to the edge of the steam room floor. As Rhett watched, the glass and metal cube slid another few inches. Instinctively, he lunged forward a step. If it fell and hit the rock-solid ground, the cube could break. When he stepped forward, though, he saw what was down on the ground *below* where the cube teetered. Or rather, who.

Mak was there, her machete whirling around her in a metallic blur. One psychon after another approached her and was quickly dispatched. She was fully focused on the battle, without any idea of what was happening above her. Rhett glanced up again as the cube was pushed farther out onto the edge. A wooden slat from the broken floor snapped away and flipped down through the air, smashing into splinters only a foot or so from where Mak stood. She still didn't notice.

"Basil, look—" Rhett said, turning to where Basil was standing. But Basil was already gone. Rhett spun around, trying to see where he could have gone. He was nowhere in sight. Rhett gave up and started running toward Mak, yelling her name. When she didn't respond to that, he started screaming it. "MAK! LOOK UP!"

A loud scraping sound roared from above. He looked up just in time to see the cube slide off the edge, a hunk of glass and metal the size of a small apartment building flipping end over end amid the blinding static of the snow. Below it, Mak was still fighting. It was racing for her . . .

Basil appeared from within the torrent of snow. He sliced through a psychon that was right behind Mak . . . and then shoved her.

Her face was full of shock as she fell forward, sliding across slippery glass, her machete lost. She turned and saw Basil down on one knee. He'd shoved her so hard that he'd lost his own balance. Rhett was frozen in place, watching Basil and Mak as their eyes found each other.

"I LOVE YO—"

The cube hit the ground, and Basil's voice was swallowed up by the sound it made crashing into the glass. The ground around it broke upward, shattering into a wave of daggers. Rhett ducked down and covered his head as they fell like hail, mixing with the blizzard.

When he stood back up, his arms were covered in gashes. He spotted Mak, who hadn't moved. Her face was lined with cuts that dripped blood. She was staring with wide eyes at the cube. It was still intact, glowing brightly behind the falling snow, dug into the crater it had made.

Basil had been right underneath it.

"NOOOOOO!" Mak screamed. She was on her feet, running toward the cube, her features lost in its glow. She pounded her fists into it, screaming, crying. She crumpled to the ground, and almost at the same time, Rhett felt himself sinking to his knees.

The battle went on without them. The monstrous spider flung house-size pieces of the ship in every direction. The psychons swarmed and clawed and the syllektors fought back. But Mak and Rhett were lost to it all. They were on the ground, Mak weeping against the cold surface of the cube and Rhett staring down at the glass under his hands, at his own reflection, still a stranger to him with its head of stark-white hair. It looked back at him with shocked, horrified eyes. Basil had pulled Rhett from this very state on the night that he had died. He wouldn't be here to pull him out of it again.

Something strange and violent stirred inside him. It was like a heartbeat but distorted, a bizarre warbling in the place where his heart belonged and, beneath that, an actual heartbeat. But not just any one heart—a collection of them, thumping in unison. He felt them down into his bones, shaking his insides, the energy they gave off coursing through him.

It was coming from the cube.

He looked up at it, the tool of his best friend's demise. It was lit brighter than ever, and he could just barely hear a humming noise coming from it. The light pulsed in time with the heartbeat that was buried in Rhett's soul. The throbbing power that came with it pushed out from Rhett's body.

Psychons had taken notice of Rhett slumped on the ground and were now moving in his direction. He could sense them in a weird way he hadn't before. He couldn't just see them out of his peripheral vision, but he could *feel* them, their life force, moving to destroy him. There was no need to be afraid now, though. Somehow Rhett understood this.

He stood slowly, calmly. And when the psychons—five of them—that were lunging toward him were only a few inches away, he clenched his fists. Something rippled out of him. The creatures fell dead at his feet, those same life forces snuffed out by just a reflex in Rhett's mind.

Life has always had a counterpart, Ními had said. *That thing is in you, too, boy. Beware of it.*

But as Rhett moved toward the cube, his steps sure, he did not beware of it. He *relished* in it. This was the power that Urcena wanted, the thing that Treeny had told them about. Not the ability to reignite life, but to extinguish it. The ability to wipe out entire civilizations in one fell swoop. And what a power it was. Another psychon collapsed at the clenching of his fist. Then another. They fell around him like sacks of meat, as if they had only ever been empty husks to begin with. His rage fueled the power, giving it the strength to slowly take him over.

Right behind him, something huge and heavy and made of metal crashed into the ground, nearly knocking him off his feet. It had been tossed by the spider, which was still towering above everything, hissing and kicking. Rhett reached out and found its core. It was ugly and afraid and hateful. Raising his fist, squeezing it, he quashed the life out of the giant monster. All eight of its massive legs curled under its body, and the thing fell to its side, smashing into the ground in a spray of metal and glass. The whole world quaked under the force of it.

"*Yes*," Urcena's voice rattled in his ear. "*Yessss. Destroy them all. Destroy everything.*"

Rhett caught his reflection again in the glass beneath his feet. It was the same, except this time his eyes were glowing purple embers. They looked inhuman, full of hate and malice, everything he'd sworn not to be in the afterlife. But he couldn't stop now. He knew what he had to do.

He closed the distance between him and the cube, standing tall above him. The footing was uneven, broken apart by the cube hitting the ground, but he had his balance. There was no way he would fall, not like this, not full of power.

Mak was there, staring into his strange new eyes, her face streaked with tears.

"Rhett?" she said. "Rhett, snap out of it. Wake up!" She had him by the shoulders. She was shaking him.

The thing of it, though, was that he had *already* snapped out of it.

Rhett put his hand up against the cool glass of the cube, feeling its chill even without his senses. The heartbeat inside him slammed like a bomb going off, over and over. His entire body was made of that heartbeat. And now, with his hand on the cube, he could hear the

voices inside, whispering. All the trillions of souls in there, talking to him.

"*Wait.*" Urcena again. There was something new in her voice, something that Rhett was sure he'd never heard before: fear. "*What are you doing?*"

On the other side of the glass, the palm of a glowing blue hand appeared, pressed right up against the spot where Rhett's hand was.

"Theo!" Rhett called over his shoulder, yelling through the blinding snow, through the war that was still raging on. He didn't need to yell, though. Theo was there. And Treeny. And Jon. His friends were with him. They had been with him from the beginning. "I need your ax!"

The big lug dropped the handle of his ax into Rhett's outstretched hand. Rhett stepped back, heaving the weapon over his shoulder.

"*NO!*" Urcena screamed, and Rhett could sense her racing through the battle, obliterating psychons and syllektors in her path. She was crawling across the ground like an animal, moving faster than Rhett ever could have imagined. She was coming for him.

Rhett swung the ax as hard as he could.

The blade connected with the cube.

He could feel the souls inside.

The glass shattered, bursting outward, and everything was blinding blue light. A tidal wave of energy exploded out of the cube. Rhett and the others fell on their backs, staring up at the light that was spilling across the frozen desert, light that started out as a single rushing mass and then broke apart into humanoid shapes. They were souls, standing and moving and fighting with the syllektors. They went after the psychons, wrestling them to the ground, seven souls for every one skeletal beast.

The power surged out of the broken side of the cube, just inches from Rhett's face. He looked up and saw Urcena still creeping across the ground, her eyes almost entirely black now, the pinpricks just tiny specks of rage. She crawled right at him, but glowing hands reached down out of the tunnel of light and yanked her back. She scrambled to get her grip again. The souls wouldn't yield.

And when all of the souls had emptied out of the cube, they spread out across the field of wreckage, changing into those glowing humanoids, and began to shift the pieces of the *Harbinger*, lifting them into the air, collecting the scattered debris. Iron groaned and screeched as the *Harbinger*'s parts were yanked up out of the solidified sand. The souls twisted pieces of metal back into their true shapes, they fused glass back together with just their hands, they reconnected wires and pulled the crystal chandelier out of the ground, lifting it back up to where the ship was. Before the syllektors' eyes, the *Harbinger* was being rebuilt by the souls it had carried for so long.

Rhett rolled over and got to his feet. Around him, his friends did the same. Including Jon, who was hunched over, coughing something up. A strong blue glow appeared in the back of his throat, and an instant later a comet of light launched like a firework out of his mouth. It grew arms and legs and joined the other souls. The syllektors watched as the souls moved around them, ignoring anything but the tasks they were focused on. They looked like humans made entirely of light. And two of them were holding Urcena where she stood. A man and a woman.

Urcena squirmed and bucked in their grip, screeching and howling as they left smoldering handprints along her arms, and she winced from the pain of them. Her eyes were full of hate as Rhett walked over to her. The glow was gone from his eyes, but he knew the power was still there. He tamped it down, though, refusing to let it take control of him.

Above their heads, pieces of the *Harbinger* rolled and turned in the air, wrapped in that blue light. Souls floated down to grab more pieces and then floated back up to the ship. The cracked chunks of iron inched closer together, looking more and more like the vessel they were supposed to be. The snow had stopped.

Rhett stared at Urcena, his friends and his crew standing behind him.

"You know what I have to do now, right?" Rhett asked the demon.

"So then do it," she spat. All the power had gone out of her voice. The two souls that held her captive were draining her. She sounded so weak without all the other voices filling Rhett's head.

Rhett just looked at her for a moment. Then he reached out and gripped both sides of her head.

He knew it was dark and that he was caught in some kind of storm. Everything else was shadows and noise.

The air was a brutal wind, whipping around him in constant, vicious gusts. Everything was living darkness. Somewhere out in the middle of that raging black fog stood a pillar of light. It glowed softly, barely penetrating the swirling storm, and Rhett could tell it was getting weaker. He struggled to get to it, pressing forward against the wind, his arms up to block his face from the knobby, twisted hands that reached out of the darkness for him. Fingers slithered across his skin. Knuckles, bony and dry, caressed his cheeks. Something yanked at his hair, pulling him back. He stumbled. Something else wrapped itself around one of his ankles. The wind almost knocked him over completely, but he only staggered, waving his arms around. He dropped to one knee amid the twisting, groping shadows. The pillar went out of view, and he was submerged in total blackness.

"You only come farther into my reaches, Soul Keeper," something growled in his ear. It was nothing like Urcena's voice at all. This was monstrous, horrible. It was a voice that sounded like it belonged to something with a forked tongue and glossy red eyes. *"My life cannot be snuffed out so easily as those of the beasts I've used against you. I am eternal."*

Rhett continued to struggle against the storm. He tried to stand but couldn't. The wind gusted into him, over and over, the force of it holding him down. He lost his balance again and dropped to all fours. His knees and hands were pushing against something that felt like grass that had been smeared with tar.

"Nothing," he said, gritting his teeth, pushing upward, "is eternal." He gave one enormous shove and finally broke through the storm of shadows, rising to his feet. The darkness rippled around him, flinching away as if it were afraid.

Just ahead, between Rhett and the pillar of light, pieces of the dark began to gather themselves together, pooling into a vortex that had no shape at first, then sprouted limbs. Legs and arms formed. A head with black horns that looked more like antlers with at least twenty points on each side. The thing rose up to its full height, almost as tall as the pillar that stood behind it. It towered over Rhett. And embedded in the face, he could see her eyes, flat, shadowy orbs with tiny white specks for pupils.

"Do not pretend to understand this world!" the thing roared. Its dark mass took a long step forward, closing the distance between itself and Rhett, who could feel the ground thrumming beneath him. *"You are a child, Soul Keeper. Nothing more. And until I get what I want, you and your friends will suffer in ways that no living human could ever imagine."*

Rhett reached for his knuckle blade but found nothing on his hip. He took one fearful step back, then another. The thing looming over him chuckled, a sound like a felled tree breaking away from its stump and crashing to the forest floor. It cocked its head, the points of its dark antlers twisting against the gray sky.

"Now you see. You were made to fear me. As I was made to conquer death and to wipe the disastrous earth clean. To give life back to those who understood its flaws and let them start again."

He understood what the demon meant. A clean slate. Get rid of all the pesky humans who have botched the world. Resurrect the ones who thought they knew what was best for it, even if that meant genocide or slavery or worse. Rhett couldn't imagine what that world might look like, and he didn't want to.

He found his voice again and spoke with his head craned back, looking up at those tiny white pupils, shouting against the wind. "And what do you get out of all this?" he asked.

The demon cocked its head again.

"Such a vile, human notion, the insistence that something should be gained from the effort of doing what is right. I thought you were better than that, Soul Keeper." Its voice was so loud that it was like a crack of thunder right above Rhett's head. *"You continue to disappoint me."*

It swung one of its monstrous fists downward, slow and lumbering, not aiming directly for Rhett but for a spot right beside him. Its great, shadow-laced knuckles connected with the ground, punching a crater a couple of feet to Rhett's right. Whatever it was that he was standing on shattered under him. He was thrown off his feet, falling backward.

It was the glass-crusted desert all over again. There was nowhere solid to stand, nowhere safe to hide, no good vantage point from which to even try to attack this thing. The only consolation was that it wasn't just Rhett and the demon here—there was still the pillar of light, stuttering somewhere out in the black mist. If Rhett couldn't kill the demon with death, then he might be able to do the next best thing: wash it out with life.

As the thing wound up for another swing, Rhett rolled onto his stomach, got up on his feet, and ran. The fist came down through the air like a massive pendulum, rushing past just as Rhett moved out of its way. The wind coming off it sent him stumbling forward, but this time he kept his feet under him.

Rhett sprinted away, with the demon stomping after him.

The pillar was in his sights, only slightly obscured by the darkness. Rhett ran for it. He could feel the demon on his back, reaching, chasing. The ground shuddered with every one of its heavy steps. The closer Rhett got to the light, the more he could reach out and feel it. He could sense the low heartbeat thumping within its sturdy form. He thought of the girl in the apartment building. The man on the train. He thought of the push and felt it tugging that invisible lasso.

As he approached the pillar, panting, feeling the pang in his lungs with every hitching breath, realizing now that his senses were fully tuned in to his body, he could see a young girl standing on top of that shaft of light. She was no older than fifteen, dressed in a clean hospital gown. She was staring down at him, her eyes wide and afraid and normal.

"There's nowhere to go, Soul Keeper," the demon said from behind Rhett. The sound of its voice was so close that Rhett could feel the hot, stinking whoosh of its breath. *"Come and meet your fate."*

Rhett stopped and turned, putting the pillar to his back, the power of the girl's light and life humming within him now. He leveled his gaze at the hollow white dots of the demon's pupils.

"Fuck you," he said.

Light and heat erupted from the pillar, radiating outward, a tidal wave. It washed over Rhett, then collided with the demon just as the wave of souls had collided with Urcena back in the desert. The demon, midstride, toppled. It fell to the ground with the force of an earthquake, startled. It tried to stand, reaching forward for anything to grab hold of. Another wave of light swept out from the pillar and slammed into it. Pieces of its fingers and antlers and face cracked, then broke apart and were carried away.

The demon roared.

Another wave pushed it back, breaking it some more. It was afraid now. Terrified. Its white pupils were smaller than ever, and the dark orbs surrounding them were huge.

"*I will end you! I WILL END YOU!*" it screamed. Rhett thought his head might explode from the force of it, but he held strong, pushing the life outward, letting it fill up the dark. It was washing out the thing that had been rotting inside the girl for who knew how long.

One wave after another, rushing out into the shadows and eradicating them, breaking them down into chipped black glass that gathered in mounds at the edges of whatever this was—the girl's soul, Rhett assumed.

The demon slid backward even as it struggled to push ahead, digging its claws into the ground and heaving its cracked mass toward Rhett and the pillar. It looked like a colossal effort. And, as Rhett watched, more and more of the demon began to break away. Its howls wiped out all other sound that there might have been, a cry of rage and anguish that would have been heard for miles in the living world.

Light throbbed outward, soothingly warm to Rhett but deadly to the demon, who broke and broke until it was only a few threads of darkness that vaguely resembled what it had been. It squealed and moaned, losing the last of its strength.

Rhett let out a long, relieved, exhausted breath.

Sure now that the demon was not going to advance any farther, he turned toward the pillar again. The girl was still there, sitting on the edge. Closer now, he could see that her face was peppered with freckles, and her face looked kind under curls of dark brown hair. Her legs dangled, looking heartbreakingly innocent.

"You shouldn't have come here," she called down to him.

"Yeah," Rhett said. "Seems that way. But somebody had to. I think you needed help."

She smiled. "I think I'm a little beyond help now. But it would be nice to finally go to sleep." Even as she spoke, something like thunder sounded in the distance. It was the rumble of this world beginning to fall apart.

Rhett looked around, nodding.

"I can probably manage that," he replied. "Are you sure that's what you want?"

"Yes," she said. "It's been a long time since I've been able to rest."

"Okay."

He stepped up and put both of his hands on the pillar. Part of him wanted to hug it, the energy it gave off was so peaceful. He focused his thoughts on the power and the heartbeat and the light. One last wave of brightness engulfed the girl's soul, obliterating the last tendrils of the thing that had taken up residence within it.

The girl spoke one last time. Rhett heard her voice but couldn't make out the words. Maybe it was "thank you." He didn't know for sure.

Then he fell into the warmth.

When Rhett regained his focus, he was standing on the glass floor of the desert, his hands outstretched. Between them there floated a gentle white wisp. It swirled around for a moment, and then it grew, just as the soul inside Jon had done, spreading out into a shape that resembled a girl made of brilliant blue light. She stood in front of him, head cocked to the side slightly, and then she turned away and floated upward to the *Harbinger*, joining the rest of the souls.

The other two souls—the man and the woman—were still there. They were watching Rhett as he swayed on his feet. He couldn't feel any weariness, but his body was clearly drained. The woman lifted her luminous hand and brushed Rhett's cheek with her thumb. The man gripped Rhett's shoulder. They were there with him, for just that tiny moment, and it was enough.

Both souls lifted up off the ground and floated into the mass of blue light and energy that coursed through the ship. It hung in the air above them, weightless, held up by some invisible force. And it *was* a ship again. There were subtle differences, things that were still missing, like one of the smokestacks, which had been broken apart and swallowed by the kymaker. But it was intact, a vessel of death pulled back together by the power of life. It was as massive as ever, and Rhett could only marvel at it, as he always had.

Someone touched his arm. He turned and found Jon standing there. Marta was behind him, and behind *her* was the rest of the crew.

"I thought we lost you there for a second," Jon said.

"I think you did. But I found my way back." He glanced past the group, at the place where the shattered cube was still half buried in the ground, empty now. Mak and Treeny and Theo were standing in front of it. He looked back at Jon.

"Go," Jon said. "They need you. I have someone else I need to find." His eyes swept over the heads of the crew, a nervousness in them that Rhett had never seen before.

Rhett nodded and made his way over to the cube, where his friends stood staring at the jagged hole he'd put in it. He could just see down to the bottom. Maybe there was a black smudge there, something that could have been ash. It was too dark to tell. The clouds were thinning out, but they were still lingering in the shadow of the *Harbinger*.

When he finally glanced at the others, he saw tears standing out in all their eyes, even Theo's. Mak was holding something—a scythe, one of Basil's. She caught him looking at it.

"I found it," she said, squeezing its handle as if she were wringing out a towel. "I thought maybe . . . maybe he'd . . . like the bridge, remember?" She was sniffling before, but now she was sobbing again.

Rhett understood what she was trying to say. They'd thought Basil was ghosted once before, in San Francisco, and he'd made his way back to them then. Rhett couldn't tell her that this time he'd actually seen the moment when Basil was no more. But he could tell her something else, something powerful, a new truth to their existence as Death. No syllektor was gone for good. Not anymore.

He put an arm around her shoulders and pulled her close. He told her what he knew. She nodded, staring down at the scythe in her hands. And the four of them stood there like that for a while.

"Uh . . . guys?" Jon said from behind them. "I think it's time to go."

Rhett and the others turned around. Standing and floating there with the crew was the massive collection of souls. They were waiting for the syllektors, a sea of blue light that stretched far and away from the glass crater.

Everybody hesitated, unsure of what to do. They looked around at one another, nervous, battle-weary.

But then Marta stepped forward, a strange confidence in her eyes.

"Mom . . . ," Jon started, reaching for her. He had found his boyfriend, the guy with the blond hair, who held on to Jon even as he tried to stop his mother. Marta only shushed her son, waving him off.

Marta walked right into the waiting arms of one of the souls, illuminated by its steady glow. The soul hugged her close . . . and then it carried her up into the air, floating effortlessly toward the hulking shape of the *Harbinger*. Marta giggled with delight. It was a bubbly sound that erased the tension in the air.

One by one, the rest of the crew stepped up and allowed themselves to be carried away, up to where the ship waited. They left hundreds of psychon corpses behind, along with the carcass of the giant spider. There were also heaps of ash everywhere. Rhett knew that this wasn't the end of psychons and enormous monsters. But it would be a break, at least.

He watched a pair of souls carry Theo and Treeny away. Then one more lifted Mak off her feet, still holding Basil's scythe, squeezing it to her with both hands. Jon and his boyfriend were whisked away, hands clasped tightly together. Then it was just Rhett, alone among the wastes of war.

A pair of warm, glowing hands gripped him under his arms. The ground shrank away beneath his feet, and pretty soon he was floating past the miles-long hull of the *Harbinger*, its black iron sweeping past in a rush. When he reached the top deck, he could see the entire desert stretching out and away. It was bright and hot in the sun that was finally showing through the clouds.

The bridge tower was there, reassembled, standing tall and true.

Its roof was detached, though, held a few feet above the tower itself by a dozen or so souls. The one that carried Rhett dropped him slowly down onto the bridge. With his feet firmly on the metal floor, the soul floated away, and the roof was lowered onto the tower. The souls hovered around the outside, welding the metal together with brilliant sparks that they created from just their hands.

Rhett stood looking out through the glass that surrounded the bridge, and his friends were there with him. The wooden steering wheel stood at the front with the lantern's pedestal. Mak stepped over to it, unclipping the lantern from her belt, and positioned it carefully on top. The flame flickered almost gleefully, as if it were happy to be home.

The last thing to be lifted back onto the ship was the cube. The syllektors watched it come floating up over the starboard side of the ship, its broken wall put back together, and already filling back up with souls. They were returning to their sanctuary, floating into it, dematerializing as they went. It vanished behind the one good smokestack, but Rhett imagined it being lowered into the newly repaired steam room, the last of the souls funneling through its door. The extension tube that connected the tank to the rest of the *Harbinger* would lock itself back into place and . . .

As if in tune with his thoughts, the distinct sound of things powering up rolled through the ship. Lights in the bridge flickered on, and Rhett could picture the power sweeping back through everything on board.

The *Harbinger* came back to life.

But the ship was still floating in the air, turning ever so slowly, giving them a panoramic view of the angry-looking desert. Rhett wanted nothing more than to be back on the waves of the river. He just didn't know how to get there.

"Where to now?" Mak asked him. "Captain?"

When Basil had made Rhett first mate, Rhett had no way of knowing that it would eventually lead to him being captain. But he supposed the same had been true for Basil. He had done everything he could to keep the crew together and safe. Rhett could only hope to be half the captain that Basil had been.

"I don't know," he said honestly. "I think . . ." Then he spotted the flame within the lantern. It was pointed downward again, its tip upside down.

All at once, the ship dropped out of the air.

The *Harbinger* plummeted, its front end tipping downward. Gravity was lost, and from the bottom of the spiral staircase that led up to the bridge, Rhett could hear the crew crying out in fear.

He held on to the steering wheel, trying to keep his feet on the ground. But everything and everybody was hovering as the ship fell.

The ground came into view, racing up to meet them as they headed stern-first for the hardened glass field that they had just left behind. Rhett had time to imagine what the silhouette of their gigantic ship looked like, completely vertical, falling with the sun glaring behind it.

A second later, they hit the ground.

The tip of the ship's stern slammed into the glass, obliterating it. Shards flew up and around the ship, clattering against the windows of the bridge. Rhett and the others were thrown down against them, and Rhett feared that they might shatter. But they held, and the ruined pieces of the glass that had once been sand engulfed the ship. It plowed through like a missile and somehow stayed in one piece.

Rhett didn't think that would last for long, though. And just when the ship was shaking hard enough that it should have been ripped apart all over again, the glass gave way to water. The *Harbinger* dove into it, the murky darkness falling in around the bridge. Gravity shifted once more, and the syllektors fell backward, away from the windows. They held on to what they could. Rhett and Treeny had the steering wheel in their grips, while Theo, Jon, and Mak clung to the staircase.

They weren't going down anymore. They were going *up*, the entire ship submerged in the water, rushing to the surface.

From down below, metal groaned and cried out against the pressure. Rhett could feel the bridge tower straining under the force of being pushed up through the water. It frothed and bubbled against the windows and along the hull. Rhett was sure the glass would break now.

"Everybody hang on!" he cried, squeezing his eyes shut against the inevitable onslaught.

But the glass held. The ship held. The crew held. And the *Harbinger* broke the surface, shooting up out of the water like some kind of metallic whale. It reached up toward the sky, still almost totally vertical . . . and then dropped back down, crashing into the water and creating a massive tidal wave that rolled away from the ship in all directions.

The *Harbinger* bobbed and shook, iron groaning, its angular metal hull cleaving in and out of the waves, its single surviving smokestack protruding from it and expelling a fresh dark cloud. Water lapped at the ship's sides, a lonely, pretty sound. Lightning danced across the horizon, jittering to the music of grumbling thunder. Gradually, the ship began to level off, floating steadily on the water for the first time in almost two years.

From inside the hull, a cheer rose up. Startled and relieved and elated. The sound of hundreds of the ship's crew returning home together.

Other than that, it could have been a ghost ship.

EPILOGUE

It was raining again.

The gravestones were dark and glistening, droplets rolling lazily across their rough surfaces. The sky was low and dreary, dribbling in preparation for another downpour. The cemetery could handle it. It wasn't the oldest boneyard in Wales, but it had still been around for a long time. It had weathered far worse than a little rain.

Mak stood near one in particular, hands buried in her coat. She stared at the name on the gravestone:

BASIL WINTHROP
1905-1923

She had been standing there for a while, but now the rain was picking up and there wasn't a lot of time left.

They had done what they came here to do, and from the other end of the graveyard, his voice carried through the rain, brightening all the best parts of her.

"Oh, come on, get away from there, love," Basil called. "Don't you know that my rotting corpse is right under your feet? That's really depressing."

She couldn't help herself—she laughed.

He was waiting for her near the gates. She turned and found him watching her. There was a touch of white hair at his temples now, but aside from that he was the same as he'd always been. Six months ago, she had been sure she would never see him again. Now, she crossed the cemetery, her feet squelching in the mud, and slipped her arms around him, felt him kiss the top of her head. Rhett had been right.

Speaking of, Captain Snyder himself came back in through the gate. He'd made some excuse about going to sightsee for a minute, said he'd never been to Europe. But Mak knew that he'd just wanted to give her and Basil their moment together. She was grateful for that. These days, she was grateful for a lot of things.

"Sorry to break up the honeymoon," Rhett said, ducking against the strengthening rain. "But I think it's time to head back."

Mak grinned at the jab. Basil chuckled at her side. Then they exchanged a serious look. Rhett looked back and forth between them.

"Listen, mate," Basil said. "We were talking, and . . . we think maybe it's best if we hang around here for a while. There are a lot of us still out there who haven't found their way back to the ship. Markeski's crew. Syllektors who've been wandering around on their own all this time. A lot of them may be dealing with the Ash. We'd like to try and find them. With your permission, of course. Sir." He clicked his heels together and made a show of saluting Rhett.

"Why are you asking permission?" Rhett asked. "*You're* the captain."

"Not anymore. You've made a much better captain than I ever did. I'm very happy to resume my former post as second mate. With my first mission being this one. This very important, very personal mission."

Rhett sighed, glancing around at the weather-beaten gravestones.

"You sure I can't change your mind?" he asked.

"We're sure," Mak chimed in. She wrapped her arm around Basil's waist again and pulled him close. "Someone's gotta keep him out of trouble."

Rhett grinned. "Well, that's true. All right. Permission granted. But I expect to see results. And a very detailed report." He was trying to sound serious, but he was already laughing at himself.

"How detailed are we talking here, mate?" Basil asked, waggling his eyebrows.

"*Ewww!*" Mak and Rhett groaned at the same time.

"Not that detailed," Rhett said.

Then they were all laughing. Until it was time to go.

"I'll see you guys soon?" Rhett asked.

Mak and Basil both nodded. Rhett pulled her in for a hug. She'd never had a brother when she was alive. She was glad to have one now. When he let her go, she felt her senses start to course through her, and tears welled up in her eyes. Rhett and Basil put their arms around each other and squeezed tight, like men who had known each other for much longer than they really had.

"Thank you, mate," Basil said into Rhett's ear.

They let go, and still they stood there. The rain pinged against the metal bars of the cemetery gates.

"If things get rough . . . ," Rhett started.

"We know where to find you," Mak finished. "Now go. The crew needs their captain." The words were heavy in her mouth, a strange way of saying good-bye to someone who had done things even Captain Trier could only have fantasized about. But he was her friend, and she was proud of him. She was also sorry to be saying good-bye.

Rhett, in his awkward, perfect way, put up a hand in a motionless wave, and he turned away.

Leaving them there was harder than he thought it would be. He stepped away from the graveyard, with Mak and Basil watching him go, and went back out through the gates. The sky was looking nasty, but they had seen nastier. He knew they'd be okay. He looked back one more time, though, quietly hoping that they'd be running after him. They weren't.

He stepped out of the grassy yard and onto the sidewalk, collar up and hands still deep in his coat pockets. He walked a couple of blocks, back to the little hat shop that he and Mak had come from. Ducking inside, he heard the bell above the door jingle quietly, and the woman behind the counter looked up. Of course, she couldn't see anything. She only *thought* she'd heard the bell.

Rhett walked to the back of the shop, where there was a door marked FITTING ROOM. He gripped the doorknob, leaning in slightly to listen, and turned it. The door swung away, and on the other side was the high ceiling and wide, ornate floor within the *Harbinger*.

He stepped through and shut the door behind him. It closed into its frame with a painful finality. There was a creeping hurt in the back of his mind, the intuition that he would never see Mak or Basil again.

Jon was there waiting for him. A sad smile crept over his face as he realized Rhett had returned alone.

"How did it go?" he asked, clearly already understanding.

"It went," Rhett replied. "Where's Treeny?"

"Up on the bridge," Jon said. "Waiting for you."

"Good." His new first mate was turning out to be almost too loyal, and Rhett had a feeling she was still trying to shake off a lot of guilt. That was okay. He was trying to shake off some of his own.

They left the room of doors and headed back up through the column, where they were met with cold blue lights and polished steel. They were a strange kind of comfort. The staircase wound up to the bridge. There was barely a fraction of the crew that had been aboard before, but they were making due. With most of the psychons killed or left behind in the desert, there wasn't an army of them to threaten the syllektors' every move. The crew members could go out and gather souls on their own. The push had returned, strong and full and begging to be acknowledged. And Rhett was glad to see that not only was everybody working hard, but they were taking pride in that work.

Because the souls they collected weren't born from death. They were the power of life, of love. And they went with a person until the end, when they were given to the crew of the *Harbinger* to protect. The syllektors weren't curating death but maintaining a version of life, one that had been willing to protect them as much as they were willing to protect it.

The spiral staircase came into view, and Jon and Rhett climbed up it. Treeny was at the top, her tablet in hand. She poked at the screen but smiled at the pair when they came up.

"Welcome back," she said. Her eyes drifted away. "Everything go according to plan?"

"Unfortunately," Rhett said, "they're staying. They have an . . . um . . . assignment."

Treeny shrugged. "I figured. They deserve a break."

Rhett couldn't argue with that. "How are the rest of the repairs?" he asked, changing the subject.

The ship had returned to the river almost entirely rebuilt, but there had still been things that needed fixing. The first of which was the second smokestack, which now stood tall with its sibling, spewing their dark atmosphere of smoke.

"On schedule," Treeny said, responding to the question as eagerly as Rhett had asked it. "A little over a month from now, she should be whole again."

Rhett nodded. "And Theo?"

"Right here, boss." The big lug was sauntering up the staircase. He was wearing a coat of his own now, with only one sleeve filled in. The other one was rolled up all the way to the stump of his missing arm.

"Okay," Rhett said. He swept his gaze around at each of his friends. "Which way are we headed?"

Treeny pointed out the window, across the churning waves. "The lantern says that way."

When Rhett looked up, a grin broke on his face. For the first time since he'd arrived in the afterlife, there was light on the horizon.

They sailed toward it.

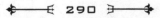

ACKNOWLEDGMENTS

Writing the acknowledgments for this book might be even more sur-real than writing them for *The Soul Keepers* was. I think there's a tiny part of every debut author that's convinced the first book will also be the last. In my case, I was fortunate enough to have the opportunity to carry the story of the *Harbinger* and its crew through to the end of this duology, and I would never have been able to do so if not for several very important people.

The Swoon Reads imprint was forged and is overseen by two incredible women—Jean Feiwel (its creator) and Lauren Scobell (its director). Without these two, my books, along with many others, prob-ably wouldn't exist. I can't thank them enough for taking a chance on my weird paranormal fantasy and for being the guiding lights of an incredible community of readers and writers.

I owe an immense debt to my fierce, persistent, and endlessly patient editor, Emily Settle. She asked very difficult questions and helped to shape this book into what I believe is the best version of itself. She's as much a fan of Rhett and the gang as I am, and there are no words to express how thankful I am to have her in my corner.

The Swoon Reads community as a whole is one that I'm overjoyed to be a part of, but I'm especially grateful to the Swoon Squad of fellow authors who lift one another up and have one another's backs on a day-to-day basis. That group continues to grow and get brighter every time Lauren, Jean, and the Swoon editors select a new list of books to publish. It's incredible to say that this gig comes with its own built-in support system, which is a rare and beautiful thing. The Swoon Squad knows who they are, and I hope they know how much I appreciate them.

I'm in a strange spot because I'm writing this just a few days before *The Soul Keepers* actually hits shelves. So as of right now, I'm not sure who, if anybody, has picked up that book and read it. But I'm going to assume the best and say thank you immensely to anybody who started Rhett's journey with that book and continued it with this one. I hope you enjoyed them both.

I want to thank Zak Bagans, Aaron Goodwin, Billy Tolley, and Jay Wasley, along with the rest of the *Ghost Adventures* crew, for putting the science into paranormal investigation, which inspired some very important parts of this story. Also for giving me the creeps every Saturday night.

There's a multitude of bands whose music inspired this series, including (but nowhere near limited to) Crown The Empire; August Burns Red; Chunk! No, Captain Chunk!; Ice Nine Kills; Imagine Dragons; Bring Me The Horizon; Being As An Ocean; I the Mighty; Dance Gavin Dance; Nothing But Thieves; and so many others from my childhood to now that would take a whole other book to list. Thank you to all of them.

I have many friends and family members I want to thank:

My best friend, Cait, who has hung with me through good times and bad and knows what hardship looks like, facing it always with a smile and a good heart.

My sister-in-law, Morgan, who is far better at braiding my daughters' hair than I am and never says no when they ask her to do it. And my brother-in-law, Michael, who is as kindhearted and fun-loving as they come.

My siblings, Kaydance, Chloe, Marcus, and Shane—we may not always be on the same page or in the same place, but our hearts are always connected. I wouldn't be the person I am today without you, and these books certainly wouldn't be the same.

My in-laws, Dynel and Eric, who are the constant buoys to their kids' (and grandkids') lives, without question or reward. They are two of the best people I know and have never hesitated to lend me a helping hand, no matter how big or small. Thank you, guys.

My mom, Mylinda, who somehow turned into the kind of mom who feeds me every time I'm at her house, which is the best thing ever. As I always like to say, that woman has seen some shit, and she's stronger and better and more amazing because of it.

My beautiful wife, Kelsey, the pillar of light in my own storm of darkness. Even when I'm as far out as I can get, you always know how to guide me home. I love you, gorgeous.

And of course, my daughters, Rylan and Norrie, to whom this book is dedicated. Fearless, joyful, intelligent, ferocious little girls. Your mama may have my heart, but you have my soul. I know you'll always keep it safe.

That's that for now. If I left you out, please don't be offended. As Christopher Robin says in his movie, "I am a man of very little brain." I hope to thank you the next time around.

With love,

Devon

P.S. There's one more very important person I almost forgot to thank: the villain of my story, Urcena. Who of course was more than just that young girl in a hospital gown. She was something far more fearsome. An entity, let's say. One that was left behind, shattered and unseen, in a glass crater in a desert on the underside of the afterlife. And even though that entity was broken down and abandoned, maybe there was enough hot wind coming off the sand dunes, enough energy left coursing through its tiny, scattered particles for some of them to be swept together among those jagged peaks. Maybe there was just enough of it left to pile those pieces into something that vaguely resembled a claw, reaching into the air and curling its horrid fingers into an angry fist . . .

But more on that another day.

DT

Check out more books chosen for publication by readers like you.

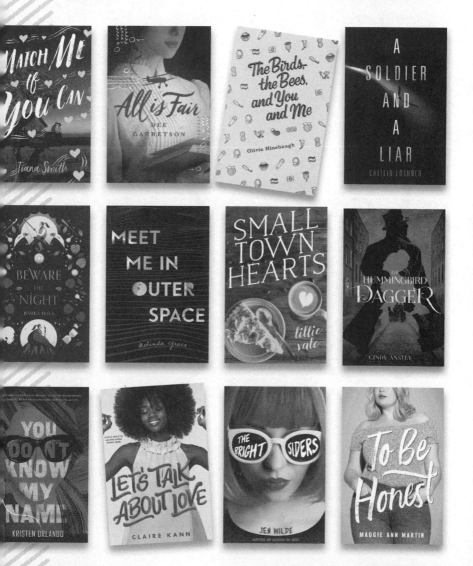

DID YOU KNOW...

readers like you
helped to get this
book published?

Join our book-obsessed community and help us
discover awesome new writing talent.

1
Write it.
Share your original YA manuscript.

2
Read it.
Discover bright new bookish talent.

3
Share it.
Discuss, rate, and share your faves.

4
Love it.
Help us publish the books you love.

Share your own manuscript or dive between the pages
at **swoonreads.com** or by downloading the **Swoon Reads app.**